THE THING IN THE DARKNESS

The sound seemed to be increasing in volume, more urgent now, hissing and rustling. He aimed the torch at the wall and at last saw where the sound was coming from. The black, fungal growth covering the walls was alive with movement, the fine, hairlike filaments waving and rippling, as if caught in a breeze. But there was no breeze. The air was still and fetid, but the growth continued to move, giving the impression that the entire wall was breathing.

He gripped the ladder with both hands and started to haul himself up. He put his foot on the bottom rung and pushed, almost crying out as a lance of white-hot pain roared up his leg from his injured ankle. He reached up to grab another rung and something cold and damp wrapped itself tightly around his waist and he was pulled bodily from the ladder.

He fell to the floor, the impact forcing the air from his lungs, the torch flying from his grip. It bounced once, then rolled across the floor, dropping over the edge of the well and down into the blackness.

He was struggling to get his breath, his hands reaching down and clawing at the thing gripping him around the middle. His fingers found something wet and slimy, almost rubbery to the touch, and it was squeezing tighter and tighter, making it hard to breathe.

And then it started to pull him across the floor toward the well....

SHELTER

L. H. MAYNARD
& M. P. N. SIMS

LEISURE BOOKS NEW YORK CITY

A LEISURE BOOK®

July 2006

Published by

Dorchester Publishing Co., Inc.
200 Madison Avenue
New York, NY 10016

ISBN 0-8439-5706-9

The name "Leisure Books" and the stylized "L" with design are
trademarks of Dorchester Publishing Co., Inc.

Printed in the United States of America.

Visit us on the web at www.dorchesterpub.com.

SHELTER

North Africa—1946

The sun beat down from an azure sky, scorching the backs of their necks as they walked across the dusty plain. The captain and the corporal, marching in unison, following the Arab dressed in his white desert robes, his swarthy features masked by a black hood. The soldiers' uniforms clung to their sweating bodies, the boots they wore no match for the hard stony ground. Flies danced at their lips, pecking droplets of perspiration that oozed from their pores. They brushed them away with quick, spiteful motions of their hands.

"Primitive country," the corporal grumbled.

"They're still living in the Middle Ages, Hooper," the captain agreed. "I thought they could have at least provided transport." His legs were aching, his feet blistering inside the boots, but he trudged on, the mountain range growing nearer with every painful step.

Shortly they started to climb. The Arab, with only camel-hide sandals to protect his feet, hopped nimbly from

1

rock to rock, guiding them farther up the mountainside. Occasionally he'd stop and wait for them, a gap-toothed smile splitting a face as wrinkled and brown as a walnut.

"How much further?" the captain said, his officer training allowing him to mask his tiredness, though it was there in his eyes.

"Close now," the Arab said. "Very close."

They had chosen him as their guide because of his knowledge of the area and his ability to speak English, a rare gift among this traditional people.

Eventually they saw the cave, a dark hole in the side of the mountain. Another Arab stood outside the entrance. His robes were grubby and ragged, and at his side, hanging from a leather strap, was a curved and wicked-looking sword. As they approached he drew the blade from the scabbard and held it aloft.

The captain instinctively reached for the service revolver at his hip, but the corporal stayed his hand. "It's a greeting, not a threat, sir," he hissed under his breath.

"You're sure?"

"They mean us no harm. They could have killed us at any time during the trek here. They chose not to."

"What do you mean?"

The corporal glanced back over his shoulder, signaling with his eyes for the captain to do the same.

Fifty yards behind them were a group of Arabs, keeping pace with them, watching them with hooded eyes.

"I didn't realize . . ."

"They've been with us since we started out. If they wanted to kill us they would have done so by now."

They reached the entrance to the cave. The Arab standing guard moved to one side to let them enter, but said something quietly to the guide, who nodded urgently and started to make his way back down the mountainside.

2

"Looks like we're on our own," the captain said, swallowing hard. Despite the corporal's reassurances, and the relentless heat, a cold sweat was trickling down his back underneath the thin cotton of his tunic.

The entrance to the cave stretched for a hundred yards, tunneling deep into the mountain. At least it was cooler here, and the ground beneath their feet was smooth rock, not the sandy, stony desert that had been so difficult to traverse. Rush torches hanging from iron brackets set into the walls at regular intervals illuminated the tunnel. The burning rushes gave off an acrid smoke that stung their eyes and irritated their throats, making them cough. The corporal took a swig from a water bottle and handed it to the captain. The captain drank deeply, wiping his lips with the sleeve of his tunic, but the water did nothing to alleviate the dryness of his mouth.

The tunnel finally widened and they found themselves in a cavern, lined with rock, with a ceiling too high to be clearly visible. The guard said something in a tongue they didn't understand, but his message was clear from his gestures. "Wait here."

The captain and the corporal exchanged uncertain glances, but they didn't have to wait long. From a gap in the rock at the opposite end of the cavern an old man stepped into view carrying another torch. He bowed a polite welcome and approached them. His robes were clean—impossibly white in this dusty environment—as was the headdress he wore. The folds of material framed a face of wrinkled leather, of great age. The nose was prominent and hooked, the lips below it thin, pressed tightly together in a hard line, framed by a straggly white beard that stretched down to his chest. But the old man's eyes were in great contrast to the rest of his face. Pale blue—the color of fine Ceylon sapphires—they shone with vitality and intelligence, and something else. The captain stared at him closely. There was something in those sapphire eyes that hinted at deeply hidden secrets, of knowledge as old as time. As the eyes were turned on him he found himself shrinking backward, away from their gaze.

The old man came closer; the flickering flame of the rush torch he carried lit various features of the darkened cavern. To one side was a slab of stone raised three feet from the floor, supported at each end by two rocks to form a crude table. To the left of the table was a small metal tank, two feet by one, filled to the brim with water, its purpose they could only guess at.

With calm resolve the old man fixed his torch to a bracket on the wall and came to stand before them. "Thank you for making the journey," he said in precise but heavily accented English.

"We're still not sure why we're here," the captain said.

The old man smiled. "That is about to become clear, Captain Charteris." He snapped his fingers, before the captain could consider how he knew his name.

Two berobed men appeared from the shadows behind him. Each held the arm of a young girl, who sagged between them. No more than seventeen and totally naked, her dark hair awry, a tangled web of black, hanging across her face like a shadow. Her skin glistened in the torchlight and her belly was distended, in the late stages of pregnancy.

The captain and the corporal moved forward as one, both recognizing the girl instantly, though it had been months since they had last seen her.

The old man held up his hand. "No further," he said. "Please."

The soldiers halted. "What have you done to her?" the captain said, staring at the girl, who looked back at him with tearful, frightened eyes. No more than a child, he thought, as a wave of guilt swept over him. He glanced at the corporal, whose brow was beading with sweat, his fingers clenching and unclenching, ready to lash out, to fight, to the death if necessary.

The old man spoke calmly. "I see you recognize the child, yes?"

Both men nodded.

"Then you both know what has happened to her and which of you is responsible."

The captain let his hand move slowly to his hip, ready to pull the revolver from its holster. This time the corporal did nothing to stop him. "Just let her go," the captain said with forced calmness. "We're traveling back to England tomorrow. We'll take her back there with us. She should be in hospital, not in some filthy cave."

The old man considered this for a moment, nodding his head sagely. "And she would be looked after? She would be treated as an equal in your society? I think not. The girl belongs here, here with us tonight. There is no future for her now. She has sinned and she knows she has to atone for her sin." He made a quick gesture with his hand and the two men holding the girl dragged her across to the stone table, laying her out on it. The girl was too weak to struggle, and in too much pain as a contraction spasmed through her body.

"Stop this!" the corporal said, taking a step forward, but before he could move again his arms were pinned against his sides by two Arabs from the group that had followed them from town, and now stood in a ragged line behind them. How did they move so silently? The captain was similarly held, but he struggled violently until he realized he was no match for the men.

The old man watched them until they were still, and then he snapped an order in Arabic. The two men with the girl moved swiftly. One of them laid his full body weight across the girl's legs, while the other lay across her chest, his sinewy hand clamping itself across her mouth. Her teeth bit deep into the bone of his hand, but he maintained his fierce grip.

The old man waited, and then, apparently satisfied that the girl couldn't move, took a curved knife from the waistband of his robe and approached her.

Mercifully his body blocked what came next, but the captain and the corporal were left in no doubt about what was happening. Even with the weight of the Arab pressing down on her, her legs thrashed, and her head twisted from side to side. The captain met her eyes as her head turned toward him and he saw a look of indescribable terror and agony written there, as well as a chilling and bitter accusation, as if her eyes were telling him, "You brought me to this. You did this to me." He looked away—away from her accusing look, away from the blood that was puddling on the floor at the old man's feet.

The sound of a baby's cry brought his head round again. He looked at the corporal, who was swaying on his feet, his face bleached to the color of ivory.

"It's barbarism," the corporal whispered under his breath.

The old man heard him and turned, holding a bloodied and crying infant in his arms. "Barbarism? I assure you, gentlemen, natural childbirth would have been much more painful." Cradling the baby in one arm, he turned back to the girl, said something soothing to her, and drew the razor-sharp blade of the knife across her throat.

The girl made a small sound, midway between a gasp and a sigh, and quietly died.

The old man moved quickly then. Carrying the baby across to the water tank, he laid it gently inside, pushing it down beneath the surface.

The captain and the corporal watched helplessly as the

minutes ticked by and the old man held the baby under the water. Finally he released his grip and turned to the other men in the room, a huge grin splitting the ancient, weather-beaten face. "Verani!" he said exultantly.

There was a murmur of approval from the others, but the men holding the captain and the corporal didn't slacken their grip.

The old man said something else to the men in their own tongue, and a ripple of laughter eddied around the cavern. "I said to them you look shocked," he said simply.

"Butcher!" the captain spat at him. "First the girl, now the child. Was what she did so very wrong? Why punish her? Why kill the child? We were the ones deserving of punishment, not them."

The old man raised his eyebrows. "But the child lives. Look."

He motioned for them to be brought forward.

They stood in front of the metal tank scarcely believing what they were seeing. The baby was floating, an inch under the surface of the water, but its eyes were open, legs kicking, arms waving, rippling the liquid in the tank.

The corporal shook his head. "I don't understand."

The old man put a leathery hand on his arm. "There is a great deal to understand if you are to care for this child."

The captain couldn't drag his eyes away from the infant—a boy child, he noticed. "Go on," he said.

"The child is Verani, like his mother. It breathes the water as we breathe the air. But unlike us it can survive in either, as you will see later."

"What's Verani?" the captain said.

"All your questions will be answered presently. I will tell you everything you need to know before you take the child back to England with you."

"But I can't . . . I'm married."

7

The old man smiled knowingly. "Ah, I see. And your colleague?"

"I'm single," the corporal said.

"Then it is for you to decide who will act as the child's father. But one of you must. When you enter into a relationship with a Verani it is for life. The girl knew this, and she knew what her fate would be. You will find both pleasure and punishment in this child's life, but you will accept it, without question, without recrimination. What's done is done, and it is within no one's power to rewrite history, or indeed, destiny. Now, I suggest we sit and talk. There is much for you both to learn."

The Arabs released their hold on them, and the captain and the corporal followed the old man to the back of the cave.

CHAPTER ONE

For Sale.

Laura Craig wandered around her tiny Abbotsbury cottage, plumping cushions, hiding magazines in drawers, making sure everything was uncluttered. That was the appearance she had been told to achieve, uncluttered. Clean and tidy, with lots of space. It sounded like a good description for the way Laura wanted her life to develop from now on. Except that mocking phrase, *For Sale,* kept popping into her mind to obliterate any seeds of hope that began to sprout. Everything seemed to be ending rather than beginning. So many loose ends had unraveled at the same time that although she was resolved to knitting them back together, she was concerned the result would be unrecognizable.

Then again though, the cottage had only been on the market for a few days and already Maggie, her best friend and owner of the estate agency trying to sell it, had lined up a prospective buyer. A professional married couple, both of whom worked in Bridport.

They were due at eight, but it was already half past. Laura checked her watch again, moved items around some more, and went into the kitchen to switch the coffee machine back on. Maggie had given her tips to make the cottage more saleable. Apparently the smell of fresh coffee was supposed to work like a charm. Unless, as Laura pointed out in her newly discovered mood of pessimism, they didn't like coffee. Not that Laura thought the cottage needed much help to sell; she'd fallen in love with it the moment she stepped through the door, and it was going to be a hell of a wrench to leave it. Not that she had any choice in the matter, not after all that had happened. *For Sale* wasn't always a sign put up willingly.

Just after nine, just as she had given up on the couple, the doorbell rang. "At last," she muttered, and walked through to the hallway, stopping to check her reflection in the mirror hanging on the wall next to the hat stand. Her makeup was subtle—just a hint of eyeliner and some blusher—and she'd tied her long chestnut hair into a ponytail and secured it with a white ribbon. It made her look almost virginal. She smiled at herself, satisfied that the buyer's first impression of her at least would be a good one.

She opened the front door and the smile dropped from her face.

"Is this your idea of a joke?" Brian Tanner stood in the doorway, dwarfing the space. He thrust the solicitor's letter at her and pushed past into the hallway. She could smell whiskey fumes on his breath and the whites of his eyes were threaded with red.

"You've been drinking," she said calmly. "Why don't you come back in the morning when you're sober and we can talk about this reasonably?"

He lashed out with his foot, kicking the door shut behind him. "Fuck that," he said viciously. "We'll talk about it now." He grabbed her arm and hauled her through to the lounge.

"Brian, you're hurting me," she said, trying to keep her feet as he dragged her.

"Not half as much as you've hurt me," he said, threw her down onto the couch, and stood over her. "Right. Explain." He was breathing hard, sucking air in through his mouth and expelling it through his nose.

Like a rampant bull, she thought. She'd experienced Brian's explosive temper in the past. She still carried the bruises to prove it. "I told you last week it was over, Brian," she said, trying to keep her voice even. *Don't let him see you're afraid.* "This . . ." She glanced down at the letter clutched in her hand. ". . . This makes it legal. I'm dissolving the partnership."

"You can't," he said petulantly. "I won't let you." He paced across the lounge to the cupboard where she kept her bottles of drink and poured himself a glass of Teachers, taking a mouthful, shuddering slightly as the neat liquor burned down his throat.

She stood up and dropped the letter down onto the table. "You can see from this that I can," she said, feeling less vulnerable standing. "It's over, Brian. Accept it."

He downed the rest of the whiskey and hurled the glass into the fireplace, where it smashed on the marble hearth, sending shards of glass flying across the sheepskin rug.

"I think you'd better go," she said.

"Like hell," he said, advancing on her again.

She backed away—the two of them moving in a

bizarre minuet danced in the cramped confines of the room. Let the couple turn up now, Laura thought, then, no, don't let them see the cottage like this, full of anger and regret.

Brian stopped, his shoulders sagging, the "little boy lost" look she'd once found so appealing creeping back into his eyes. "What about *us?*"

"There is no *us*, Brian. There never was. It was only ever *you* and what you wanted. I, like a fool, fell for it."

"It wasn't like that. You wanted it too." He had begun the pleading stage of his strategy sooner than she thought he would, but once she had learned to see through his ploys none of his charm worked on her.

"At first, yes, I did. Until I learned what you were really like." She found she didn't have to work as hard on being tough, as she once might have done.

"You make me sound like some kind of monster." The face of a reasonable man.

She sighed. "I'm sorry, Brian, but I've made my decision. The partnership is over. Our relationship is over. You'd better go."

He lowered his head, tears in his eyes. Laura relaxed and took a step toward the door. Before she could take another he lunged at her, grabbing her by the hair, his fingers closing around her thick ponytail. "You're not going to do this to me," he hissed in her ear and pulled her backward through to the kitchen and forced her head down onto the work top. With his free hand he grabbed a carving knife from the wooden block on the side.

She saw the blade glinting in the sharp light of the overhead halogen spots and gasped. "Brian, no!"

The rage was back in his eyes and he stroked her cheek with the knife. "I could kill you," he said.

"Easy. I could cut you so badly . . . You bitch! You're not going to dump me. Who the hell do you think you are? Without me you'd still be selling space on the local rag. I made this company. I made *you*."

Laura said nothing, her head still pinned to the work top by his grip on her hair.

"I'll show you," he said and moved the knife away from her face and began sawing at the thick rope of her ponytail. The razor-sharp carving knife cut through it in seconds. She felt the pressure ease as the hair came away. When the ponytail was all but severed she jerked upright, reached out, and grabbed a Pyrex measuring jug from the draining board, spinning round and catching him a glancing blow on the side of the head.

He staggered backward, dropping the knife. She scooped it up, holding it out in front of her. "Get out!" she said. "Get out now!"

The fire in his eyes dimmed and he looked down at the hank of hair still grasped in his fist. He frowned in confusion, as if wondering how it got there.

"Laura, I'm sorry," he said, his voice soft, contrite. "I don't know what came over me."

"Go!" She screamed the word, jabbing the knife at him.

He shrugged and walked through to the hall, still staring at the trophy in his hand. "I always loved your hair," he said, dropping the severed ponytail onto the couch, where it lay like a dead animal. He opened the front door. "It didn't have to be like this," he said, looking back at her.

Laura still held the knife out in front of her, but her hand, her whole body, was starting to shake.

"Good-bye, Brian," she said, trying to keep the tremor from her voice.

His mood switched again and he smiled at her. "I'm going to destroy you, Laura," he said. "I'm going to take away everything you've ever cherished." He took one step out through the door and she dropped the knife, ran forward, and slammed the door shut.

It was then the tears came. She leaned her back against the door, her fingers touching the jagged ends of her hair, and she began to cry, sliding slowly down to the floor, bringing her knees up to her chest and hugging them.

She sat like that long into the night.

CHAPTER TWO

A late spring afternoon and the café was packed to capacity, customers spilling out onto the handful of tables and chairs clustered on the pavement, where they sipped at their lattes and put the world to rights. Laura pushed her way inside and looked around. She spotted Maggie almost immediately, sitting at a table in the far corner, her fiery confusion of copper curls haloed in a wreath of cigarette smoke. She weaved her way through, pulled up a chair, and sat down. Maggie looked up from the paperback book she was immersed in. Her eyes widened in surprise. "Nice crop," she said. "New image, eh?"

Laura ran her hand self-consciously through her freshly cut hair. It had taken the hairdresser less than an hour to repair the damage from last night. "Time for a change," she said. She couldn't bring herself to tell Maggie the real reason, just as she couldn't involve the police, even though common sense told her it was the right thing to do. For some reason she felt ashamed. As if in some way Brian's attack on her was *her* fault.

"So how did it go last night? What did they think of the place?"

"They didn't show."

"You're kidding. Fuck them! I wondered why they hadn't got back in touch with me. I'll call them. Have a go."

Laura shook her head and took a mouthful of the coffee Maggie had thoughtfully ordered for her. "Don't bother. I'm sure there'll be others."

"Of course," Maggie said. "It's just that they sounded so keen."

"So, what have you got for me?"

Maggie dragged her voluminous bag from the floor and set it on the table in front of her. She dropped the paperback inside and rummaged through the contents, bringing out three sheets of A4 paper, and spread them on the table. "Three to choose from, all within your price range, all with vacant possession; those two there"—she indicated two of the sheets with a finely manicured but nicotine-stained finger— "those two are so new the advert only just went into the newspaper. So you've got a couple of days' grace before it hits the streets."

Maggie had been running her own estate agency for five years, and in that time Laura had bought several properties with her friend's help. It was an aspect of the friendship that suited them both perfectly.

Laura studied the details for each of the houses in turn. "This one looks interesting. Four bedrooms, two receptions, kitchen . . . what about the outhouses? It says three. Is that right?"

"Agent-speak; so don't get your hopes up. From

what I remember they're three brick-built sheds, ramshackle and dilapidated. Oh, and that one hasn't got a bathroom. The toilet is in one of the sheds. The old boy that lived there couldn't be doing with modern conveniences. There's a tin bath hanging on the back of the door, and the kitchen has an old-fashioned copper for boiling the water. You have to see it to believe it."

"You'll be telling me next there's no mains electricity."

"The place has its own generator in—"

"One of the outhouses?"

Maggie made a gun with her extended index finger and mimed pulling the trigger. "Bull's-eye! Interested?"

"At that price? No way. Now if they were to drop by several thousand I *could* be. The location seems right, lashings of land and the house gives me plenty of scope for renovation."

"I could have a word. It's some distant relative of the old boy who's selling the place. She wants to hold out for the full asking price, but her husband's more pragmatic. I think he just wants rid of it. What about the others?"

Laura shook her head. "No, I think this could be the one. I've got a gut feeling about it, and you know I always trust my instincts. Shall we go and have a look?"

"Shortly," Maggie said. She gathered up the papers and slipped them into her bag, dropping it back down to the floor. Then she leaned forward conspiratorially. "But first things first. Tell me, have you heard from Brian?"

Laura avoided her friend's eyes. "My solicitor has

written to him. I think it's best not to have any direct contact. It only ends in recrimination and grief. His I don't care about, but I'm developing a well-overdue sense of self-preservation." Her fingers went to the nape of her neck. She imagined she could still feel the blade of the carving knife pressed against her skin. She shuddered involuntarily. It was only hair, she thought. It would grow back. It could have been so much worse.

"Could have been worse," her friend said, unknowingly echoing her thoughts but in a completely different context. "You could have married him. It's not as if he didn't ask you enough times."

"When the relationship was strictly business it worked fine," Laura said. "But once it became personal, once sex reared its ugly head, the whole relationship was on the slippery slip. I knew the first time we slept together I'd made the biggest mistake of my life, but by then it was too late to slam on the brakes. I had no idea what I was getting myself into. As for marriage . . ."

"I tried to warn you," Maggie said.

"I should have listened."

"Just think of it as a lucky escape."

"I haven't escaped yet. Once the solicitors dissolve the partnership I'll sleep easier."

They talked in a similar vein for the next half hour, Laura catching up with Maggie's news—new boyfriend, excitement—ditching new boyfriend, depression. The usual news, the usual Maggie.

"One day you'll meet the right one, get married, and have hundreds of kids," Laura said.

"Yeah, right, when hell freezes over. I think I'm destined to remain spinster of this particular parish."

She laughed bitterly. "Come on then. Drink up. I'll take you over and show you the house."

Maggie's car, as usual, was filled with cigarette smoke. Laura wound the window down, letting the slipstream fan her face. There was always a sense of completeness when she was with Maggie. She could relax in a natural way that she never could with other people. It was the nearest she felt to being on her own, but more secure.

Maggie stubbed a cigarette out in the ashtray.

"Much farther?" Laura asked.

Maggie indicated and turned off the main road onto a narrow winding lane. "Almost there," she said, then reached for her cigarettes on the dashboard and lit another.

The car shuddered and jolted over the potholes in the macadam. Laura braced herself. "I thought you said access wasn't a problem."

"It's a road, isn't it?"

"Only just," Laura said. Through a gap in the trees she could see a house in the distance. Redbrick, slate roof. "Is that it?"

Maggie nodded, sending a column of ash tumbling down the front of her shirt. "Impressive, huh?"

"It's big but I'll need a closer look."

"God, you're such a pessimist these days." Maggie indicated again and pulled off the lane. There was a break in the hedgerow and what remained of a five-bar gate hung limply askew from a rotting post. There was a long winding drive leading up to the house, little more than a mud-track, though the mud was baked to hard rough ridges by the summer sun. Now in full view Laura could see how badly the place was in need of restoration. There were slates missing from the roof, paint had peeled from the window frames, revealing the timber beneath, and the bottom six inches of the front door had simply crumbled away.

Maggie parked and climbed from the car, grabbing her clipboard from the backseat and a bunch of keys from the glove compartment. Laura followed, her eyes drinking in every detail, a curious thrill of excitement running the length of her spine. Despite Maggie's assertion, she wasn't a pessimist, not a fully paid-up member yet anyway. You couldn't enter into a career like this without a boundless sense of optimism. To most people this house would be a complete disaster, but she was already formulating plans. New windows, a new roof, and certainly a new front door. She could see it in her mind's eye clearly. It needed work—a lot of work—but the house had an undeniable charm. And she hadn't even looked inside yet. Renovated to holiday accommodation, the sale or rental potential was limitless.

As if reading her thoughts Maggie said, "We'll do out here first, and then I'll reveal the delights within."

They circled the house, Laura noting that all the guttering and downpipes needed replacing. They came across one of the outbuildings almost immediately. "This is where the generator lives," Maggie said, and pulled open the door, brushing away thick cobwebs with her hand, ignoring the spiders that darted for cover in the shadows.

"Does it work?" Laura said, eyeing the antediluvian contraption skeptically.

Maggie shrugged. "Doubt it. But who knows?"

Laura closed the door and followed her friend around to the back of the house.

There were two more brick-built sheds, one a lot smaller than the other. "The small one's the loo," Maggie said. "We'll give that one a miss. Too easy to conjure images of the old boy sitting there straining for my liking."

"Maggie, that's disgusting." But Laura was only half listening. Her attention was captured by the garden. It was a riot of color. Lupins and delphiniums jostling for space with huge rosebushes and great clumps of spirea and hydrangea. Beyond the formal beds was a row of fruit trees—apple, pear, plum, and greengage—and beyond them a meadow area. Gravel paths led through the profusion of plants, badly overgrown and weed-strewn.

"Well, he was a keen gardener if nothing else," Laura said, then opened the door of the larger of the sheds and stepped inside. As if to confirm her observation the shed was crowded with gardening implements. Spades, forks, hoes, and rakes, three large sieves, and an antique lawn mower with rusting blades and a broken handle. There were shelves along each side of the shed, crowded with terra-cotta pots of every imaginable size, and a pair of leather gardening gloves tossed casually beside them, as if the owner had just popped into the house for a cup of tea and left them there. Laura felt a sudden and almost overwhelming sense of sadness. She was surprised to find tears misting her eyes.

There was something unimaginably sad about the place, a deep melancholy that stirred emotions in her she thought were long buried. She remembered her grandfather, pottering in the garden at home. A man so vital and full of life that even now she found it hard to think that he'd lost his long and desperate battle with cancer. She rubbed away the tears pricking at her eyes.

"God, what is wrong with me?" she said under her breath, and stepped back out into the sun, closing the door behind her, but not before a soft, whispering sound came from inside the shed. It sounded like the wind blowing through long, dry grass. She opened the door wide and looked in, but nothing was stirring. Laura shook herself and closed the door. Get a grip! she thought. Then to Maggie she called, "Come on, let's go inside."

Maggie was yards away walking through the flower beds, bending to sniff a rose, brushing her hand lightly over the thick lavender bushes. Even from where she stood Laura could see the beds were fast running to weed. Thistle, nettles, and dock were squeezing their way into the gaps left by the flowers. Bindweed was spiraling up the stems of the taller plants while couch grass was starting to choke out the smaller perennials. Maggie looked around at her friend, shielding her eyes from the sun, which hung low in the western sky.

For an instant there seemed to be someone beside Maggie. It could have been only the play of shadow from the position of the sun, but to Laura it seemed as if there was a figure next to Maggie, arms raised ready to drape them over her. She nearly shouted out to her friend, but then a cloud passed in front of the sun and Maggie was walking toward her, fumbling in that bottomless bag of hers.

Maggie found the front door key on the bunch and slipped it into the lock. It turned stiffly. Inside, the air was musty and damp. The hallway was dark and gloomy, almost swallowing the sunlight that poured through the open door. A rank gray carpet covered the hallway floor and extended up a narrow staircase, but where the hallway turned into a passage leading to the ground-floor rooms there was no carpet at all, and the bare boards were stained and scuffed.

Laura frowned. Professionally she could see a lot of work was needed.

"Not very welcoming, I'll grant you . . . but a lick of paint here, new carpet and curtains there, and you won't know the place," Maggie said.

Laura shook her head, opening the door to one of the rooms and stepping inside. The room was bare. The walls were papered in a floral pattern, but had faded over the years. Here and there were patches of brighter paper where pictures had hung. The picture rail that ran around the top of the wall was thick with dust and the windows were grimy—one pane cracked—the bottom corner of it missing completely. From the birdlime that speckled the carpet she could tell that the window had been broken for some time. There was an old cast-iron fireplace set into a chimney breast, its tiled surround begrimed with soot and dirt. And in one corner green mold covered the wallpaper.

"Damp," she said. "That would explain the smell."

The kitchen was in a similar state. There was an old Belfast sink, an ancient gas cooker with grease-encrusted rings, and a cupboard, circa 1950, with reeded glass doors and a pull-down flap that served as a work top. Hanging from a hook on the back door was the tin bath Maggie had mentioned. The fireplace had been removed and in its place was the copper, a self-contained boiler in an enameled metal jacket. She lifted the lid and peered inside at the metal drum that held the water for washing clothes and bodies. A filthy rag sat at the bottom of the copper, dry and dusty, a home for a family of wood lice. She dropped the lid back into place with a shudder.

The last room downstairs was once the dining-cum-sitting room. There was a large window overlooking the garden, but that was its only attractive feature. The fireplace was missing and in its place was a rusting paraffin heater.

"How could he have lived like this?" she said, more to herself than to Maggie, who was leafing through a sheaf of papers in her hand.

"Sorry," Maggie said. "What did you say?"

"I was just thinking aloud," Laura said. "Let's have a look upstairs."

The boards on the staircase creaked ominously as they ascended. Once at the top the stairs gave onto a long landing with doors leading from it. These were the bedrooms—all of them a good size but nothing to distinguish one from the other. Peeling wallpaper, bare boards; an overwhelming sense of decay and neglect. That sense of sadness permeated the whole place.

As she emerged from the last room Laura said, "I think I've seen enough."

"I'm sorry if I've dragged you out here under false pretences. This is my first time here. I sent one of the lads at the office out here to check it over. He didn't tell me quite how bad it was. I'd better get you back."

Laura smiled. It was a sad little house, filled with melancholy echoes of the previous occupants. It needed care and attention, more than just a lick of paint and a cosmetic makeover. It needed to be loved. "I'll take it," she said.

"Pardon?"

"It's a lovely house. Oh, I know it's a mess now, but I've tackled worse. Six months time you won't recognize it."

"You're serious?"

"Never more so."

Maggie stared at her friend thoughtfully. "Okay then. Make me an offer."

They walked back to Maggie's car.

"You're sure about this?" Maggie said. "It's a big job for your first solo effort."

"I'm certain. Of course it depends on me selling the cottage. I'm relying on you there. I've got to start over. If I don't, then Brian's won . . . and I won't allow that to happen."

"Right," Maggie said, secretly pleased to see the weeks of oppressed Laura starting to dissipate.

Laura climbed into the car next to Maggie, a knot of excitement twisting in her stomach. She couldn't wait to get started. Maggie eased the car gently out through the broken gate.

From a vantage point hidden by the trees of the wood on the other side of the track, Brian Tanner took the binoculars away from his eyes and smiled to himself. "Oh no, Laura. It's not going to be that easy," he said softly and made his way back to his car.

CHAPTER THREE

"Bad news, I'm afraid," Maggie said, a few days later.

Laura pressed the phone closer to her ear. "Go on." Upstairs the professional married couple, who had turned up a day late, but who had immediately agreed on a price to buy Laura's cottage, were measuring for curtains.

"I've had another offer on the house. Full asking price."

"Shit!" Laura said. "Who from?"

Maggie hesitated. "You're not going to like this."

"I'm a big girl now. Tell me."

"Brian Tanner."

Laura felt like she'd been hit in the stomach. "The bastard! It's not a coincidence. He must have known I was going for it."

"Well, he didn't find out from me. You know what a small world the property game is round here. It'll be one of his mates from the golf club, I expect. How are you fixed? Can you raise any more money?"

Laura shook her head, then realized her friend couldn't see her. "I don't know," she said. "I was banking on using the equity from this place. I thought it would be enough. It bloody would have been if this offer hadn't come in." She thought for a moment. "I don't suppose there's any way you . . ."

"I wish I could, darling. You know I'd help you in any way I can, but I've got to present the offer to the vendor. It would be unethical not to."

"Of course," Laura said. "Sorry. I didn't mean to put you on the spot. But surely my offer was accepted days ago. Doesn't that make it binding?"

"You know better than that. Nothing is settled until contracts are exchanged, and even then . . . well, anyway. The fact is the old couple selling the house are bound to want to play you and Brian off against each other. You'll need to come up to the full price yourself. You're well advanced on survey and searches, so it'll just be the extra few thousand."

Extra few? Laura breathed deeply. That extra few made all the difference. "I'm not sure I can come up with it."

"But I don't have to present the offer straight-away," Maggie said. "Would twenty-four hours help?"

Laura hesitated. There was one possible place she could raise the extra cash. "Possibly. Look, I'll ring you back in the morning. And, Maggie, thanks. I really appreciate it."

"That's what friends are for. I saw what that bastard did to you emotionally. I don't want him to get it. You'll exchange on the cottage in about four weeks, I should think, so you're well advanced on that side as well. You'll sort it out, I know you will."

Laura rang off and ran her hand through her hair.

She might have known Brian would pull a stunt like this. The dissolution of the partnership had been bloody, and thanks to the very clever lawyer Brian employed it left her far more short of funds than she'd anticipated. She needed this project. She needed the income the lets would bring in. There were other properties she could go after, but it would take time to track them down, and it was unlikely they would be as suitable as this one. And if she did find one the chances were she'd find herself back in the same position with Brian trying to scupper her plans.

She poured herself a stiff vodka tonic and made a decision. It went against everything she believed in, but her back was well and truly against the wall. She'd run out of options. She picked up the phone and dialed.

"Hello," a familiar voice said.

"Mum, are you in tonight? I'd like to come over. There's something I need to discuss."

George and Barbara Craig owned a bungalow in a quiet residential street a stone's throw from the seafront at Bournemouth. Barbara greeted her daughter with a hug and a kiss on the cheek. Her father was up in the attic room playing with an elaborate train set—a passion since his retirement from the civil service.

"Shall I tell him you're here?" Barbara said to her daughter.

"No, let him play. He'll only be grumpy if you disturb him."

Barbara smiled. "That's true. He's like a big kid. He spent all those years holding down a senior position at work, running an office with thirty people under him. He retires and reverts to a second childhood."

She laughed fondly. "At least if he's up there with his trains he's not getting under my feet."

"I heard that," George Craig said from the top of the stairs. "Hello, kitten, I thought that was your car pulling onto the drive."

Laura hugged him as he reached the bottom of the stairs.

"Come through to the kitchen and I'll pop the kettle on," Barbara said. "Are you staying for dinner?"

"Yeah," Laura said. "Why not?"

George Craig was sixty-six, but looked ten years younger. His salt-and-pepper hair was cut in a fashionable style and the clothes he wore belied his years. Today it was denim jeans and a Grateful Dead T-shirt. His wife was ten years younger and clung to her youth with a tenacity Laura could only admire. As parents went, they were the best she could have hoped for.

Once the tea was made they sat around the table in the kitchen. "So," Barbara said. "What brings you down to see us?"

"Money," Laura said bluntly. She could have tried to dress it up, but knew her parents wouldn't appreciate any subterfuge. "I've run out."

Barbara and George exchanged looks.

"I was wondering how long it would be," George Craig said. "I can't believe you let that Tanner get away with so much."

"You never liked him, did you, Dad?"

George shook his head. "Both of us had reservations when you tied yourself up with him. Your mother's a pretty good judge of character and she never took to him, did you, pet?"

Barbara shook her head. "I always thought he was

a slippery one. Always a little too charming. A little too . . . neat."

"He's put in an offer on the place I'm trying to buy. Full asking price. It's pushed it out of my reach."

George Craig frowned. "I wondered if he might pull a stroke like that. How much do you need?"

She took a deep breath and told them. "I could pay you back. It would only be a short-term loan. Just until the project's finished and I start collecting the rent."

"What about the partnership's other properties? Aren't you receiving any income from them?" Barbara said.

"She walked away from them," George said. "That's what I meant when I said I couldn't believe she let him get away with so much."

"It was worth it just to be free of him," Laura said. The agreement was very one-sided, her lawyer pleaded with her not to accept, but she was adamant. A clean break both professionally and from the personal relationship that had intruded.

"Yes, I can see that," George said. "At least I can see why you thought like that. If you'd have gone to see Peter Franklin like I suggested, you might have come away with more." Franklin was the Craig's family solicitor and one of George's closest friends—another model railway enthusiast.

"Now don't start all that, George," Barbara said. "Laura wanted to do it her way, using her own people."

"Maybe so," George said. "But Peter—"

A look from his wife silenced him. "Of course you can have the money," she said to Laura. "And don't break your neck to pay it back. It's only sitting in the bank doing nothing except financing your father's obsession with trains."

"Dad?" Laura said.

He smiled ruefully. "Your mother's right. And it will make me feel better to know that we've done something to get back at that bastard Tanner."

"So, about that dinner," Barbara said. "It's only beef casserole, but I can stretch it to feed three."

"Sounds good to me," Laura said.

"Come on then, you can give me a hand with the potatoes."

"My cue to make myself scarce," George Craig said. "I'm going back to my trains."

"Typical man," Barbara said, smiling at her husband fondly. "Is everything else all right?" she said to Laura once they were alone.

"Yeah, fine."

"You've lost weight. And I must say, that haircut makes you look . . . well, vulnerable."

Laura ran her fingers through her cropped hair self-consciously. "Needed a change," she mumbled.

Her mother put an arm around her shoulders. "I know you're a big girl now, but you would tell me if there was anything—"

"Really, I'm fine." She kissed her mother on the cheek. "Thanks," she said.

"What for?"

"Being there."

"At least I know I'm not redundant in the parenting stakes."

"Oh no, you'll never be that."

It seemed like an age ago, a different life, that Laura and Brian Tanner had worked together in the advertising department of a large provincial newspaper. Thinking up original slogans and ideas for local businesses had long since paled when she and Brian started having lunches together and talking about ambitions. She couldn't even remember now whose idea it was to start the business. Reading the adverts for houses and the letting agencies prompted the idea that money could be made buying dilapidated houses, refurbishing them, then letting them out as holiday homes. They set up business together after quitting their jobs on the same day. Their first venture was a derelict farmhouse just outside Bridport. Both of them were single and had enjoyed a few years of a reasonable income. Both of them had money in the bank to invest in the project. And the result was a beautiful site set in a picturesque landscape. The house was converted into four flats, the part sale and part rental income from which financed their next project.

The business grew quickly with Brian looking after the letting and Laura concentrating on engaging the architects and builders, dealing with the local authorities on planning matters, and generally overseeing the projects. But, as she'd told Maggie, Brian was always eager to take their relationship to, as he saw it, the next level, with the proposal of marriage. And while, in her heart of hearts, she knew there could never be any long-term romantic attachment between them, her resolve wavered slightly after a particularly boozy end-of-project party in a Dorchester hotel and restaurant.

The project team drifted away one by one or in small groups until only Laura and Brian remained, surrounded by pillows of cigarette smoke, empty plates, and discarded glasses. Even though she had drunk as much as the others, there was a clarity about her thinking that made her feel initially guilty as though she was manipulating the situation. Brian was mumbling to her, stroking her leg, telling her how great they were together. Suddenly she felt an over-powering range of emotion from lust to pity, from empathy to superiority.

"Come on," she whispered to him, grasping his tie and pulling him up from his chair. She noticed a couple of the waiters smiling as she led him out of the restaurant. Your room or mine? she thought as she collected both keys from the front desk.

"Laura, love you . . ." Brian told her continually as the lift silently colluded in their liaison.

His room. She pushed the card into the security slot, pushed the door open, and pushed Brian inside.

"Oh, Laura . . ."

Even as she stood before him, unzipping her dress, countless misgivings were circling her thoughts, like vultures above her head. She certainly felt sensuous as she undressed him, letting his hands wander over her body. It was inevitable; she had always known they would spend at least one night like this. He was erect as soon as she held him in her hand. As her underwear was pulled off, his fingers, his mouth, were more delicate than she could have imagined. The actual act of sex that followed that night was a clumsy hurried affair, he far more drunk than he should have been, and she far too preoccupied with the wider aspects of the relationship.

In the morning with Brian in bed beside her, her head ached as the vultures of doubt feasted on her feelings. The human psyche allows myriad thoughts and emotions to roam together in harmony or in discord. Laura felt shame for acting so wantonly; she felt guilt at letting Brian think she might feel for him as deeply as he obviously felt for her, she felt selfish for wondering how it might affect the business partnership. She never asked Brian how he felt, but things were never the same again.

From that point on the relationship fell into a downward spiral of petty squabbles and, sometimes, decibel-shattering shouting matches. She only encountered Brian's violent side toward the end of the relationship, but by then she'd already decided that their relationship, both business and personal, had to end.

But now she was free of all that. This house was not only going to be her first solo project, but it would also stand as a symbol of her newfound freedom. It was going to be daunting flying alone, with nobody there to pick her up if she crashed, but it was exhilarating in a way she could never have dreamed possible. It was as if her life suddenly had wings.

Dunbar Court, England—Summer 1950

Ryder, the maid, stood with her ear pressed to the bathroom door, listening to the sound of retching coming from within. She hesitated before knocking, not really sure what to say. This was the seventh day running that she'd brought Lady Helen breakfast, only to listen to her throwing it up minutes later. Elizabeth Ryder was in her early twenties and had been in the Charteris family's employ since leaving school at fifteen. There had never been a man in her life and as such she was still a virgin, but coming from a family of nine children and helping her mother through five of her pregnancies, she knew full well what Lady Helen was experiencing.

She tapped on the door lightly. "Is there anything I can do, ma'am?" she called.

There was a pause in the retching. "Just go away, Ryder, and leave me alone," came a strained voice from within. Elizabeth pulled back slightly from the door, but it would be a dereliction of duty to do as Lady Helen requested.

Minutes later the door opened and Helen Charteris emerged, pale-faced, trembling slightly. Elizabeth offered her arm and the other woman took it gratefully. Together they walked back to the bedroom. Once inside, Helen flopped onto the bed and lay there staring up at the ornate rose that decorated the center of the ceiling. "I'm sorry," she said. "I shouldn't have snapped at you like that."

"It's all right, ma'am. My mother was the same during her confinements."

Lady Helen looked at her sharply. "What do you mean? It's a stomach upset, nothing more."

Elizabeth bowed her head slightly. "As you say, ma'am."

From the bed Lady Helen sighed deeply. "Oh, who am I trying to fool? Myself, I think. I keep telling myself it's not happening, but all the signs are there."

"Have you told the master?"

Helen's face hardened, her lips becoming a thin line, closed in bitterness. She remembered vividly the moment of conception. She and her husband, William, had been sleeping at opposite ends of the house since his return from North Africa. It was an arrangement she'd initiated the day he arrived back at Dunbar Court with Tom Hooper in tow, and the child. The argument that followed his arrival was fierce and acrimonious, and she almost packed her bags and left that day, but a compromise was reached to avoid a scandal. They would live together as husband and wife in name only. The child would be seen by the world as a result of Tom Hooper's dalliance while abroad on active service. He was a bachelor and as such had no reputation to lose. But from that day Helen denied William access to her bed, and life returned to as near normality as could be reasonably achieved in the circumstances.

Until one night two months ago.

She'd gone to bed early and was reading when the door to her bedroom burst open and William stood in the doorway, swaying slightly. From the bed she could smell the whiskey fumes, but she said nothing, trying to ignore him by concentrating hard on the page of her book. What happened next she couldn't ignore.

Some would have called it rape, if in law a husband could rape his wife. William explained it coldly as a husband exercising his given conjugal rights, and they never spoke of it again.

But now the results of that night were becoming evident, and she knew she could no longer pretend otherwise.

"Get my clothes," she said to Elizabeth. "I can't lie here all day."

"Forgive me for asking, ma'am, but have you seen the doctor?"

"I suppose I should, shouldn't I?" Helen said, pushing herself up into a sitting position. "I'll telephone him and make an appointment."

"And if there's anything I can do, ma'am, anything at all, you will say."

Helen Charteris ran her fingers through her disheveled hair and smiled at her bleakly. "What would I do without you, Elizabeth?"

Elizabeth started slightly. It was the first time since coming to work here that Lady Helen Charteris had ever called her by her Christian name. "Anything at all," she said softly, and went through to the dressing room to get her mistress's clothes for the day.

In the morning room the french doors were open to the garden and the sound of a child's laughter floated in on the mild summer breeze. Helen got up from the table, walked across, and looked out at the garden.

Tom Hooper was there, digging in one of the flower beds.

Her husband was on all fours on the grass, the child, the reason for the gulf in their relationship, perched precariously on his back. "Horsey!" the child cried, digging his feet into William's sides, and holding on to the collar of his shirt. To the left of them a middle-aged woman sat, sewing. Mary was the child's nanny, and her olive skin glowed richly in the morning sun. Of course her name wasn't really Mary. That was given to her just for convenience because nobody could pronounce her real Arabic name. She was another of the intruders William had brought back with him.

Whenever Helen came into contact with Mary the mutual dislike that bristled between them was almost tangible. The woman's hooded eyes flashed dangerously, and her protective manner toward the child became even more evident. Helen had no doubts that if the occasion arose, Mary would sacrifice her own life for that of the boy. And should anyone threaten her charge, then she would react with all the savagery inbred in her.

Helen closed the french doors, shutting out the noise, and went back to reading the newspaper. Later she telephoned the doctor and made an appointment to see him that afternoon.

She had to stop crying. She'd done nothing else since receiving the confirmation from the doctor. The doctor himself thought they were tears of happiness and offered his congratulations and a handkerchief, but there was a terrible hollowness inside her—as if someone had just ripped out her heart.

She tapped on the glass separating herself from the chauffer and gestured for him to pull over to the side of the road. Once the car stopped she opened the door and stepped out into the afternoon sun. They were midway between

Dunbar Court and Dorchester and they'd pulled into an entrance to a farm. In the distance she could see fields of sheep, grazing contentedly. Beyond them a tractor trundled across a field. Above her head gulls swooped and dived, calling to each other, their strident voices filling the air.

She walked up and down a few times, trying to compose herself, ignoring the curious looks she was getting from the chauffer. No doubt he would report back to her husband, telling him of her strange behaviour. Apart from Elizabeth, there was no one in the house she could trust not to go running to William. He paid their wages and demanded absolute loyalty. She wondered now why she married him. Was he so very different before he went away to war? She couldn't believe he was, but since his return to civilian life their relationship had foundered. They no longer conversed as they once did, and when he looked at her now there was no love in his eyes, only a sort of half-hidden contempt.

She had done nothing wrong. She'd sat at home while he was away fighting, eschewing a social life, waiting patiently for him to return, the loving and dutiful wife.

And this was how he repaid her. No reward for the loyalty he set such store by. Not even the common decency to hide the evidence of his philandering. Instead he'd brought the child into their midst, paraded him under her nose like some kind of trophy. She felt sorry for the poor bitch of a mother—God alone knew what happened to her.

Anger was starting to replace self-pity, and the tears were drying on her cheeks. No more tears, she thought. He would never again bring her to such a state of despair. And one day she would have her revenge. One day she would make him pay dearly for planting his unwanted seed within her.

* * *

"I thought you'd better know, I've just got back from the doctor's," she said. William Charteris was sitting at his desk in the study, working on some papers. He didn't even look up to acknowledge her presence. She continued, undaunted. "I'm pregnant."

He shuffled the papers in front of him. "Is it mine?"

She felt the anger pierce her composure like a hot wire, but she suppressed it. "I won't even dignify that remark with an answer," she said calmly. "The child is due in February next year. I will expect the finest medical care. I wish to have the child at home and you will employ a full-time nurse for the last two months of my confinement. And when the baby is born you will hire a nanny to look after it, because I certainly will not. Afterward I will be going away for a while. A cruise possibly, or maybe a tour of Europe."

Finally he looked around at her. The contempt in his eyes had deepened, making them seem like dark and dangerous pools. She almost flinched under his penetrating gaze, but she stood her ground, chin raised defiantly, daring him not to agree to her terms.

"Anything else?" he said.

"I'm sure there will be, but I'll tell you as and when I'm ready."

He nodded slowly and went back to shuffling his papers. "Very well," he said.

"And that's all you're going to say?"

"I think you've said enough for the both of us, don't you? I've agreed to your terms, now go away and leave me to my work."

The anger she'd been holding down finally erupted. Tears filled her eyes and her hands curled themselves into fists. "No," she said. "You'd like that, wouldn't you, for me to pack my bags and just slip away, like some thief in the night? Well, I'm sorry, but I'm not going to give you that satisfaction. I'm still your wife, and it's a role I'm going to play to the hilt. I'm going to drag every last shred of courtesy and consideration from you, and I'm going to make you pay for what you did to me. If you don't want me in your life anymore, then you go. Leave this house and take your precious bastard with you." She stormed from the room, slamming the door behind her, then leaned against it, letting the tears flow once more. Something stirred in her stomach and she threw her hand across her mouth and ran to the bathroom to be sick.

CHAPTER FOUR

Laura stood in the shadow of the house and watched the lorry maneuver the caravan up the winding lane. She couldn't believe that more than three months had gone by since the meeting with Maggie in the coffee shop. It had been a long struggle to get to this point, and without her parents' injection of cash, and Maggie's willingness to compromise her ethics enough to ensure that her offer was the one to be accepted, she would never have made it.

The lorry was struggling around a bend in the lane that led up to the house. She'd watched for thirty minutes while the driver negotiated the narrow tree-lined lane, towing the caravan that would be her home for the next three months while she oversaw the renovation work.

"He's making heavy weather of it, isn't he?" Shaun Egan was standing at her side, watching the lorry's progress. Shaun was her project manager—a master builder who had been with her since her first house. He was a tremendous asset. A superb craftsman who put his heart and soul into every project, and ran the building operation like a military campaign, bringing in carpenters, plumbers, bricklayers, and electricians only when the project required them, and making sure they all worked to his exacting standards. He was also a marvelous interpreter of working drawings, bringing out facets of the architects' work in a way that often surprised the architects themselves. Dublin-born with a mischievous twinkle in his tourmaline-green eyes, and a sharp tongue to unleash on those he thought weren't pulling their weight. Laura had come to rely on him heavily. Losing Brian from the business would be difficult, but not insurmountable. To lose Shaun would have been a disaster. But he'd made it clear when the first threads of acrimony had appeared in her and Brian's relationship that he would stick by her, irrespective of the dissolution of the partnership. And it heartened her to know that Shaun respected her as much as she respected and valued him.

"How's the demolition coming along?" she asked him. It was the first job on the project, getting rid of the crumbling outhouses that Maggie's agency had set such store by.

"I've got Pat and Dean working on it. Should be finished by lunchtime. Then, if you've no objection, we'll burn the timber in the field back there. The bricks we'll save for the time being. They match the bricks of the house, so they might come in handy. Besides, it'll save on the number of skips we need. I figure we'll try and keep traffic to a minimum until we get a few dry days, else that lane will end up as little more than a quagmire, and we'll get nothing up here."

"Good idea," she said. "Now who's that?"

A green Range Rover had appeared at the end of the land and was driving up it slowly. The lorry towing the caravan finally passed through the gateway and drew alongside them; the Range Rover was just behind.

It pulled up a few yards away from them and a young man stepped out, saying a few words to the large and shaggy Irish wolfhound that was occupying the passenger seat. The man was tall, dressed in country tweeds with a bright blue shirt and a knitted tie. On most people the attire would have looked absurd and pretentious, but the young man carried it off with aplomb. His face was lightly tanned and aristocratic, his fair hair swept back from it, shining in the early morning sun.

He approached Laura, hand extended. "Sorry to arrive uninvited," he said as Laura took his hand and shook it. "Richard Charteris. I'm your closest neighbour. Thought I'd better pop over and introduce myself."

"Laura Craig. This is Shaun . . ." But Shaun had moved across to the Range Rover and was peering in through the side window. The dog responded with a bout of ferocious barking and Shaun took a step backward.

"Don't worry about Socrates. He's a noisy bugger but quite harmless. Quiet, Socrates!" Richard called. The dog silenced immediately, his long tail beating a tattoo on the leather upholstery. Richard turned back to Laura. "Sorry about that; he loves making new friends. Not unlike his master. So, what do you think of the old Hooper place? Bit of a wreck at the moment, but not so bad that it can't be put right."

Laura smiled. "That's what I intend," she said.

"I'm sure."

Richard Charteris was handsome and utterly charming, and Laura found herself glancing down at his left hand, checking to see if anyone had already laid claim to him. There was a large gold signet ring on the middle finger of his left hand, but the wedding finger was bare.

"So which is your house?" she said, racking her brain to try to remember the surrounding dwellings.

"Dunbar Court. Just over the rise." He gestured airily away to the east.

"I'm impressed," she said, and immediately regretted the choice of word. She'd passed Dunbar Court a number of times in the months she'd been coming up to look at the house. It was a sprawling Regency-style building with later additions, sweeping landscaped gardens that included a lake, and its own maze. She often looked longingly at the place as she'd driven past, wondering what it must be like to actually live in such a grand setting.

"It's a house," he said. "Much like any other."

"Not in my experience," Laura said. His modesty seemed natural; otherwise she would have instinctively found it annoying.

"Oh, it's big all right, but the upkeep has its own share of drawbacks. I have an apartment in London, and given the choice I'd spend most of my time there. Unfortunately Dunbar Court has a very large estate and my mother finds the running of it rather taxing. So I find myself spending more time here in Dorset than I'd like."

Laura found herself warming to him. His manner was self-deprecating and very attractive. "Would you like a coffee, Mr. Charteris? I'm afraid the kitchen's a disaster area, but the builders have a primus and a jar of instant. Best I can do in the circumstances."

"Sounds wonderful." He had the ability to concentrate fully on what she was saying, but at the same time she gained an impression that he had taken in the whole site with an all-encompassing gaze. "Oh, and please, call me Richard."

For the next thirty minutes, both of them clutching mugs of steaming instant coffee, she took him on a guided tour of the house, explaining her plans for renovation, pointing out the finer period details that she intended to keep and elaborate upon. He was enthusiastic about her plans, and full of admiration for her design conceits. "So you plan to live here while all this work is carried out?"

They'd emerged at the front of the house and Laura had just outlined details of the ornamental carp pond she planned to build here. "Oh yes," she said. "I'm going to live on-site while the work's being done—hence the caravan. That way I can keep an eye on things, and I'm always on call if Shaun—you met him earlier—has any problems with the plans."

"On-site? A strange choice of phrase . . . unless of course you don't intend to live here once the house is renovated."

"I don't," Laura said bluntly. "I specialize in taking old properties and turning them into holiday lets. It's my business," she added proudly.

A cloud passed over Charteris's face, muddying the bright blue eyes, making them look hooded and slightly dangerous.

"You seem to have a problem with the concept,"

she said. She found herself hoping she hadn't alienated him before she had even got to know him.

He shook his head. "Not me. I'm all for free enterprise. But you might encounter problems with some of your other neighbours. They're not all so progressive as Mother and me."

"I'd like to meet her," Laura said. She said it simply as a polite reaction to his words, and was surprised to find she meant it.

"I'm sure she'd like to meet you too. She has a bit of a soft spot for this place. Old Tom Hooper, who lived here, was head gardener at Dunbar Court until his death. My mother and he were as thick as thieves, always planning new improvements to the gardens at the Court. She was delighted when she heard this old place was to be sold. She likes to think of the house being inhabited again . . . as if it will bring back just a little of old Tom. Since his death Mother's interest in gardening has waned somewhat. I think she's lost heart." He paused for a moment, running a hand through his thick blond hair. "Just a thought," he said, "but it's Mother's birthday on Friday and we're having a few friends over for drinks. You'd be very welcome to come."

She walked with him to the Range Rover, not sure she was ready for that kind of socializing just yet.

He sensed her hesitation. "You could bring someone with you. Shaun perhaps?"

She laughed. "I don't think his wife would be impressed if I brought him along. Nor would his three kids. No, you're very kind to invite me . . ."

"I sense a but."

He opened the door of the Range Rover and the wolfhound leaped out past him, knocking him to one side. It made straight for Laura, tail wagging furiously, saliva dripping from jaws that had framed themselves in a canine version of a smile. It bounded up to her and reared up, placing paws as big as fists on her shoulders, a great floppy tongue dragging up her cheek.

"Down, Socrates!" his master shouted, moving forward to grab the dog's collar.

Laura was laughing, ruffling the dog's neck with her fingers. "Well, you're just adorable, aren't you?" she said.

The dog panted at her happily until Charteris grabbed the collar and pulled him away. "Sorry about that," he said to her. "He seems to have taken to you."

"I'm flattered."

"So you'll come on Friday? I assure you Socrates, like his master, does not take no for an answer."

She didn't reply, but crouched down and let the dog lick her again. At that moment, from the back of the house, came a thunderous crash and a scream. "Oh my God! What on earth was that?" She sprang to her feet and raced around the side of the house to be met with a scene of total devastation.

CHAPTER FIVE

The largest of the outbuildings had completely collapsed. Dust rose from a pile of debris almost waist high. Two of the workers were pulling at the timbers and bricks with their bare hands, with an urgency that had Laura fearing the worst. There was an ominous silence over the scene. Laura felt the worm of fear wiggling in her stomach.

"Is anyone hurt?"

"Dean was working in there when it went," one of the men said without looking at her, his whole attention focused on the job of heaving the debris out of the way.

Laura looked around frantically. "Where's Shaun?" she said, but just at that moment Shaun ran from the back of the house and lent his weight to moving rubble. Richard Charteris had thrown off his jacket and was helping the others.

When they'd cleared enough of a space Shaun held up his hand, motioning them to stop. "Quiet," he said. "Listen."

"Get me out of here, will you?" The voice was plaintive and seemed to be coming from a long way away. Over the top of it was the sound of splashing water.

"Dean!" Shaun called. "What's happened? Where are you?"

"Bloody floor gave way," came the reply. "I'm up to my neck in water down here and it's bloody freezing. Jesus, it stinks too. Hurry up and get me out."

As one they moved forward and started hauling the wreckage out of the way, taking care not to send any bricks or timbers down the black hole that had been hidden up until now by a section of tiled roof.

Laura spun round at a sound behind her. Socrates was sitting back on his haunches—teeth bared, growling deep in his throat.

"Get that bloody animal out of it, will you?" Shaun snapped at Richard. "We've got enough to do here without worrying about that great beast taking chunks out of us."

Laura turned to Richard. "Would you mind?"

He called the dog to heel. It obeyed reluctantly. "Is there anything else I can do?"

"We'll manage," Shaun said.

"Well, in that case . . ." Richard made to walk back to the car.

Laura stopped him. "Thanks for your help."

He smiled at her. "No problem. And Friday?" he said.

"I'll ring you, if that's okay?"

He smiled at her, nodded his head slightly, and walked back to where the Range Rover stood, Socrates keeping pace beside him, hackles raised, the growling continuing like a low note on a double bass; focusing on something none of the humans could see or hear.

Shaun found a length of rope from somewhere, tied one end around his waist, and lowered the other end into the hole. Someone else had found a torch and was shining it down into the blackness. Laura looked over the edge and saw McMillan struggling to keep afloat in a pool of inky water, his face white and panic-stricken.

"Hurry," she urged them.

Shaun's mouth was set in a hard, grim line. He called down to McMillan, "Grab the rope and I'll haul you out."

As the rope dangled close to his fingers the terrified workman made a grab for it, missed, and sank beneath the oily water. He resurfaced, spluttering, gasping for air, tried again, missed again, sank again.

Shaun swore savagely and waited for the man to reappear. And waited. After what seemed an age McMillan's head broke the surface. He drew in a deep breath and looked up at the ring of faces staring down at him.

Laura watched the expression on his face turn from panic to terror. "There's something down here," he said, his voice rising to a scream. "It's got my leg!" With a splash of flailing arms he disappeared under the water again.

Shaun untied the rope from around his waist and handed it to another of the men, kicked off his heavy work boots, and with a glance of resignation to Laura, dropped down into the pool.

"Hold that torch still," Laura snapped at the workman who was holding it, then reached across and grabbed it from him. "Here, let me."

She shone it down into the hole but could see neither McMillan nor Shaun and a hollow feeling of dread filled her stomach. A full minute later both men broke the surface, Shaun holding on to McMillan by the collar of his jacket. He reached up and grabbed the rope. "Right, pull!" he shouted.

A moment later both men were lying on the ground at the side of the hole, exhausted and gasping for air, coughing to clear their lungs of the foul, stagnant water.

Laura felt wetness on her cheeks and realized she was crying. She crouched down next to Shaun as he sat up. "Thank you," she said, feeling the words were totally inadequate.

"All in a day's work," he said with a grin. Then the grin turned to a look of concern as he turned to McMillan. Thankfully, the other man was breathing easily. He was still whey-faced and kept glancing back at the hole with an expression of dread.

"We should get him to hospital," Laura said. Shaun nodded in agreement, but McMillan struggled to his feet, his sodden clothes hugging his body, his wet mousy hair flattened to his head. Without a word he stumbled away, reached his van, and opened the door. With a final look back at them he gunned the engine.

Shaun started to run after him. "Dean, don't be a bloody fool! Come back here!" But McMillan let in the clutch, and with wheels spinning on the muddy ground, shot forward, swerved, and headed for the lane. Seconds later all they could see were his brake lights through the trees as he slowed to negotiate a bend in the road.

Shaun stood at the gate, hands on hips, shaking his head. "Idiot," he said as Laura came up beside him.

"I'll go and see him tonight after work—try to calm him down a bit."

"What did he mean? 'There's something down here.' "

Shaun shrugged. "Search me. Mind you, it's pretty disgusting down there. He probably snagged his foot on something. The question now is, what are we going to do about the hole? From what I could see it's brick-built down there, a cellar of sorts. It was too dark to see exactly, but it seems fairly large. What bothers me is that the water may have come from an underground spring. If it has, then there's every possibility the spring extends right under the house, which is not good."

They turned and walked together back to the demolished outhouse. The excitement over, the other men returned to their appointed tasks. Laura picked up the torch and shone it down the hole again. Crouching down on her haunches she could angle the beam to see the walls of the cellar. As Shaun had said they were brick, but covered with a thick coating of black, slimy weed.

"I'll hire a pump and drain the water out," Shaun said. "Then we'll have a better idea what we're dealing with."

She looked round at him. "Hadn't you better dry yourself off first?"

He glanced down at his sodden clothes. His plaid work shirt was ripped and stained, his jeans sticking to his legs like a second skin. "Siobhan's going to kill me when she sees the state of these clothes." He smiled ruefully.

"Tell her I'll buy you a new wardrobe. You deserve

it after today. It was very brave, jumping in after him like that."

He shook his head. "The great lummox wasn't going to get out by himself, and the last thing I want is for this project to be delayed by Health and Safety inquiries. As I said, I'll go and see Dean tonight, to make sure he has nothing stupid in mind, like paying a visit to his solicitor."

"Perhaps I should go with you. Offer him some kind of compensation."

Shaun shrugged. "As you like, but I think it's better I go alone, at least initially."

In a spontaneous move Laura hugged him and planted a kiss on his cheek. "I still think you were brave," she said, and went to inspect the newly installed caravan. It was small, and although her needs were modest she found the interior oddly depressing. It was neat enough, and clean, and certainly uncluttered enough, but the thought of living in it, after the last few years of relative comfort, brought a sadness to her. Still, it was a beginning.

By seven o'clock the site was deserted. Light was beginning to fade from the sky, bathing the area in a murky twilight. Laura sat in the caravan, reading a sheaf of regulations thoughtfully supplied to her by the planning department of the local council. The legal-speak was giving her a headache. She reached across to switch on the reading lamp, but the electric illumination did little to aid comprehension, and nothing at all to ease the dull throbbing behind her eyes. Throwing down the papers in disgust she walked to the door, pulled it open, and filled her lungs with fresh Dorset air.

She stared across at the house, standing silhouetted by the gradually darkening sky, its blank empty windows staring back at her challengingly. She couldn't shake the feeling of unease that had been creeping up on her steadily all afternoon. The accident was unsettling. It was the first serious incident she'd encountered since going into this business. There had been minor accidents in the past—the occasional hammered thumb, an errant saw slicing unsuspecting skin—but nothing of this magnitude. Had it not been for Shaun's quick thinking and his boldness, Dean McMillan might have died. And how would that have sat on her conscience?

She stepped out of the caravan and walked across to the hole. Someone had covered it with a sheet of chipboard and scrawled DANGER in bright red paint. She stared at the sign and bit her lip. Was it a well, or more seriously, as Shaun suspected, the outpouring of an underground spring? Until the hole was pumped out she wouldn't know for sure. Neither would she know just how far beneath the ground the area extended. If it carried on under the house it could be a disaster. There was no room in her budget for underpinning the property, but with dubious foundations she might be left with no choice but to find the money to do it.

With a sigh she trudged back to the caravan. Her mobile phone was ringing. She checked the caller ID.

"Hi, Shaun," she said into the phone.

"I've been to see Dean, but he wouldn't speak to me." His tone suggested an understated fury, even though she knew he hadn't been that hopeful. Dean would still be in the first throes of anger about the accident, and to expect him to listen to reason yet was probably hoping for too much.

"I see," she said glumly. That still didn't bode well.

"I spoke to his wife. She said he came home in a right state—soaking wet and shaking. He took a shower, took two more, then locked himself in their bedroom. She's absolutely furious, and she's baying for your blood. The words negligence and compensation were mentioned more than once."

"Shit!" Laura said, though she wasn't surprised. "Give me his address. I'll go round and see them in the morning."

"Is that wise?" Shaun said cautiously.

"Better than waiting for some hotshot ambulance-chasing lawyer to arrive on my doorstep."

Shaun told her the address and she wrote it down on the cover of the planning regulations.

She switched off the phone and stared at the address, trying to place the street in her mind. Then she picked up the phone again to ring Maggie. If ever she needed cheering up, it was tonight, and Maggie, with her effervescent personality and couldn't-give-a-damn attitude, was just the tonic she needed.

CHAPTER SIX

The phone was picked up on the second ring. "Hiya, stranger," Maggie said. "How's the latest mansion coming along?"

"What kind of bitch-friend are you?" Laura said. "Selling me a shit-heap like this?"

"Going well, then, is it? Do you want to tell Auntie Maggie all about it?"

Laura spent the next ten minutes recounting the events of the day, spurred on by encouraging noises from Maggie. When she finally paused to draw breath Maggie said, "So, you've met the Honourable Richard. Lucky girl."

"Maggie!" Laura said in exasperation. "I could be facing a lawsuit here for negligence, and that's all you can think of to say?"

"You worry too much. You weren't to know the floor was going to give way. You didn't know about the well, or whatever it is. No court in the land would find against. No, meeting Richard Charteris is far more interesting. That was one of the local delights

57

the selling blurb didn't cover when the house went up for sale. Have you met his mother yet, Lady Catherine? Now there's a formidable lady."

Laura realized she wasn't going to get any sense out of Maggie until they discussed it. "Go on then," she said. "Tell me all about them."

"Richard's grandfather was William Charteris— Lord Dunbar, army officer in the Second World War, chairman of several companies, member of the House of Lords. His family can be traced back to William the Conqueror. Fabulously wealthy. Dunbar Court, the family seat, has entertained several members of the Royal family, and Lord Dunbar was supposed to have the ear of a number of prime ministers. Lady Helen Charteris was the typical lady of the manor. The only official child of the family is Catherine and she inherited the lot when her father died, though by all accounts it was touch-and-go for a while whether she would."

"Now I'm really intrigued," Laura said. "What do you mean 'official?' "

Maggie chuckled mischievously. "Catherine was a fifties child and grew up into a sixties rebel. She ran away from home at sixteen and fell in with some dubious characters. She bought into the whole flower power thing—drugs, orgies, the complete rock-and-roll lifestyle. I heard she even went out to India to study with the Maharishi, that charlatan who hoodwinked The Beatles, among others.

"She eventually returned to Dunbar Court, with a baby in tow—Richard—but things carried on much the same as before. She'd hold wild parties, sometimes lasting for days. Meanwhile, Lord Dunbar set about raising Richard as his own—having another crack at parenting after making such a pig's ear of it the first time round. Then another scandal hit the family. I'm not sure of the details, but it concerned a brothel in London that had a pretty exclusive clientele—minor royalty, pop stars of the day, that kind of thing."

"She was running a brothel?" Laura said, aghast. She pulled her legs under her on the sofa.

"I said she was wild, not stupid. The press had been sniffing around the perimeters of the story for a while, getting nowhere, but then Catherine sold her story to one of the Sundays, naming and shaming several VIPs, and at least one high-ranking member of the clergy.

"After that she disappeared completely from the scene. Rumor had it that Lord Dunbar paid for her to go abroad, but nothing was heard from her until the early eighties. Lady Dunbar had died, the lord's health was failing, and Catherine suddenly reappeared on the scene. She quickly established herself as lady of the manor, the dutiful daughter returned from exile to nurse her ailing father."

"You sound skeptical." A picture of Richard driving away in the Range Rover was hovering in her mind.

"Given her track record I'm more than a little cynical. Anyway, the old man finally died and she inherited everything, and she's been there ever since."

"And what about Catherine being the only 'official' child of the family? What did that mean?"

Maggie's laugher echoed down the telephone line, and Laura could imagine her with her feet up on her desk, cigarette in hand and gin and tonic waiting. "Nothing recorded, as if there would be, you know how it is in these landed families. There's talk of a son born outside wedlock, as they would have said in those days, a brother to Catherine. There are probably dozens of the Charteris bastards floating about, born to poor serving wenches. You can ask Richard when you see him!"

"How do you know all this?" Laura said. It was as if Maggie was reading from a history book.

"You probably won't have come across it, unless your solicitor did some digging, but the house you're renovating was once part of the Charteris estate. They, well, sort of bequeathed it to the Hooper family. It's them you bought it from, though indirectly through the Probate. When Brian Tanner was sniffing around I wanted to make doubly sure there were no legalities he could exploit. Our legal people checked to make sure the title was kosher. While they were doing that I checked out the family history. Just being nosy, you know me!"

"Maggie, that's really good of you, thanks. What about Richard? Any dark secrets?" So far Richard had escaped any criticism in Maggie's story, although his family certainly sounded colorful.

"No, I've never spoken to anyone who has a bad thing to say about him. I've met him only once, at a chamber of commerce dinner and dance. We were introduced, and he seemed perfectly charming, but I'd only just opened the agency and my name didn't mean squat then. Different now, of course, but our paths haven't really crossed since, except at the odd networking event."

"He's invited me to drinks at Dunbar Court on Friday," Laura said.

"You lucky cow!"

"I haven't accepted yet."

"But you will?"

"I don't know. I said I'd call him."

"Laura, listen to me. You put this damn phone down straightaway, and you call Richard Charteris and tell him you'll be delighted to come for drinks on Friday. Good God, girl, are you mad? Invitations like this don't fall into your lap every day, and when they do, you grab them with both hands and you don't let go. Richard inherits the lot when Catherine—"

"Maggie! That's enough. I still don't know," Laura said, but found herself warming to the subject and spent the rest of the conversation with Maggie discussing it.

When she switched off the phone she was feeling brighter than she had all day. She could always rely on Maggie to make her see the silver lining on the most thunderously gray clouds. She made herself a coffee, laced liberally with Tia Maria, switched on the CD player, and let the soothing music of *Adiemus* lull her into a state of total relaxation. It had been an awful day. Tomorrow could only be better.

The sound of a heavy motor being started woke her from a deep and dream-free sleep. She looked at the clock on the wall and swore. Nine thirty. She should have been up two hours ago. She crawled out of bed, groaning at the nagging headache that beat a tattoo behind her eyes, and swore for the umpteenth time never to touch liqueur coffee again. She pulled back the curtain.

The site was busy. Scaffolders had arrived and were busy erecting a steel exoskeleton around the house; several of Shaun's team were engaged in tearing down the toilet at the end of the garden, and Shaun himself was laying out a thick rubber pipe that led to a large water pump. The other hose from the pump was already snaking its way down into the recently exposed pit in the ground.

She threw on her jeans, pulled a jumper over her head, and slipped her feet into a pair of Reeboks. She brushed her teeth quickly, ran her hand through her hair, and went out to face the day.

"I've run the hose from the pump down to the drainage ditch at the end of the garden," Shaun told her when she inquired about his progress. "This beast shifts a lot of water very quickly, so hopefully we should have the place drained within a couple of hours."

"I wasn't expecting you to move so quickly on this," she said. She was impressed with his speed.

"Imperative," Shaun said. "We have to find out what exactly is going on down there. We don't want a repeat of yesterday. Luckily I have a mate who had the pump. He brought it round last night."

"I'll leave you to it. No sign of Dean this morning?"

Shaun shook his head. "Haven't heard a word," he said.

"I'll put my face on, and then I'll pay him a visit."

Shaun arched his eyebrow. "You sure?"

"I don't see I have any choice in the matter."

She had no choice, but she was dreading the encounter.

Dean McMillan lived on a council estate on the fringes of Bridport. Most of the houses were now privately owned, as the diversity of double-glazed windows and UPVC doors bore witness. Not so the McMillan house. The front door was still a dull Corporation blue, and the paint on the aluminum windows was yellowing and peeling. A child's tricycle was lying on its side on the scrubby front lawn, and there was a sticker of a German shepherd dog stuck to the front door bearing the legend I LIVE HERE! As a warning to would-be burglars. Though the implication was that it served as a warning to keep anybody and everybody out.

Laura knocked on the door and waited. An ice cream van pulled into the street, its cacophonous chimes playing a murderous rendition of "Greensleeves." The front door burst open and a small boy, no more than eight, rushed past her, clutching a five-pound note in his grubby hand, and ran across to where the ice cream van was waiting.

Laura waited for a few moments more, then stepped inside and called, "Hello."

The hallway was cluttered with children's toys and a bookcase chockablock with cycling magazines and paperback western novels, with the occasional Stephen King and Dean Koontz to add variety.

Laura called out again, and this time the call was answered. A woman's voice called back from somewhere deep in the house. "In the kitchen, come on through."

Laura followed the voice through to the back. She pushed open a door and found herself in an untidy kitchen. A young woman was on her knees in front of an ancient washing machine, mopping up a large puddle of gray soapy water. "Bloody thing's always leaking," she said, then glanced round at Laura, her eyes widening in surprise. "Who the hell are you? I thought you were the health visitor. She always comes on Tuesday morning. Jamie has asthma."

Laura stepped forward and held out her hand. "Laura Craig. Your husband works for me."

The other woman peeled off her rubber gloves with a snap and threw them into the cluttered sink, but ignored Laura's outstretched hand. "Used to work for you," she said. "There's no way he's coming back to that place. Bloody death trap. You should have seen the state of him when he came home yesterday." The woman's badly highlighted hair was piled high on top of her head like a pineapple. A scraggly, greasy fringe hung down past her eyes. She pushed it away from her face with the back of her hand. "I'll be seeing our solicitor about it, that's for sure."

Laura doubted the couple actually had a solicitor, but she let it ride. "Mrs. McMillan, I agree it was an unfortunate accident, but I'm sure we can settle this without involving lawyers. I've already taken advice and there doesn't seem to be much of a claim." The last was just Maggie's opinion, but the woman wasn't to know that. "If I could have a word with Dean I'm sure we can settle the matter here and now."

The woman frowned suspiciously. She reminded Laura of a pig, pale eyelashes framing watery blue eyes. Her body was slipping into pig shape as well, and fat would soon be her natural self if she didn't take care.

"If I could see Dean?"

The frown deepened but eventually she seemed to reach a decision. "All right. He's in the lounge, though whether or not he'll speak to you is another matter. He certainly isn't speaking to me." She pointed through the kitchen door to the small hallway. "That door there."

Laura thanked her and walked through to the hall, glad to be out of the woman's company. She knocked on the lounge door.

"Just go in," Mrs. McMillan called out. "It's not locked," then laughed as if she'd just made the joke of the century.

Dean McMillan was sprawled out on a cheap settee, watching a daytime soap opera on an expensive wide-screen TV. He didn't look away from the set as Laura entered the room.

"Hello, Dean," she said. "How are you feeling now?"

McMillan said nothing but picked up the remote and increased the volume on the set.

There were two other chairs in the room. Neither of them matched the settee or each other; both were crowded with old magazines and on one a pair of muddy football boots. She perched on the arm of the least cluttered chair. "Can we talk?"

"Nothing to talk about," McMillan grunted.

At least it was a start.

"About what happened yesterday. It was a complete accident, you know? There was nothing in the deeds to tell us there was anything under the outbuilding. Nothing at all."

"Perhaps you should have checked harder," he said, his eyes still not leaving the exploits of an emotionally retarded Australian family.

"There was no way we could have known. I'm sure it must have been a shock to you—"

He laughed harshly. "A shock? Plunging into some filthy cesspit? You bet it was a shock. I could have died . . . and when it grabbed my leg . . ." His face paled and she noticed the hand holding the remote control was shaking slightly.

"That's what you said yesterday, but the hole must have been covered up for years. How could there have been anything down there? Perhaps you snagged your foot on something. Perhaps the shock of falling made you imagine something grabbed you."

For the first time he looked at her, and his eyes still carried the expression of dread and terror she'd seen in them yesterday.

"So I imagined it, did I?" He dropped the remote onto the cushion beside him and leaned forward, rolling up the leg of his tracksuit bottoms. "Then how do you explain this?"

Laura leaned forward to look at McMillan's leg and winced. Encircling his ankle was an ugly red weal, the center of it deep crimson, the sides puckered and blistered. "Have you seen a doctor about that? It looks nasty. There could be a chance of infection."

"What did you do, come round to cheer me up?" He laughed bitterly. "I'll tell you what you can do. You can go back to that bloody site and wait for my solicitor's letter. Jen's going into town later. She's made an appointment."

Jen, she supposed, was his wife. "I've just been speaking to her and I'll tell you what I told her. If we involve the law, the only people who'll benefit are the lawyers, and neither of us want or can afford that." She reached into her jacket pocket and brought out her checkbook. "I appreciate that were it not for the accident you would have been working for the duration of the build. I'm willing to pay you the money you would have earned during that time."

"Very generous," McMillan said sourly. "Thanks

but no, thanks. I reckon we can squeeze you till your pips squeak. I could close down that site, you know? Then where will you be?"

Laura took a deep breath. She could feel her hackles rising. Perhaps Shaun was right and it wasn't such a great idea coming here.

McMillan said, "Of course, if there was more money on the table, then I might be inclined to reconsider."

So that was what it came down to. "Had you a figure in mind?"

"A thousand," his wife said from the doorway. Laura had no idea how long she'd been standing there. Laura glanced around at her and saw the cold, calculating look in the woman's eyes. McMillan had gone back to watching the television. "A thousand," his wife repeated. "Plus what he would have earned on the job."

"Mrs. McMillan . . ." Laura began, then shrugged and got to her feet, dropping her checkbook back in her bag. "I'm sorry," she said, "but I don't do blackmail." She turned on her heel and walked past the woman in the doorway, noting with satisfaction the vague look of panic in her eyes. "Call me when you're ready to accept my offer. Oh, and I really would get that leg seen to before it becomes infected. I'll see myself out."

She closed the front door. The McMillans' son was standing in the front garden, licking at an ice cream cornet. He didn't even glance at her as she walked past him to her car.

CHAPTER SEVEN

She arrived back at the site early in the afternoon and sought out Shaun. He was up in one of the bedrooms laying some new floorboards to replace the woodworm ravaged ones that presented a serious safety hazard. Bent over an electric saw, he was cutting a board to size. As Laura entered the room he switched off the machine, bringing an almost preternatural silence to the room. "Well?" he said, breaking the silence. "How did it go?" A light covering of sawdust coated his hair.

She told him quickly, describing in detail what she would like to do to Jennifer McMillan.

He raised his eyebrows at the violence of her language. "I did warn you," he said.

"I know. Why are people so unreasonable?" she said. Her anger was on different levels; the turning up of the volume on the TV as annoying on a human level as the threat of lawsuits was on the business side.

"Human nature, I'm afraid. We're getting as bad as America. Everyone thinks litigation first and compromise second. Still," Shaun added, laying the sawn floorboard on the workbench. "It's not all bad news. I've cleared the water out of the hole."

"Thank heavens for that. So what's down there?"

"Come on. I'll show you."

All the remnants of the shed had been cleared away, leaving a rectangle of concrete, the exact dimensions of the building. To one end of it was a perfectly square hole in the ground. Lined with wooden lintels, the opening was obviously purpose-made. Shaun stood at the edge of the hole. "There was a wooden trapdoor covering it. It must have been rotten and gave way when Dean stepped on it."

"But the whole shed collapsed," Laura said. She could still picture the scene of chaos as the dust overwhelmed everything and everyone.

"I know. I'm still trying to work that one out. Dean was demolishing it, but when I last checked him he hadn't got very far. He obviously did something to bring the whole lot down, but until I speak to him I won't know. It was just lucky for him he fell through the trapdoor when he did, otherwise he would have been crushed when the roof caved in. Look, down there."

Laura followed his pointing finger. Set in the wall was a rusting iron ladder leading down.

Shaun said, "It was covered in weed, but if he'd seen it all he had to do was reach out and he would have found it. He could have climbed out himself and saved me from a soaking."

"He was in a state of panic," Laura said fairly. "He wouldn't have known the ladder was there. I certainly didn't see it when I looked down."

Shaun shrugged his wide shoulders. "Maybe. Anyway, come down and have a look." He climbed down first, beckoning her to follow.

They stood in a brick-lined room about fourteen feet square. Shaun had rigged up two hurricane lamps that lit the place with an orange glow. There was an iron-framed bed standing against the left hand wall, the frame thick with rust and supporting a sodden, rotting mattress. The wooden headboard was swollen and split, veneer peeling from it like sunburnt skin. Against the left-hand wall was a bookcase, the books bloated with water, brown and unwholesome. Thick black weed covered the walls, slimy and sickly looking. The smell was appalling, overpowering—like the smell of a stagnant pond. Laura wrinkled her nose in disgust. But it was the floor of the room that caught her attention. It was flagstoned with puddles of water in the dips and crevices. In the center of it was a circular hole, three feet in diameter. To one side of the hole was a flat square of rusting steel, large enough to cover the hole, and scattered around the steel were a number of heavy concrete blocks.

Shaun had brought a heavy-duty torch with him. He shone it at the hole. "A well," he said.

"How deep is it?" Laura asked, hanging back, not wishing to venture too close to the circular edge.

"I couldn't say. I pumped out as much water as I could, but the hose wasn't long enough to get to the bottom. It must be fed from a spring, and a pretty powerful one at that. It's already filling up again. But this isn't the source of the flood. Like all wells the surface of water must level out naturally at the height of the water table. It's impossible for it to rise any higher than that. So my guess is the room was flooded deliberately."

"But why?" The thought of a carefully constructed area belowground such as this being built, and then filled with water, made no sense to Laura.

He shrugged. "Who knows?" He walked across to it and shone his torch down. Reluctantly she moved forward and stood next to him. She peered down. As Shaun swung the torch she could see the beam reflected on the surface of the water a few feet below.

"Is this good news or bad news?" she said. Her voice was echoing eerily from the walls.

"For you, only good. The spring must be so far down that, even if it runs directly under the house, it wouldn't present any problems."

Laura looked from the wellhead to the bookcase, to the bed. "It looks as if someone spent quite a lot of time down here. Extraordinary. Who would want to sleep down here in this dingy room when there's a perfectly good house above?"

"Search me," Shaun said. "But look at the walls, the bricks."

The black weed stopped three-quarters of the way up the walls. Above it the bricks were clearly visible. She stared at them, but didn't know what she was meant to be seeing, and said so.

"That's because you're not a builder. But I would say those bricks are more than four hundred years old. So this place, this cellar or whatever it is, has been here quite a time, a lot longer than the house. I'd like to check back in the records to find out what stood on this site before the house went up. But I suspect that a much larger, grander place stood here. I figure this would have been the cellar and the house was built over the well to provide the occupants with fresh water. From an archaeological point of view

71

this place is quite a find." He shone the torch at the ceiling. "Concrete—the base of the shed—much later. I suspect the original ceiling was wood. Just as I suspect there are other rooms connected to this one. This could only have been a part of the whole thing."

Laura moved back toward the ladder and the pool of daylight that was pouring down from the opening. She needed to feel the sunlight on her skin again. There was something not quite right about the cellar, but she couldn't identify quite what it was. The damp and cold had seeped through her clothes, chilling her to the bone. She shivered.

"Not very pleasant down here, is it?" Shaun said.

"No, not at all." She reached out and with her finger she prodded the weed clinging to the bricks. It sank in up to the first joint. She withdrew it quickly. "Disgusting," she said. "This is where the smell is coming from. This weed. I've never seen anything quite like it. Come on," she said, moving back to the ladder. "Let's go back to the house and decide what we're going to do about it." She climbed the ladder quickly, drawing in a deep breath of fresh air. She couldn't really explain it to Shaun, but she'd been very uncomfortable down there. The subterranean hole had a grim, oppressive atmosphere—an atmosphere that made her skin crawl. She was relieved to be back aboveground.

Later she telephoned Dunbar Court to confirm she'd be there on Friday. There was nobody but the butler to take her call, but he assured her he'd pass the message on.

She left the site and drove into Dorchester to find something to wear. She wasn't sure whether or not the evening would be formal or casual, but either way her usual attire of jeans and sweatshirt would be unsuitable.

After searching a number of shops she settled for a long crushed velvet skirt and a lacy top, nothing too sheer—she didn't want to create the wrong impression.

She stopped for a cup of coffee at one of the tearooms that proliferated in the high street, found herself a corner table at the back, and took a magazine from her bag. She felt slightly guilty, like a schoolgirl playing truant, but she was sure work wouldn't grind to a halt in her absence.

She was lost in an article about handmade kitchens when she became aware she was no longer alone at the table.

"I thought it was you," Brian Tanner said. "Hair's a lot shorter, but it suits you," he added with a smirk.

She looked at him coldly. "I don't remember asking you to join me," she said.

He feigned a look of hurt bewilderment. "Surely we can at least be civil to each other," he said.

"Why?" She was remembering the violence of their last meeting. If she lived to be a hundred, she wouldn't forget that night. Now, looking at him sitting across the table from her, she felt revulsion and loathing for him. And something else. Fear.

"Look, Brian, you got what you wanted. You got your pound of flesh, and more besides. Why don't you just go away and pester someone else?"

He ignored her. "Congratulations on your new purchase," he said. "Though I must admit I didn't think you'd get it."

"Well, it was no thanks to you, was it?"

"Must have stretched you. Going to the full price like that." He smiled. "I instructed my solicitor to clear you out. How on earth did you raise enough capital to beat my offer?"

She returned his smile with a bitter one of her own. "That's none of your damned business." She swallowed the last of her coffee. "You'll have to excuse me," she said, dropping the magazine into her bag. "I've got more important things to do."

"So soon? That's a pity. I was enjoying our chat." He stood up. "Shame about that accident," he said quietly. "Something like that could finish you off. Dean McMillan, wasn't it? Crippled for life, I'd heard, and with a wife and sick child to look after. Criminal."

She glared at him. Where did he get that piece of information? "Well, you heard wrong," she said.

He grabbed her arm. "Look, Laura, I hate all this unpleasantness between us. Come to dinner with me. There's a lovely restaurant in Weymouth. Scallops, mussels to die for . . . and oysters. You always loved oysters," he added with a hint of lasciviousness.

"Get your hand off my arm," she said evenly, even though her heart was racing. Surely he wouldn't try anything here. Not in public.

He let his hand fall away and made an apologetic shrug. "Come on," he said. "Let's put everything behind us. Start again, on the right foot this time. Come out to dinner."

"I'd rather stick needles in my eyes than share a meal with you. In fact I don't even want to share the same air as you," she said. "Now excuse me. I have to go." She spun on her heel and headed for the door. She was determined not to look back at him, but at the door she glanced back over her shoulder. He was standing there, a smug smile playing on his lips, as though he had been waiting for her look. As she reached for the handle of the door she saw her hand was shaking. Was she never going to be free of him? She walked out into the bustling street and hurried back to her car.

CHAPTER EIGHT

Shaun refilled the oil in the hurricane lamps and put a match to the wicks, watching them flicker into life again before replacing the glass covers. The orange and blue flames spluttered and hissed, reflecting from the wet weed on the cellar walls and spreading a dim glow over the ancient and rusting bed.

"How do you want to handle this?" Pat said. Pat Donnelly had been with Shaun for nearly five years and was, in effect, second in command; an efficient and industrious worker whom Shaun entrusted with all but the finer details of the build.

Shaun pointed to the bed. "You grab one end and I'll take the other. We'll drag it over and then get a rope on it and haul it out."

Pat regarded the bed. "Is it heavy?"

"Won't know till we try to move it."

"Glad I kept my gloves on. What is that slimy stuff?"

Shaun shrugged. "Who knows? Come on, grab an end."

Pat grumbled darkly but went across to the head of the bed and took a firm grip on it. He wasn't happy being down here. He'd seen the look of terror on Dean McMillan's face when they'd dragged him out of here yesterday, and whatever it was that had scared the man so severely, he certainly wanted no part of it. It was cold and dank down here, and smelled atrociously. The slimy weed that covered the walls, and much of the bed, looked unwholesome and felt unpleasant to the touch. He wanted to get this job done as quickly as possible and then get out, back up into daylight and the fresh air. Shaun didn't seem bothered by the place, but Pat had profound misgivings.

"On three, and watch you don't fall down the well, "cause I'm not coming down to get you," Shaun said, taking hold of the other end of the bed. "One, two, three!"

They lifted together, raising the bed a foot from the floor. Pat struggled with the weight. It seemed remarkably heavy for such a small bed and, even though it had an iron frame, the weight of it seemed out of proportion to its size—almost as if the legs were rooted to the floor. Sweat popped out in small beads on his forehead, and his fingers hurt with the effort. He felt weak, as if the oppressive atmosphere of the cellar was draining his strength.

"Come on," Shaun said sharply. "Move it!"

Pat took a step to the side, then slipped on the wet floor. He threw out an arm to balance himself, letting go of the bed. It crashed back to the floor and Shaun swore, releasing his end, but not before the weight of the bed had nearly wrenched his arms from their sockets and strained his back. On its descent the bed skidded against the wall, peeling off a large swathe of weed.

"Sorry," Pat said. "Lost my footing. Can't we just slide it across the floor?"

Shaun had his hands pressed into the small of his back and was cursing and stretching, trying to relieve the ache that nagged at the base of his spine. "Might be best," he said at last, and grabbed the bed again. Then he stopped and stared hard at the wall. Where the weed had been stripped away the wall beneath was revealed. Block work. Where the rest of the room was constructed in ancient, russet brick, this area was dark gray concrete. He said nothing about it to Pat, but started to slide the bed across the slippery floor.

With the help of several others they secured a rope around the bed and hauled it up into the daylight.

"Can I get back to work now?" Pat said, clearly relieved to be out of the hole.

Shaun nodded, but his mind was distracted. He went back to the house, found his tool kit, and a few minutes later, clutching a wallpaper scraper, descended the ladder once more to the cellar. Using the area stripped by the bed as a starting point, he maneuvered the scraper under a fresh area of weed and started peeling it away.

The Bell Public House stood on the high street in the market town of Bridport. Late afternoon and the bars were all but empty. A couple of diehard drinkers were standing at the dartboard enjoying a competitive game, but the bar staff looked bored as they dried glasses and prepared the pub for the bustling evening trade. One of the bar staff was Jenny McMillan. Dressed in regulation white blouse and black slacks, hair washed and tied back, makeup artfully applied, she looked a far cry from the harassed housewife Laura had encountered earlier that day. But a smile was missing from her face and had been for the past two days.

Her thoughts were occupied by her husband's accident and the way he'd virtually retreated into himself, snapping at Jamie, and almost completely ignoring her. And the constant scratching of his injured leg was driving her mad and keeping her awake at night.

The visit by Laura Craig only added to her irritation, planting as it did, seeds of doubt about the compensation claim they intended to make against her. Jenny was thinking now they should have accepted the woman's offer, paltry though it was. It might have been better than nothing at all.

No reason to smile then. But that was about to change.

Brian Tanner sat at a small circular table in the corner of the pub, nursing a pint of bitter, smoking a cigarette, and watching Jenny McMillan as she polished glasses. He'd been in the pub the evening before when Jenny had given vent to her feelings, telling anyone who'd listen about Dean's accident and how she was going to make Laura Craig pay dearly. He'd said nothing then, despite an almost overwhelming curiosity to find out more about his ex-partner. Coming back today in daylight, when the pub wasn't heaving with customers, would make it easier to engage the woman in conversation and satisfy that curiosity. He finished his beer and took the empty glass up to the bar.

"Pint of Bass," he said to Jenny, who looked at him bleakly and took the glass to fill it from one of the three pumps in front of her. She poured the pint expertly in two long pulls and set it down in front of Tanner, took his money, and handed him the change.

"Jenny, isn't it?"

Jenny regarded him suspiciously, taking in the expensive leather jacket and stylishly cut tawny hair. "Who wants to know?" She'd been born and bred in a tough area in the East End of London, only coming to live in Dorset when she met and married her husband. Country life didn't suit her and rubbed against her prejudices. Despite the common belief of the rough-and-tumble camaraderie of London life, the complete opposite prevailed, at least in the area of Walthamstow that was her home for twenty-three years. She still hadn't got used to the Dorset way of saying good morning to complete strangers on the street, and of engaging in conversation with people you didn't actually know.

"Brian Tanner," he said.

"Tanner," she said, backing away from the bar slightly. "You used to be that bitch Laura Craig's partner. Did she send you here to try to get me to change my mind?"

Tanner smiled. "No, she didn't send me. And you're right, she is a bitch; an absolute bitch with no feelings for anyone other than herself. That's why I broke up the partnership. I couldn't carry on working with someone as self-centered and as unpleasant as her. I came to see you, Jenny, because I overheard what you were saying last night about your husband's accident."

"So?"

"So, I might be able to help. Is there somewhere we can talk?"

"I'm working," she said, the aggression still there in her voice, but tempered slightly by vague hope.

Tanner shrugged. "Shame," he said. "I know Laura Craig very well. She always tends to get what she wants and doesn't mind who she walks over to get it. I thought we could put our heads together; work out a plan to see that she doesn't get away with this. Criminal negligence, I would call it. Wouldn't you?"

She placed the glass she was polishing on the shelf above her and checked the clock on the wall. "I'm finished here in ten minutes," she said. "You can buy me a coffee if you like. Then we can talk."

He smiled. "I've just got time to drink my beer then," he said and went back to his table, tracing with his fingernail the warm wet ring left by his glass.

Back at the site the scaffolders had finished and gone and the roofer was already at work replacing damaged slates. One of the workmen was filling a cement mixer with sand. "Where's Shaun?" Laura said.

"Down the hole," the man said without breaking rhythm. She walked across to the hole in the ground, and then detoured as she noticed something in the garden.

She walked slowly around the four island beds, looking at the plants carefully. Everything was wilting. Leaves had turned brown and were falling from the roses and other shrubs. Even the evergreens, the camellias, and the laurels were showing signs of distress, their foliage shriveled and sickly looking. Autumn was approaching, but it was still a month before the leaves on the trees would start to fall. The entire garden looked as if it had been sprayed with a particularly virulent weed killer.

She scratched her head in puzzlement and went back go speak to Shaun. She hesitated at the ladder. She had no real desire to go down into that dank, inhospitable cellar again. "Shaun," she called. "Are you down there?"

His face appeared out of the gloom at the bottom. "Glad you're back," he said. "Come down, I've something to show you."

She grimaced, but steeled herself and let herself down slowly into the hole.

"Over here, look."

She followed him across the gloomy room to the far wall. The bed was gone, as was the bookcase, she noticed, and Shaun had cleared a patch of brickwork, a mound of slimy weed in a wet pile at his feet. Was it her imagination or was the weed on the walls thicker than it had been earlier? She shook off the impression as just fancy and looked closely at what Shaun was showing her.

"If I hadn't cleared the weed away I wouldn't have found it," he said. He was pointing to a large rectangular patch of concrete blocks, starkly outlined by the surrounding brick. "It's a doorway, see? I'd be interested to see what's behind it."

She was suddenly and irrationally irritated. Why was he spending time down here when he should be aboveground supervising the building work? He knew she was working to a tight schedule, one she couldn't afford to go over if she wanted to realize enough capital to pay her parents back the money they'd lent her.

"Aren't you interested to know what's behind here? My bet is another room like this one. Maybe more than one. Like I said before, this can only be part of the original cellar."

"Quite frankly, Shaun, I think your time would be better spent getting on with the job in hand, rather than wasting it on this."

Her annoyance was unmistakable and uncharacteristic. He raised his eyebrows. "You're not in the slightest bit curious?"

"No," she snapped, then caught herself. It was unfair to take out on Shaun the anger that should be directed at Brian Tanner. She sighed. "I'm sorry, Shaun. I've had a bit of a day. First McMillan and his wife trying to blackmail me. Then I bumped into bloody Brian in a tea shop in Dorchester. He knows about the accident! We must have a mole—someone feeding him information."

Shaun swept a callused hand through his long and untidy black hair. "Tell me what he said."

Laura recounted the conversation in the tea shop. "You see what I mean? Someone's feeding him this information."

He nodded his head slowly. "So it would seem. But not one of my boys. They've all been with me quite a time now, and we've all worked together on your houses. None of them cared much for Tanner and we were all relieved when you split up the partnership. Most of us thought he was a complete arsehole."

"Seconded," Laura said with a grin. "But he's getting the information from somewhere."

"Then it's probably from Jenny McMillan. She was on her way to work when I went round there last night. She works as a barmaid at the Bell in Bridport.

It's very possible she told some of the regulars about the accident. Has a loose tongue, does Jenny, and she wouldn't think twice about trying to stir the shit if she thought she could do you some damage. She's always had a problem with you. I think your success highlights the failure to get on in her own life. People like that can be quite poisonous."

"But I don't even know the woman; I only met her for the first time today. Okay, she didn't welcome me with open arms, but consider the circumstances. Would she really be that vindictive?"

Shaun nodded. "Oh yes. You don't know Jenny; she wouldn't think twice about it. I'll never understand why Dean married her, but I suppose it takes all sorts. Wouldn't do if we were all the same."

"Then that's probably the answer." She sighed again. "People! Why can't they just let me get on with my life?"

"Jealousy, envy, call it what you will. Nothing stirs up the bile quite as much as another's success."

She looked at him frankly. "Where would I be without you and your Irish wisdom?"

"Standing in a hole, up to your neck in water," he said with a smile.

She prodded the pile of stinking weed with the toe of her trainer. "How has this stuff got so thick, especially down here in the dark?"

"I was thinking that myself, but having spent the last hour scraping it off the wall, I'm not sure it's a weed. I think it's a type of fungus. If you look you can see it's spread into the bricks themselves. It's something like dry rot, but I've never come across anything like it before."

"It's pretty disgusting."

"It is that." He paused, waiting for her to say something else. Finally he broke the silence. "So are you going to let me satisfy my Celtic curiosity and have this wall down?" He tapped the concrete blocks with the handle of the scraper he'd been using to attack the weed.

She knew when she was beaten. "Oh, I suppose so . . . but just make sure no other jobs suffer. If I can't settle with McMillan and it goes to court it's going to cost me whether I win or lose. I really need to finish this place as soon as possible."

"I'll tackle it when I've got a moment," he said.

CHAPTER NINE

Shaun arrived home thirty minutes later to find his house in darkness. Normally this would be his children's bath-time, and Siobhan would be getting them ready for bed. He parked his van on the drive of their suburban semi and let himself in the front door. There was a soft glow coming from the dining room at the back of the house and a delicious smell of garlic-cooked mushrooms filling the hallway, but the kitchen door was closed.

The table in the dining room was set for a candlelit dinner for two, a bottle of Chianti standing in the center, uncorked to let it breathe. He opened the kitchen door and put his head round. Siobhan stood at the cooker dressed in a sexy low-cut black dress, her fiery red hair swept up elegantly, revealing her creamy swan's neck. She glanced around at him, her brown eyes twinkling in the overhead halogen lights. "Just in time," she said, smiling.

She was wearing makeup, something she never did during the day, and looked stunning; as beautiful as the first day they'd met in a Dublin bar. He scratched his head in puzzlement. "Have I missed something?" he said. "Birthday, anniversary? Where're the kids?"

"Mum's got them for the night," she said and tossed the mushrooms in the pan. "And yes, it's our anniversary."

His confusion deepened. "But we married in June."

"Not that anniversary. But it's ten years today that we first . . . well, you know?"

Enlightenment dawned. He went across and slipped his arms around her waist, drawing her into him and kissing her neck. "Trust a woman to keep a note of something like that," he said.

"Go and have a shower. We've got steak, sauté potatoes, mushrooms, and baby corn. Ring any bells?"

He laughed. "The Paradiso. That was our meal that night. I remember it well." The Paradiso was the first restaurant to which he'd taken her. They'd eaten well that night, and drunk far too much. After the meal they'd gone back to the flat in Aungier Street Siobhan shared with two other nurses from the hospital where she worked, and made love with a passion that remained undimmed, even after ten years. "I'll go and get cleaned up," he said, kissed her again, and went upstairs to the bathroom.

Later they lay in each other's arms, stomachs full, passion spent. "As good as the first time?" Shaun said.

Siobhan giggled and nestled closer. "Better," she said. "Sex is one thing that definitely improves with age."

"Like a good wine."

"Or Stilton."

"Stilton?"

"Shut up, it's the only other thing I can think of."

He laughed and pulled her tighter. He couldn't remember the last time it had been just the two of them. The demands of three young children meant that for years their private life was compromised. Tonight was a rare treat and the fact she'd organized it only deepened his love for her. "Would you like a coffee?" he said.

"Sounds wonderful."

He disentangled himself from her and swung his feet to the floor, sitting on the edge of the bed and reaching for his T-shirt. She reached up and touched his shoulder. "What's this?" she said, her fingers tracing the outline of a black patch the size of a penny on the smooth tanned skin at the top of his arm. "I thought you'd showered."

He glanced down. "Must have missed a bit." He stood up and went across to the dressing table mirror, twisting his body in the light to get a better view of the mark. He frowned, running his finger lightly over his skin. The black patch was slightly raised from the surrounding skin and felt vaguely slimy. He grabbed a tissue from a box on the dressing table and rubbed at the mark. "Can't seem to shift it," he said.

"Here, let me do it." Siobhan rose from the bed and came across to him. He watched her nakedness in the mirror and felt his passion stir again. She took the tissue from him and started to rub the mark.

"Ouch!" he said. "Not so hard."

"Ah, my big, brave man. Don't be such a baby."

He watched her work, a frown of concentration creasing her pretty face. "It's coming," she said. "Bloody obstinate though. What on earth is it?"

Absently he stroked the alabaster skin of her thigh, sending a shiver through her body. She slapped his hand. "Let me concentrate," she said. "There. Gone."

He twisted and looked again. Where the patch had been the skin was inflamed and, when he touched it with his finger, sore. He made coffee, made love again to his wife, and went to sleep.

In the morning he showered, dressed, kissed Siobhan good-bye, and set off for work. The black patch on his skin was all but forgotten—just a slight irritation on his shoulder but nothing to give him pause for thought. As he drove through the sleepy Dorset streets he wasn't even aware that underneath the thick plaid of his work shirt the patch had returned, slightly larger this time and growing imperceptibly with each mile he drove.

Shaun spent much of the morning shoring up the ceiling of the cellar with carefully positioned steel jacks. He'd learned from Dean McMillan's experience about the risks of demolition from the inside, and had no wish to be buried under several tons of reinforced concrete. He worked alone, all of his team to a man reluctant to join him, but that suited him. He preferred to work alone down here. There was something about the dark room he found strangely peaceful.

He took his lunch with the others in the house and when he'd finished walked around checking progress. Blown plaster had been stripped from two of the bedrooms, revealing the bricks beneath. The damp spot in the sitting room was being attended to; the cause of it, a broken and blocked downpipe that ferried water from the gutter above, had been renewed.

The roofers were making short work of replacing the slates, and outside footings were being dug for the new building that would house the state-of-the-art generator to provide the house with electricity.

Over the next few weeks fresh plaster would be applied to the walls, the carpenters would be brought in to repair the interior woodwork, and new double-glazed windows would be fitted. The next major development would be the arrival and installing of a new septic tank to handle sewage.

As he carried his mug of tea back to the cellar he was satisfied that the build was on schedule. They'd achieved a lot already in a very short space of time, and he was pleased for Laura. He wanted this to be a success almost as much as she did. He admired her enormously and would do everything in his power to see that the building work went smoothly and that the finished house lived up to her expectations.

He was about to descend the iron ladder when a lorry swung into the lane. On its flatbed trailer was the new bathroom suite, heavily wrapped in cardboard and polythene. Shaun frowned. The suite wasn't due to arrive on-site for another week. Pulling the delivery schedule from the pocket of his work shirt, he went across to have words with the driver. The cellar would have to wait, at least for the time being.

Laura spent the morning trawling around kitchen showrooms and secondhand furniture warehouses, checking prices and making orders. It was the part of the refurbishments she most enjoyed, and the sheer pleasure of it drove all thoughts of Brian Tanner and the McMillans from her mind.

At one warehouse in Blandford she found a superb

antique pine bed for the master bedroom and a Welsh dresser that would give the kitchen the country cottage look she wanted. In Poole she visited a kitchen manufacturer who specialized in working with reclaimed pine, building units that looked traditional but had all the benefits of modern technology.

With orders placed and deposits paid she drove down to Bournemouth to visit her parents to bring them up to date with what was happening.

They sat in the kitchen eating smoked salmon and cream cheese bagels. As they ate Laura told them about the accident at the site. They took the news calmly. George Craig started to make suggestions as to how she should handle it, but Barbara Craig glared at him as he interrupted. "I'm sure it won't present too much of a problem," she said to Laura. "You must be insured for such an eventuality. Employer's liability?"

Laura flushed and stared at the floor. "Actually . . ." she began.

Her father sighed loudly. "Not very prudent, kitten." He glanced at his wife. "If you don't mind me saying so."

Laura shook her head. "No, you're absolutely right. I really meant to get round to it, but it's been such a whirlwind since I exchanged contracts it completely slipped my mind."

Barbara Craig cut a slice from a rich Dundee cake, put it on a plate, and slid it across to her daughter. "You're not worrying about our investment, are you? Because if you are, don't. As I told you before, it's only money. I think the important thing here is that nobody was seriously hurt. And, if nothing else, you've learned an important lesson. More tea?"

After lunch her father took her upstairs to look at the new layout he'd designed for the railway. "It's based on a section of the old Great Western," he said proudly.

"Did you make all this yourself?" she said, genuinely impressed.

"Of course. Mind you, a lot of it comes in kit form. Next year I intend to start making the rolling stock as well. A friend of mine has a small machine shop in Boscombe and he's told me I'm welcome to use it at weekends. Don't tell your mother though. I haven't mentioned it."

"I won't say a word," Laura said and patted his arm reassuringly.

"You're really worried about this claim, aren't you?" he said, changing tack abruptly.

"Yes," she said. "I am. It could wipe out everything I've worked so hard for. I mean, Brian Tanner tried his best to destroy me and I've bounced back. It would be ironic if I fail because of my own stupidity."

He wrapped a comforting arm around her shoulder. "You won't fail. You can't. You're a Craig. Have I ever told you how proud I am of you? Even more so now you've ditched that deadweight of a partner of yours."

She watched the trains make convoluted circuits of the track, her father handling the controls deftly, a look of sheer delight in his eyes.

"Have you ever heard of the Charteris family? They own a massive house out my way—Dunbar Court."

"William Charteris, Lord Dunbar? Yes, I've heard

of the family. Met him a couple of times back in the seventies. Strange sort of chap, I thought, but then I find a lot of people strange."

"In what way was he strange?"

Her father was negotiating a train over a set of points. He shrugged. "Nothing I could really put my finger on. Just a feeling really. He loved that grandson of his though. Absolutely doted on him. I hear there was some kind of scandal concerning the boy's mother, but I was never that interested to probe too deeply. Why the interest?"

"I'm having dinner there tomorrow night."

"Dinner? Where?" Barbara Craig entered the cramped attic room clutching two steaming mugs of tea.

"Dunbar Court," Laura said. "Richard Charteris invited me. Maggie persuaded me."

"You still see Maggie?" George said delightedly. "Always had a bit of a soft spot for that one. If only she'd give up the cigarettes."

Barbara Craig wasn't smiling. In fact she was frowning deeply. "Mind how you go," she said. "There's bad blood in that family."

"Mother!" Laura said, faintly outraged. "That's a terrible thing to say."

"It's true though. I could tell you stories . . . Lady Dunbar, that poor woman. I served on several committees with her. Her husband led her a dog's life. A whole string of mistresses. And that daughter of hers . . . well, I've heard talk."

"Yes," Laura said. "So have I. And it appears it was true. I'll watch my step."

CHAPTER TEN

Late on Friday afternoon the site had another visitor. The man was smartly dressed in a pin-striped business suit and highly polished black slip-on shoes. He picked his way cautiously across the site to the hole in the ground and stood at the edge making notes in fountain pen on the clipboard he carried. He was there for ten minutes before anybody challenged him.

Laura came out of the caravan, saw the man, and experienced an uncomfortable sinking feeling in her stomach. "Can I help you?" she called when she'd halved the distance between the stranger and the caravan.

The man turned. He had a sharp, ratty face with narrow black eyes and a thin mouth that he twisted into the semblance of a smile. "Ms. Craig?"

"Yes," Laura said, noticing the powdering of dandruff on the shoulders of the man's otherwise immaculate suit.

"Simon Lawson," he said. He reached into his inside jacket pocket and handed her his business card.

"And how can I help you Mr. . . ." She glanced at the card. "Mr. Lawson?"

"My company is investigating a claim made against you by a Mr. Dean McMillan," he said charmingly. "I take it this is the site of the incident?"

Their conversation was drawing attention from a number of the workmen who'd stopped what they were doing and were listening intently.

"We'll discuss this inside," Laura said and led him back to the caravan. "And it was an *accident*, not an incident."

Half an hour later the man emerged and headed back to his car, picking his way across the site as fastidiously as before. Laura sat alone in the caravan, seething quietly. The amount of compensation the claims company was demanding was so excessive it had taken her breath away. She knew companies like this existed—people who specialized in finding other people with grievances and then fighting their claim for them for a hefty commission—but it was her first experience of them. And it wasn't an experience to savor.

There was a tap at the door and Shaun stuck his head inside. "So how much do they want?"

She told him and he gave a low whistle.

"It's ridiculous. I certainly can't afford to meet a claim like that."

Shaun scratched his shoulder and said, "So what are you going to do about it?"

Laura shook her head. "I really don't know," she said. "What I do know is that I'm going out to dinner tonight and I need to start getting ready. I'll think about Mr. Lawson and his claim in the morning. Tonight I'm going out to enjoy myself."

Shaun smiled sympathetically and scratched at his shoulder again. "Good for you," he said and made to leave.

"Shaun, are you feeling all right?"

He paused and lowered his eyes. "Yeah, fine. Why?"

"Nothing. It's probably just me. I thought you looked a little off-color, that's all."

"I would have thought you've got enough on your plate without worrying about me. I'm fine, honestly." He smiled again, unconvincingly this time, and closed the door. Outside the caravan he scratched at his shoulder savagely. Over the last two days the black patch had doubled in size and was almost too painful to clean off. He'd managed to keep it hidden from Siobhan by scrubbing it off in the shower and then wearing a T-shirt in bed in case it grew back in the night, but he knew he should tell her, show her; knew also he should go to the doctor and show him, but there was a sick feeling of dread gnawing away in the pit of his stomach.

The patch was no longer smooth, but was now growing thin fibers that looked like hair but were slimy to the touch. He knew without doubt that the black patch was the same weed or fungus that was growing on the walls of the cellar. Somehow, when he'd been scraping it from the walls, some of it must have got inside his clothes and taken root on his skin. He'd try again tonight to clean it off, perhaps use something stronger than plain water—surgical spirit perhaps—and if it came back tomorrow, then he'd go and see his doctor.

He took a step forward and swayed dizzily. And that was another thing. He was starting to feel dreadfully weak. Laura was right; he was beginning to look ill. But he didn't want to add to her problems right now. This job was too important to him. He had responsibilities—a mortgage and bills to pay, hungry mouths to feed. He simply couldn't afford to be ill. He steadied himself and went across to check how the plasterer was progressing on the landing.

Laura checked her reflection in the mirror. The new clothes she'd bought looked good, and she'd gelled her hair into a sleek cap. The effect was sophisticated but with a bohemian edge. Satisfied with her appearance she locked the caravan and went to her car. She should have found the time to take it to the car wash. Mud from the site was splattered up either side, but she couldn't worry about that now. It would be dark by the time she reached Dunbar Court, so no one would notice. She drove out into the lane, turned right, and headed toward Dorchester.

Had she turned left she would have passed a dark blue BMW parked in a gateway a hundred yards from the house. Brian Tanner sat at the wheel, a pair of binoculars in his lap. From the gateway he had a clear view through the trees of the site. He'd been watching the comings and goings there for two days now, seeing how the dilapidated building was being stripped down to its bare bones in order for it to be recreated as a desirable residence. He couldn't quell the sense of loss he felt. Once it would have been him and Laura working together, sharing the excitement, the problems. Now she was on her own and he resented it bitterly.

Earlier he'd seen Simon Lawson arrive for the meeting with Laura. Simon was an old school friend and was the first person he thought of once he'd spoken to Jenny McMillan. Simon, of course, was delighted by Brian's phone call and agreed to take on the case at once, promising Brian a percentage of the commission. But it wasn't the money that interested Brian Tanner. What drove him now was a need to damage Laura Craig. To hurt and humiliate her, the way she'd hurt and humiliated him. He'd been her partner, for God's sake! They'd started the business together, shared the ups and downs, and the profits. Was it his fault he'd fallen in love with her? Any man in his position would have felt the same. Working day in, day out with a beautiful woman with whom you shared so much in common, falling in love with her was inevitable. And she'd responded, letting him share her bed, giving him access to her wonderful body, giving him every impression she felt the same about him as he felt for her.

He had no idea where Laura was going this evening, nor how long she would be away from the house, but this was the first time in two days the site would be completely deserted, and being opportunistic in nature he took a torch from the glove compartment, got out of the car, and walked down the lane to the house.

Daylight was starting to leach from the sky. He switched on the torch and shone it over the site. The first thing the beam illuminated was the garden, now a brown and dying wilderness. Even the grass had succumbed, reduced to little more than pale yellow scrub. He swung the beam and lit the crazy-paved path that led up to the house. He followed it and checked the door. Of course it was locked. He would have been surprised had it not been. But the windows were a different matter. Most of them had been removed in preparation for the installation of the double-glazed units that were stacked along one wall. The gaps were filled with heavy-duty polythene.

He took his penknife from his pocket and slit one of the polythene sheets, peeled it back, and climbed up onto the sill. From there it was only a two-foot drop down to the floor of the sitting room.

He moved the torch, taking in the bare brick walls and the stripped pine doors. He was impressed. The room was bigger than the outside of the house led him to expect, and the renovation work was progressing quickly. He knew what an excellent site manager Shaun Egan was. He'd never taken to the man, and was sure the feeling was mutual, but he couldn't fault his expertise.

He moved through the house slowly, taking each room in turn, climbing the stairs and having a good look round up there too. There were three bedrooms, all of a reasonable size, and another room that looked as if it was going to be a bathroom judging from the free-standing rolled-topped bath—still in its wrappings—that was occupying much of the space. He approved of the specification, but then Laura prided herself on always fitting the best.

He wasn't actually sure what he expected to achieve by coming here. Satisfying his curiosity, certainly, but there was also a need to see how Laura was coping. He was mildly irritated that she seemed to be coping very well without him. Except for the accident the other day everything seemed to be progressing smoothly.

Thinking of the accident reminded him that he wanted to see for himself the hole Dean McMillan had so conveniently fallen into. That really was satisfying. Simon Lawson was a terrier when it came to claims like this; worrying away at them until he got a result. He'd seen the man's home, a large Georgian house in the Cotswolds, paid for by the commissions from his successful cases. If anyone could throw a spanner in Laura Craig's well-organized works it was Lawson.

He climbed back out the way he'd come and swung the torch beam around until he found what he was looking for. He shone it down at the DANGER sign and smiled to himself. He slid the sign out of the way and shone his torch down into the gloom, but could see nothing of any interest. The light from the torch was reflected back at him from several puddles of water on the floor, and as he raised the beam he saw the fungus-lined walls.

There was an evil smell emanating from the hole. He remembered smelling something like it before when he'd found a moldering lettuce in the bottom of the fridge. The lettuce had turned to a blackish slime and stank—a smell very much like this. He wrinkled his nose and drew back, pushing the signboard back across the opening. He was about to turn and head back to his car when a noise stopped him. It was a soft, whispery sound like paper being torn into tiny pieces. He cocked his head to listen and the sound came again.

It was coming from below him, from the hole. For a moment he was going to ignore it; then curiosity got the better of him and he slid the board back again, switching on the torch and shining it down.

There was nothing to see, but then he hadn't expected anything else. He swung the beam around the walls again, and was about to switch off the torch when it slipped from his grasp and tumbled into the blackness below.

He swore. He couldn't leave it there. It would show that someone had been nosing about, and he didn't really want to put Laura on her guard just yet. He liked to think he would be able to come back here from time to time, to check things over and, if circumstances dictated, indulge in a little sabotage.

With a sigh he put his foot on the first rung of the ladder and climbed down into the cellar.

The rungs were slippery with the black fungus and halfway down his foot slipped and he fell the rest of the way, his ankle twisting as he landed.

He winced with pain and reached out, trying to find the torch. His fingers closed around the cold metal cylinder and he fumbled with the switch. A pale light spilled from the torch, much weaker than it was before, but strong enough for him to get an impression of his surroundings. The floor was wet, the walls slimy, and the place stank. He listened for the sound of approaching footsteps, but all he could hear was the soft whispering sound he'd heard when he was standing at the edge of the hole.

The sound was down here with him. He swung the torch in an arc. He noticed the circular wellhead and limped across to it, shining the torch down the hole, but there was nothing to see.

The sound seemed to be increasing in volume, more urgent now, hissing and rustling. He aimed the torch at the wall and at last saw where the sound was coming from. The black, fungal growth covering the walls was alive with movement, the fine, hairlike filaments waving and rippling, as if caught in a breeze. But there was no breeze. The air was still and fetid, but the growth continued to move, giving the impression that the entire wall was breathing.

He hobbled back to the ladder, not wishing to spend another second down here. He gripped the ladder with both hands and started to haul himself up. He put his foot on the bottom rung and pushed, almost crying out as a lance of white-hot pain roared up his leg from his injured ankle. Quickly he changed to his good foot, supporting his weight with his hands. He reached up to grab another rung and something cold and damp wrapped itself tightly around his waist and he was pulled bodily from the ladder.

He fell to the floor, the impact forcing the air from his lungs, the torch flying from his grip. It bounced once, then rolled across the floor, dropping over the edge of the well and down into the blackness.

He was struggling to get his breath, his hands reaching down and clawing at the thing gripping him around the middle. His fingers found something wet and slimly, almost rubbery to the touch, and it was squeezing tighter and tighter, making it hard to breathe.

And then it started to pull him across the floor toward the well.

He was gasping for breath, trying to draw air into his lungs. He wanted to cry out, to scream, but all he could manage was a strangled moan. A second later something wrapped itself around his neck. He scrabbled with his fingers but couldn't get a purchase on the wet, fleshy band that was slowly closing his windpipe. Lights were flashing in front of his eyes, blue and silver, like swirling illuminated dust motes, and the precious air he had sucked in was now threatening to burst his lungs as it sought a passage out of his body.

He was aware of the rough flagstones scraping the skin from his hands as he tried to halt the inexorable journey toward the well, and he flapped and twisted, trying to break free. Slowly the lights in front of his eyes popped out, one by one as his body used up its oxygen, and he sank into unconsciousness.

Slowly and methodically, without ceremony, he was dragged down into the well.

CHAPTER ELEVEN

As Laura drove up the sweeping gravel drive to Dunbar Court she could see the house was alive with light. Through the line of poplars that edged the drive she glimpsed row after row of parked cars. She gave a low whistle. If this was Richard's idea of a few friends, she'd hate to see what he called a full-scale party.

Secretly she was delighted. She'd found the thought of a small, exclusive cocktail party intimidating. This was going to be much easier than she'd imagined. Her skin was covered in a light coating of goose bumps, partly from the cooling night air, but also from excitement. After all the problems of the recent year, and the past few days, she was ready for some unadulterated enjoyment.

It took a while to find a parking space, finally squeezing her Peugeot into a tiny gap between a Bentley and a Jaguar. At the door she was greeted by a middle-aged man in butler's livery who took her coat and deposited it in the cloakroom. Laura stood in the huge hallway waiting for the butler to return, admiring the paintings on the wall and the small sculptures set in small recesses along its length. From the depths of the house a dog barked, and a second later Socrates was bounding down the stairs toward her. She sank to a crouch and spread her arms out toward the approaching dog.

The butler rushed forward to intercept the dog as Socrates reached her in a flurry of wagging tail and sweeping tongue. "Don't worry. Socrates and I are old friends, aren't we, boy?" she said, grabbing the dog's ruff and tickling him behind the ears. The dog panted happily, allowing Laura to pet him.

The butler ignored her and called the dog to heel. "I apologize," he said formally. "Someone must have left a door open." Gripping Socrates firmly by the collar, he half led, half dragged the dog to an adjacent room and shut him inside, then returned to Laura. "This way, miss," he said stiffly.

He led her toward the doorway of a huge room heaving with partygoers. Smiling unctuously he ushered her inside. A few people glanced at her as she entered, but her presence didn't seem to generate much interest. The great and the good, she thought. In the room she spotted several politicians, a couple of actors, and half a dozen other faces she recognized vaguely but had no idea who they were.

A few waiters in white shirts and black waistcoats circulated, bearing silver trays of drinks, and at a long table at the end of the room was a buffet of well-laid-out and colorful food. To the left of the buffet, on a raised dais, a jazz quartet was playing its way through an eclectic mixture of Brubeck, Gershwin, and Biederbecke.

Laura helped herself to a glass of champagne from a passing waiter and peered through the crowd, hoping to catch sight of Richard, or anyone else she knew. She eased her way through the throng toward the buffet. She hadn't eaten since lunchtime and hunger pangs were beginning to gnaw at her stomach. Halfway across the room she saw Richard. He was standing in the far corner engaged in conversation with a man she recognized as a local councillor. Hanging on the wall above his head was an oil painting, a portrait of Richard, standing with Dunbar Court in the background, at his side a dog—not Socrates, but a black Labrador. As Laura stared across at him Richard glanced round and smiled at her. A minute later he'd disengaged himself from the councillor and was crossing the floor toward her.

"Laura," he said as he reached her. "So glad you could come." He leaned forward and planted a kiss on her cheek. It was if he were greeting an old friend rather than someone he had only just met. The breeding always shows through, Laura thought to herself, determined to keep her feet on the ground and not be overly impressed by her surroundings or her host.

"I was admiring the portrait," Laura said. "The artist captured your likeness very well."

Richard looked puzzled for a moment, and then glanced behind him. "That's not me. That's my grandfather. I must admit, though, there *is* a family resemblance."

Laura stared hard at the portrait. "The likeness is remarkable."

Richard grimaced, as though it was not a compliment. "It's been said before. So, how's the house coming along?"

"Slowly, but it's getting there."

"No more accidents, I hope."

Laura shook her head. She didn't want to think about things like that tonight. "I hadn't expected so many people," she said, changing the subject smoothly.

"Mother's friends," Richard said. "I must admit the size of the guest list surprised me. Speaking of Mother, I'll have to introduce you." He took Laura by the arm and led her through the partygoers to the corner of the room where Lady Catherine Charteris was holding court.

Laura wasn't sure now what she'd been expecting, but she wasn't prepared for the reality. Elegantly dressed in charcoal-gray slacks and a crisp white shirt, secured at the neck by a sapphire and diamond platinum clip, Lady Catherine Charteris was a stunningly beautiful woman. She looked barely a handful of years older than her son. Her skin was lightly tanned and flawless. A few faint laughter lines radiated out from her hazel eyes, and there was just a hint of silver in the blond hair tied neatly back in a ponytail. The hand that brought the ivory cigarette holder to her beautifully formed mouth was slim, adorned by a simple diamond solitaire ring.

"Mother," Richard said, butting into the conversation the woman was having with an elderly dowager. "I'd like you to meet Laura Craig. Remember I told you about her? Laura's renovating the old Hooper place."

Laura stuck out her hand. "Lady Catherine," she said.

The older woman looked her up and down, then smiled and took her hand. "Oh, Catherine, please. I haven't got a lot of time for titles. Delighted to meet you, Laura," the woman said in a voice as thick as honey. "Richard tells me you plan to let the old Tom's house to holidaymakers. Is that true?"

"That's the idea," Laura said, trying to gauge whether the woman approved of the plan or not, but Catherine's face was inscrutable.

"Richard, Laura's glass is almost empty. Fetch her another, would you?"

Laura started to protest, but Catherine stopped her. "Richard doesn't mind."

Richard smiled. "No problem."

Once they were alone—the dowager having moved on to a fresh conversation—Catherine said, "I'm so pleased something's happening with the old house again. Richard might have told you but Tom Hooper was the head gardener here at Dunbar Court, and I was very fond of him. I was devastated when he died, and every time I drive past his house I'm reminded of him. Watching it stand empty for so long has been very hard. I must come along to see how things are progressing. How about tomorrow? Or do your builders work at weekends?"

Laura was slightly taken aback. Catherine was nothing if not direct. "No," she said. "I mean, no, they don't work at weekends, and yes, please come."

Richard returned with the drinks and handed one to Laura.

"I've just invited myself over to see how Laura's renovation work is progressing," Catherine said.

"Have you indeed?" Richard said with a wry smile. "Why am I not surprised?"

"I spent so much of my childhood with Tom Hooper," Catherine said. "He seemed like an old man even then, but what he didn't know about plants and gardening wasn't worth knowing. He certainly taught me everything I know. It's a shame it's a bit too dark now to appreciate the borders, otherwise you could see for yourself just what he achieved.

"Daddy and Tom Hooper were in the army together. Tom was my father's batman, and when Daddy was decommissioned, just after the war, Tom left the service too and they traveled back to England together. Daddy had just inherited Dunbar Court from his father and the place had deteriorated a little. My father was determined to restore the place to its former glory, especially the gardens, which were quite renowned in Victorian times. He wanted to reward Tom for his loyalty during the countless campaigns together but wasn't sure which position to offer him. I think he had it in mind to give Tom the job of estate manager, but once Tom saw the garden he was besotted and persuaded my father that the position of head gardener would be better suited to his talents.

"Then, of course, the estate was much larger. In fact my father owned the house and grounds you're restoring. I think the Charteris family chapel once stood on the site where the house is now, but I couldn't swear to it. Anyway, he installed Tom there as tenant. But by the early fifties he was so impressed with what he'd achieved that he made a gift of the house to him, getting his lawyers to draw up fresh deeds, annexing off the land and putting it in Tom Hooper's name."

The woman's flow was interrupted by the butler, who bowed slightly before whispering in her ear.

"Thank you, Payne," she said to him, then turned to Laura. "You'll have to excuse me but a friend's calling from America to wish me happy birthday. I'd better go and speak to him or I'll never hear the last of it. Don't go without seeing me first and we'll discuss a time for tomorrow."

She swept away from them, stopping now and then to exchange pleasantries with the assembled guests.

"Sorry about that," Richard said, frowning. "I can't believe she's got the cheek to just invite herself. I'm afraid she's never been one to stand on ceremony."

"I don't mind," Laura said. "Weekends alone on-site can be incredibly boring. Having a visitor will make a pleasant change. And it will be great to give her a guided tour and show her what I intend to do with the place."

The band launched into a jazzy rendition of "Autumn Leaves." "This is going to sound awfully trite, but would you care to dance?" Richard said.

Laura looked around the crowded room. "Is there space enough for that?"

Richard smiled. "Not in here, but there's the terrace." He gestured across to the open french doors. "And it's a lovely night. Seems a pity to waste it. Before we know it winter will be here and we'll all be huddled up in our greatcoats."

Laura smiled back at him. "Put that way it would be churlish to refuse."

The dance finished and Laura moved across to the balustrade. Parts of the garden were floodlit. The lake, the maze. "You're so lucky," she said to him. "Living in a place like this. It looks beautiful."

He stared out at the rolling expanse of lawn to the high-clipped yew hedges of the maze. "I suppose I am," he said. "Sometimes you have to distance yourself from it to really appreciate it. It helps seeing it through another's eyes. Come on." He took her arm. "Let's walk."

"Won't your guests miss you? I feel I'm monopolizing your time."

"They're Mother's guests, not mine. And I hate making small talk. Some of these people are so boring."

He led her down the stone steps to the garden. She felt a small thrill as his fingers closed around hers. "I'm glad you came tonight," he said as they walked the gravel path to the lake.

"So am I," she said.

They stopped at the edge of the lake. The effect of the lights bouncing off the surface of the water was nothing short of breathtaking. She remembered a holiday with her parents to St. Wolfgang in Austria where they'd spent an evening watching virile young men parasailing across the black water of the Wolf-gangsee accompanied by soft piano music drifting out from speakers set around the lake. To her ten-year-old mind the effect was nothing short of magical. The effect here was similar. There were no brightly colored parachutes gliding through the air, but the combination of lights, water, and the distant echo of music from the party transported her back to that time in Austria. She smiled at the memory. Happy, innocent times, secure in her parents' love.

Richard stood beside her, still holding on to her hand, silent, reliving his own set of memories.

"What was it like, growing up in a place like this?" she said, breaking the easy silence that had settled between them.

"Lonely," he said wistfully. "Being an only child was hard enough. Being an only child in a place like this was desperately lonely. Occasionally my grandfather would ferry in some of the local children to play with me, but I never made friends with any of them. Our backgrounds were so different. We had nothing in common. I was at a private school in Dorchester, and they were mostly from the local comprehensive. I think they thought I was stuck-up, so they took advantage of my grandfather's hospitality, boating on the lake, playing hide-and-seek in the maze, but I was never really included in their games."

"That's so sad," she said. "What about your mother? Couldn't she—"

"Mother was rarely here," he said bitterly, cutting across her words. "And if she had been it really wouldn't have made any difference. It didn't really matter. I got used to being on my own. I'd read a lot; adventure stuff mostly. The books gave me an escape, at least in my own mind." He stared out at the lake, a faraway look in his eyes. Then he seemed to shake himself and smiled. "But that was a long time ago. Ancient history. Come on. I'll show you the maze."

The path leading to the maze swept past three island beds filled with perennials, a kaleidoscope of color, pink roses jostling for space with towering spikes of hollyhocks, purple and white lupins underplanted with clouds of lilac geraniums.

"What was yours like?" Richard said when they'd covered half the distance to the maze.

"My childhood?" She thought for a moment. "Safe, secure, and very happy."

They reached the entrance to the maze and stopped.

The yew hedges were taller than both of them and precision clipped; solid walls of deep, dark green.

He took her in his arms and kissed her; a brief, tender kiss, their lips continuing the dance begun on the terrace.

She broke away, staring deep into his eyes. He was smiling slightly, the corner of his mouth upturned slightly.

"Did you used to play in the maze when you were a child?" she said, leaving the kiss unacknowledged.

"All the time."

"When was the last time you went in there?"

He looked at her, puzzled, not sure where the conversation was leading. "Ages ago. Not for years."

"So you wouldn't be able to find your way around it?"

"Unlikely after all this time."

She spun away from him. "Race you to the middle then," she said and ran into the maze. He called after her, but she had already taken two turns and had no intention of stopping.

She'd learned about the configuration of mazes many years ago from her father. He'd taught her that if you walked with your left hand always touching a hedge, you could find your way around them easily. He once tried to explain the geometry of maze making, but those details had sailed straight over her head. The rule was lodged very firmly in her thoughts and as she ran she let her left hand brush over the greenery, taking her deeper and deeper into the warren.

In the deep shadows of the trees that bordered the edge of the garden at Dunbar Court a figure watched them as they walked from the lake to the maze. It had found its way to the Court by instinct, walking through the wood that separated it from the Hooper house, driven by the need to return home. As it reached the perimeter of the grounds, a hundred memories burst into its mind. This was all so familiar, so much a part of its short human life. The overriding emotion was one of loss and sadness. How much time had elapsed since it was confined to that dark wet coffin? What had happened to its human father, to Tom Hooper, to Catherine? And then the couple walked into a pool of light by the maze, and the other mind sharing this body roared to the forefront, swamping all thought as it recognized Laura Craig.

Its own thoughts were buried under wave after wave of pain and jealousy, as Brian Tanner reasserted control over his body. The couple kissed and pain and jealousy transformed themselves into a cold black rage. Tanner moved forward, closing the distance between the trees and the maze in seconds, following the couple into the labyrinth of tall yew hedges.

It took Laura very little time to realize that her father's theory about the geometry of mazes did not apply to this one. She found herself in a dead end, with no option but to retrace her steps. Another turn, another dead end, and the first hint of misgiving started to insinuate its way into her mind.

The floodlights above the maze illuminated the paths clearly, but she might as well have been walking in the dark as all the paths looked identical. She walked a few more yards and stopped, straining to hear how close Richard was to her. Away to the left she could hear a solid footfall coupled with a rustle of greenery as he brushed along one of the hedges. A second later similar sounds came from the right.

Confused, she started walking again and soon found herself at the end of another long corridor of yews. She started to run, eager now to be out of the maze and to be reunited with Richard. To the right of her she heard the sound of someone running, keeping pace with her, separated from her by the high hedge.

"Laura! Where are you?" Richard's voice, coming from way over to the left.

Then who was it keeping pace with her? Who was to her right?

At the end of the corridor she was forced to turn left, and then sharp right. The runner stopped, and she imagined she could hear his breath, panting, ragged. She turned again. Another corridor, but this time she caught a glimpse of a figure turning at the end. Richard? No, not Richard. Richard was dressed in an evening suit, and she caught the glimpse of denims and a sneakered foot.

She spun around and ran back the way she'd come, something close to panic surging through her. It was so difficult to decide which way to run; so hard to determine where the sounds were coming from. It was obvious she and Richard weren't alone. There was someone else in the maze with them. Someone who seemed determined to catch up with her.

She reached a fork in the path but couldn't decide which way to go.

Right or left? *Think!* And then Richard called again.

"Laura!"

Right. She turned and ran, faster this time.

Another corner and she found herself in the center of the maze. It was a small square area with a fountain in the middle and wooden benches set against each hedge, a resting point for those who, like her, were lost.

She stood, straining to hear, but the maze was silent. Eventually she reached a decision. "Richard? Help! I'm lost."

He called back, nearer this time. "Where are you?"

"I've reached the middle, but I can't find my way out."

"Stay there. I'll come and fetch you."

And from the opposite direction came the sound of running again, of someone crashing through the hedges, drawn by her voice.

She couldn't stay here. She had to get as far away from the center as possible. She started to run again, trying to place in her mind from which direction Richard's voice had come. She turned, turned again, and arms closed around her, holding her tightly, forcing the breath from her lungs.

"I told you to stay where you were," Richard said. "I would have found you."

She put a finger to his lips. "Shh. Listen," she said.

"Listen to what?"

"Shh!"

The maze was silent.

"Are you all right?" Richard said.

She strained her ears to catch any sound, but there was nothing, only the sound of their breathing.

"You spooked yourself," Richard said with a smile, stroking her hair.

"Guess I did," she said after a moment. "I could

116

have sworn . . . No, it's nothing. Get me out of here," she said, taking his hand.

"That might be more difficult that it sounds," he said. "It's been a long time."

"I hope you're joking," she said.

He smiled and led her back through the maze.

Minutes later they reached the exit and walked back to the house. Laura caught herself glancing behind her, but there was nothing to see. No one dogging her footsteps now.

They reached the terrace. "Wait here," Richard said. "I'll go and get you a drink. You look as if you could do with one."

"Thanks," she said and leaned against the baluster.

CHAPTER TWELVE

Waiting for Richard to come back, she felt a hundred different emotions. She almost wished she'd brought her phone along with her—she couldn't wait to ring Maggie to tell her about the evening. She was enjoying herself more than she had in months, and in Richard she'd found the perfect man with whom to share such a wonderful evening. In fact he'd spent so much time with her that people were beginning to notice and she was starting to feel slightly self-conscious.

Her luck with men was notoriously bad. Brian Tanner being just the latest in a string of poor judgment calls and, as far as she was concerned, the nadir. It affected her so badly that she'd gone out of her way to avoid relationships since the bitterness exploded between them.

With Richard Charteris she felt relaxed and entirely natural. He was warm, funny, very good looking, and she was beginning to feel her defenses slipping a little. Live a little, she said to herself. You deserve it.

It was getting late and the balmy Indian summer evening had developed a chill. She shivered slightly and turned to go back inside and meet Richard when a slight movement on the terrace distracted her.

Standing no more than six feet away, partially hidden by a large bamboo plant, was Brian Tanner. She felt a weight drop heavily in her stomach. Her impulse was to turn and run, but then realized that Tanner hadn't noticed her. He stood, staring into the house through the french doors. Silent, unmoving, unblinking. He was disheveled, his clothes grubby, his hair windswept, and there was a faraway look in his eyes, as if he was lost in some private world.

She moved slightly, anxious to be inside, and he turned at look at her. She met his gaze but there was no spark of recognition in his eyes. He simply stared through her, as if she didn't exist.

"Brian?" she said. And the sound of laughter from inside the house made her turn. Richard was sharing a joke with one of the guests. He glanced at her, frowned, and came out onto the terrace, holding two glasses of champagne. "Is everything all right? You're as white as a sheet."

Laura opened her mouth to speak, looked back at the bamboo plant, but Brian Tanner had gone. She looked to the garden, but there was no sign of him.

"Laura?" Richard said.

She shook herself. "Sorry," she said. "Miles away."

He noticed the goose bumps on her arms. "But you're freezing." He took off his jacket and wrapped it around her shoulders. "Come back inside," he said, taking her arm gently and leading her back to the party.

"I was worried about you out there," he said a little later. "You looked like you'd seen a ghost."

They were sitting together on a low, leather couch. The party was drawing to an end and many of the guests had already left, only the die-hard party animals remaining. Catherine was over on the other side of the room, surrounded by a group of men who hung on her every word, laughing a little too loudly at her jokes.

"Your mother's very popular," Laura said.

"I wasn't talking about Mother. I was asking you if everything was all right."

Laura sipped her drink, her brow furrowed in a frown as she decided whether or not to mention the incident on the terrace. At last she said, "Do you know Brian Tanner?"

Richard shook his head. "Not that I'm aware."

"Would Catherine know him?"

"It's not a name I've ever heard her mention. Why?"

She bit her lip. "Brian was my business partner up until a few months ago. The partnership was dissolved. It wasn't pleasant—in fact it got downright nasty."

"I see . . . in fact I don't see. What has this got to do with anything?"

"He was here earlier," Laura said. "Out there on the terrace. I just wondered if he'd been invited to the party."

"Then the answer's no. I checked through the guest list myself. I would remember if his name was there. Why didn't you tell me sooner?"

Laura shrugged. "I guess I was so shocked seeing him there. And by the time you came out he'd gone."

She checked her watch. "I really should be going myself," she said.

Richard looked disappointed. "Look, I'm sorry if anything has happened here to upset you, but I can assure you, this Tanner chap wasn't invited to the party. He must have gate-crashed. Must you leave so soon?"

Across on the dais the band had finished playing and was putting the instruments back into their cases. "The party's almost over," Laura said. "And it *is* late. I'd really better be making a move."

Richard looked troubled. "I'm sorry the evening has finished on such a sour note. Let me have a word with Security. I can find out how this Tanner got in."

"Security? I didn't notice anybody."

Richard smiled. "No, you wouldn't have. They're very discreet. Some of the waiters, a couple of the *guests*. I'm afraid it's necessary when you gather a handful of influential people together under one roof these days. There are so many cranks around you simply can't take chances. We've installed state-of-the-art surveillance cameras all over the place and everything is monitored in a room upstairs."

"I had no idea," Laura said.

"Well, that's as it should be." He stood and held out his hand to her. "Come on, I'll get your coat."

As she reached up to take his hand an idea struck her. "There are cameras everywhere?"

"Pretty much."

"Even out there on the terrace?"

"Very much so. All the entry points to the house are well covered."

"And I suppose everything is videotaped."

"Of course. Look, I don't mean to be rude, but where are these questions leading?" Then he smiled as realization dawned. "Come with me," he said and, taking her hand, led her from the room and up the stairs.

The surveillance room was situated at the end of a long landing on the first floor. Richard ushered her inside. A uniformed guard looked up at her curiously as she entered, saw Richard, and relaxed. The badge on his chest carried the logo for RAYMOND SECURITY. Underneath it a name: MAX. Fixed to the wall above a plain pine desk were four television screens, each showing a different view of the house. The pictures changed at random as the cameras switched from one to another.

"Sorry to trouble you, Max," Richard said. "But would it be possible for us to see some footage taken earlier this evening?"

The guard, a portly man in his late fifties with thinning hair and ruddy skin, nodded slowly. "Which area?"

"The terrace. About two hours ago."

The guard pushed his office chair away from the desk and wheeled himself across to a cupboard set into the wall. He opened the door to reveal a bank of video recorders, LEDs flashing, and timers counting off the passing minutes. He pressed a few buttons, waited for a few moments, pressed a few more, and then glanced back over his shoulder. "Monitor three," he said.

Laura and Richard watched as the screen changed from a picture of the drive to a crisp recording of earlier that evening.

Laura watched herself dancing with Richard, noticing how close he held her, how his hand stroked her back with intimate tenderness. She felt herself blushing as she saw herself move in closer to his embrace and rest her head on his shoulder. "It's further on," she said. "Can you fast-forward about thirty minutes?"

The guard looked round at the screen and pressed another button. A few seconds later the picture had changed and Laura was now standing alone on the terrace. They watched as she stared out across the garden. Minutes passed.

"Where is he?" Laura said. She could plainly see the bamboo plant, but so far there was no sign of Brian Tanner.

Richard's attention was riveted to the screen. "There," he said, pointing to the image. "What's that?"

It appeared to be a shadow moving across the lawn, but the image was fuzzy, out of focus. The shadow approached the house and slid through the stone balusters of the terrace. The bamboo plant rustled violently, as if caught in a strong breeze, but there was still nothing to show what was moving it.

Laura watched herself turn. "But he was *there*," she said. "Standing just behind the bamboo."

"Well, there's something there, look," Richard said.

All three of them stared hard at the plant, but the image was infuriatingly blurred.

"Can't you get a better resolution?" Richard said to the guard.

"There's nothing wrong with the definition," Max said to him. "Look at your friend. She's perfectly in focus."

"But I don't understand," Laura said. "I could see him as plainly as I can see you two."

They looked closer. There was a definite darkness just behind the bamboo—a deep shadow that seemed to swallow the light around it. The videotape ran on. Richard emerged from the house, said something to Laura, and took off his jacket, slipping it around her shoulders.

"It's gone," Max said. "The shadow's gone."

"Run it back and play it again. This time don't watch me. Watch the plant."

Max rewound the tape and pressed PLAY.

This time as Richard emerged from the house they watched the shadow. It seemed to expand and quiver slightly, and then it slid back through the balusters and back across the garden.

"Strange," Richard said.

Laura was trembling. "But he *was* there," she said in little more than a whisper. "I didn't imagine it."

Richard put his arm around her shoulder and pulled her close. "I don't think for one moment you did," he said soothingly.

She pulled away from him sharply. "Don't patronise me!" she snapped.

"Laura, I—"

She shook her head to silence him. "I don't want to hear rational explanations. I don't want to know about faults with the camera, glitches on the tape. Brian Tanner was standing there, just a few yards away from me. I could have stepped forward and touched him."

"What did he say to you?" Richard said. "He must have spoken, once he realized it was you standing there."

Laura bit her lip pensively. She was very close to tears and kept blinking to keep them at bay. "Nothing," she said quietly. "He didn't say anything—even when he was staring straight at me. It was as if he didn't recognize me."

"Can I switch back to the drive now?" Max said.

"Yes, switch back," Richard said. "There's nothing to be learned by watching it through again."

With a half-choked sob Laura ran from the room. Richard stared at Max, who raised his eyebrows and pursed his lips in a low whistle, but said nothing.

Richard caught up with her at the top of the stairs. "Listen to me," he said, taking her arm and turning her to face him. Laura kept her eyes downcast. She couldn't bear to let him see her cry. "I can't come up with a rational explanation for what we just saw . . . or didn't see, and I'm not going to try."

"You probably think I've had too much champagne."

"I think nothing of the sort. In fact I think you're pretty wonderful, and I would really like to see you again."

"What, and spend another evening chasing ghosts?"

He pulled her toward him, kissing her hair. "This will all seem better in the morning."

She laughed harshly. "I doubt that."

"It will. You'll see. What are you doing tomorrow night?"

"Nothing, why?"

"I'm going back to London. I've got to check the mail at the flat and deal with a few business matters. Come with me. I'll take you to dinner. Maison Novelli in Clerkenwell. Beautiful food, wonderful atmosphere. It will help you unwind."

"I'm seeing your mother tomorrow morning."

"Then we'll travel up in the afternoon. We can be at my flat by four. What do you say?"

She hesitated, desperately wanting to say yes. But it was too soon . . . much, much too soon.

"Look," he said. "Just give it some thought. Sleep on it and give me your answer tomorrow."

She smiled and nodded her head slightly. "Okay."

"Talking of sleep. I really don't think you should be driving home tonight. A few of the guests are staying over. I'll check with Payne, but I'm sure we can find you a bed for the night. Tomorrow you can take Mother to the house, let her nose around, then bring her back here and we can drive up to London."

She didn't know quite what to say. "Do you always move this fast?" she managed after a few moments.

"As a rule, no, I don't. But, and it may be the champagne talking, I'm willing to throw caution to the wind." He grinned at her. "Sometimes I even surprise myself."

She thought about the drive back to the site and another night spent in the draughty caravan. "Thank you," she said. "I accept . . . but just the offer of a bed for the night. As for London, I'll decide that when I'm more sober."

"Deal," he said. "Now, let's go and find Payne."

The room the butler found for her was on the second floor. It was relatively small compared to some of the other bedrooms in the house, but the bed was comfortable and there was an en suite shower room. She'd seen Catherine briefly before coming up and the older woman was delighted she was staying.

"What fun," she said, kissing Laura briefly on the cheek and wishing her good night.

Now, in the silence of the bedroom, she wondered whether or not she'd made the right decision. The evening had been unsettling in more ways than one. She had been really frightened in the maze. Then the incident with Brian on the terrace bothered and puzzled her. But almost sweeping that to one side in her mind was the awareness of the growing relationship with Richard. She found it hard to believe things had progressed so quickly in just an evening.

She liked him, yes, but the prospect of going away with him to London was unnerving. Would he expect her to sleep with him? Did she expect herself to sleep with him? She remembered the video, watching the black-and-white image of the two of them dancing. The body language was obvious. There was a definite mutual attraction there. And that realization scared the life out of her.

She showered quickly, washing the gel from her hair and rubbing it dry with a towel. Then, wrapping a bath towel around her, she walked across to the window, switching off the light as she passed, and lifted the curtain to peer out.

She had a view of the drive. A car was making a three-point turn and another was heading down toward the main gate—the last of the guests departing. She heard Catherine call a farewell, the honey voice slurring the words slightly, and then the sound of the front door closing.

Somewhere out there, she thought, was Brian Tanner. Perhaps sitting in his car, out of sight of the house, perhaps standing in the shadows of the trees that bordered the perimeter of the grounds. But he was there. She was certain of it.

But what the hell did he want? And why hadn't he said anything to her? She'd find the time tomorrow and call him.

She let the curtain fall and crossed to the bed, slipping beneath the sheets. Her head touched the pillow and within minutes she was asleep.

Richard paused outside her door and pressed his ear to the wood. He heard nothing. Shaking his head thoughtfully he turned away and went down to the next floor. "You can call it a night, Max," he said as he entered the surveillance room.

The guard was eating a cheese roll, his feet up on the desk. "If you're sure."

"The last of the guests have gone and Payne's going around switching off lights and locking doors. I don't think there'll be any problems tonight."

Max swung his feet to the floor, stared at the roll in his hand, took one last mouthful, and dropped the remainder in the bin. "I'll turn in then," he said. He picked up the paperback novel he'd been reading during his breaks. He noticed Richard hadn't moved. He was hovering at the door like an errant schoolboy waiting for an audience with the headmaster. "Was there anything else?" Max said.

Richard rubbed his chin as if considering something. "The tape," he said. "The one we viewed earlier. Do you have it to hand?"

"Sure." The guard reached into the cupboard, pressed EJECT on one of the players, and handed him the cassette.

Richard slipped it into the pocket of his dinner jacket. "Thanks," he said and left the room.

The drawing room was empty. Even his mother had exhausted herself and gone to bed. He slid the cassette into the video recorder, poured a large scotch, picked up the remote control, and settled himself down in a high, wing-backed armchair in front of the television.

Dunbar Court—December 22, 1953

The guests had been arriving since late afternoon. Dunbar Court was bedecked in decorations, loops and swags of glittering festive chains hanging from the ceilings, holly and ivy filling large jardinières placed at intervals along the long walls of the hall. In the corner of the dining room was a Christmas tree, heavily decorated and reaching up to within inches of the ceiling.

Christmas parties at Dunbar Court were a highlight of the Dorset social season. This year was slightly different in as much as the guest list was grander than usual. As well as celebrities from the world of film and sport, several of William Charteris's fellow lords from the second House had been invited along with their wives.

Cocktails were served in the drawing room, and Charteris, the attentive and ebullient host, was circulating, stopping every now and again to exchange pleasantries and to see that his guests' needs were being attended to.

Helen seemed to be playing the part of hostess with good

grace, which surprised him as they'd had a string of blaz-ing rows about the party over the past few days.

A number of children had been invited to give the place a true festive spirit—Christmas was, after all, for children—and the guests who had been asked to bring their offspring along seemed grateful that for once they could go to a social gathering without worrying about arranging babysitters.

Tom Hooper was standing alone in the corner, trying as hard as possible to seem insignificant. He was a fish out of water here, uncomfortable in what he called his "monkey suit." The collar of the starched shirt was chafing his neck, and his bow tie was threatening to choke him. He'd hated ceremonial dinners during his service days—hated dress-ing up even then—but at least he'd been in uniform along with all the others and as such had blended in with the gen-eral melee. Here he was aware that his suit was old, thread-bare at the cuffs and shiny on the seat of the pants, and the polished shoes that pinched at his toes had made many trips to the cobbler's in their thirty-year life.

He'd been requested to attend the party by William Charteris, and to bring the boy along too. It was only natu-ral Charteris should want his son there, even if he couldn't acknowledge David as his own. The peculiar charade the two men had played since '46 was still current, like a long-running Aldwych farce. As far as the rest of the world was concerned he, Tom Hooper, was David's father and William Charteris their benefactor, giving them a house to live in, and Tom a job. Not that Hooper minded the subterfuge—better that than the truth becoming common knowledge. But he couldn't help but wonder how long they would be able to keep up the pretense. With each passing year David grew more and more like his real father. He had the slightly hooked Charteris nose, and his eyes were the same rich brown as William's. One day the similarities would become evident to even the most casual observer, and the charade would be over. And when it was, Tom Hooper would breathe a huge sigh of relief.

He was drinking wine slowly, taking small sips from his glass every now and then. He hated the stuff, preferring a pint of brown ale. But tonight etiquette demanded wine, so wine he drank. As he raised his glass to his lips he caught sight of Helen Charteris across the other side of the room. In his opinion the woman deserved a medal for her stoicism in the face of a dreadful domestic situation.

William Charteris came back from North Africa a changed man. Some would have put it down to his experiences in the war, but Hooper knew differently. Their experiences in that murky cave, watching the birth of the child now known as David, and the butchery of his mother, had scarred both of them, but more so William, who felt directly responsible for the Arab girl's death. He carried the burden of guilt with a heavy heart and a bitterness that seemed to grow on a daily basis. It was made worse by the fact he could not acknowledge the boy David as his own and shower him with the love a father should show a son.

That bitterness manifested itself in the deliberate destruction of his relationship with Helen, and in the coolness that had developed between himself and Hooper. Tom Hooper had felt the acid sting of resentment from his former commanding officer on numerous occasions, and it was only a deeply rooted sense of loyalty that kept him at the Court. Many times in the past seven years he'd been tempted to pack his bags and go, but duty kept him there. Not only a duty to William Charteris, but also to the boy who was growing up to be a fine lad, filled with a boundless enthusiasm for life. As far as David was concerned Tom Hooper was his father and Charteris a kindly uncle who showered him with gifts and always had time for an en-

couraging word and a carefree laugh. But for how much longer?

Hooper watched Helen Charteris as she helped herself to another glass of champagne from a passing waiter. He could see she was slowly getting drunk. She was hiding it well, but Hooper could read the signs—the slightly dazed look in her eyes and the vaguely uncoordinated movements of her body.

"Come on, Tom, mingle a little. At least look like you're enjoying yourself." William Charteris was at his elbow.

"Easier said than done, sir," Hooper said. "Not really my kind of thing, this."

Several of the children had formed themselves into a human train and were weaving their way through the guests, David as the driver, the slight form of a three-year-old Catherine bringing up the rear, holding tightly on to the shirt of a much larger boy lest she be left behind.

"The children seem to be enjoying themselves enough for all of us," Hooper said.

Charteris was watching David, a look of pride in his eyes. "They certainly do," he said. "But then look who's leading them. If only . . ." His voice trailed off as he struggled with the impossible.

Many of the guests had moved to the sides of the room, leaving the floor clear for the children to play. They watched the train as it hurtled down between them, David leading it in a tight arc at one end of the room and back the way they'd come. Catherine, tiring of the game, let go of the boy's shirt and went in search of her mother.

Helen stood talking to a small group of women over by the french doors. When Catherine came up behind her and tugged at her dress she glanced down, a look of irritation in her eyes.

"Mummy," Catherine said. The child's face was flushed and she looked close to tears.

Helen tried to ignore her, turning back to the women. Catherine tugged again. "Mummy! I feel sick."

Helen wheeled on her. "Can't you just leave me alone?" she snapped savagely. "Can't you see I'm talking?"

The shocked expressions on the face of the women and the other guests in the room were lost on Helen, who was now so drunk she had to concentrate just to stand upright. Since the day her husband had raped her she had loathed the outcome. When Catherine, "the child" as Helen consistently referred to her, was born Helen carried out her promise to her husband and had as little to do with her as possible. Nannies and maids cared for Catherine, who was thankfully too young to fully appreciate that not only did her parents have a loathing for one another but also a total disregard for her.

"But, Mummy—"

"Oh, for God's sake, why can't you just go away and leave me alone? Go and play with your brother!"

It took a moment for her to realize what she had just said, but then the words floated through her mind like an echo and she found herself smiling. She looked around the room. All eyes seemed to be on her. William was coming toward her, but he seemed to be moving in slow motion.

"But of course none of you know, do you, about my husband's little secret?" she continued, talking to the room now.

"Helen, that's enough!" William was at her side, making a grab for her arm. She pulled away and swung her hand, catching him across the face.

"Don't you dare touch me!" she said coldly. "Are you so afraid of people knowing the truth?"

William Charteris put his hand to his stinging cheek. He stood there, helpless.

Tom Hooper moved forward and took David by the hand to lead him from the room.

"Tom," Helen called. "Where are you going?"

"I'm taking the boy home," Hooper said evenly.

"But surely, this is his home. Here with his father."

David looked up at Tom Hooper, confusion in his eyes, wincing with pain as Hooper's fingers tightened around his arm.

"That's enough, Helen!" Charteris said.

In a welter of embarrassed coughs and uncertain laughter the guests looked away from the scene, some engaging in strained small talk, others sipping their drinks nervously while they awaited further developments.

"No, William, it's not nearly enough. I want them all to know the truth. I'm sick of the pretense. Perhaps I should also tell them the circumstances of Catherine's conception."

At the sound of her name Catherine looked up at her parents, said, "Mummm," and vomited.

William Charteris called one of the waiters over to him. "Get Ryder down here now to look after the child." He grabbed Helen by the wrist and dragged her from the room. David prized Hooper's fingers from his arm and went across to Catherine, wrapping an arm around her shoulders. He took a handkerchief from his pocket and wiped his sister's mouth.

Halfway up the stairs Helen gripped the banister rail, pulling them to a halt. "I said I'd make you pay," she said.

He hit her then. A closed-fist punch to the side of her head. There was no one to witness the blow, and he wouldn't have cared if there were. Her eyes registered surprise; then her legs buckled and she pitched forward into his arms. He carried her the rest of the way and dropped her unconscious body onto his bed. He looked down at her—anger

*and hatred making his eyes glow as if lit by an inner fire—
then he left the room, locking the door behind him.*

*On the way back down the stairs he passed Elizabeth
Ryder leading Catherine gently by the hand. The maid
avoided his eyes, keeping up a steady stream of comforting
words to the child. Tom Hooper and David stood by the
front door, Hooper hesitant, not knowing whether to stay
or go.*

*"You'd better go, Tom," Charteris said when he reached
the bottom.*

*"Yes," Hooper said. "I think I'd better. Come on,
David."*

*"No," Charteris said. "She was right. The boy belongs
here."*

*Tom Hooper looked at him steadily, and then he said,
"As you wish," and slipped out through the front door.*

*Charteris crouched, bringing himself down to the boy's
eye level. "Come here, David."*

David looked apprehensive.

*"It's all right. Soon we'll sit down together and talk
about all this, but first . . ." He took the boy by the hand and
led him back to the drawing room.*

*As they appeared in the doorway the room fell silent, all
eyes watching them expectantly. William Charteris cleared
his throat. "Ladies and gentlemen," he said, his voice steady.
"May I introduce you to my son, David?"*

CHAPTER THIRTEEN

As soon as they arrived back at the site Laura went into the caravan and changed into jeans and a sweat-shirt. She dialed Brian Tanner's number and waited, tapping her foot impatiently as the phone at the other end went unanswered. "Damn it!" she said and then went to join Catherine in the garden. This morning Catherine was dressed casually and wore very little makeup, just a hint of eyeliner. If anything she looked younger than the night before. She walked around the flower beds, reaching out occasionally to pluck a withered leaf from a bush or to crush a desiccated flower head between her fingers. "What on earth has happened here?" she said as Laura joined her on the path. There was more than a hint of accusation in her voice.

"I was going to ask you the same thing," Laura said. "I'm no gardener, but even I can see that things shouldn't be like this."

Catherine frowned. "All the plants seem dried out, as if they've had all the moisture, all the goodness drained out of them. I've never seen anything quite like it."

"I think it must be me," Laura said with a smile. "When I first came here the garden was glorious, a bit neglected maybe, but everything seemed to be growing healthily. This has happened in the last week." Since the accident, she realized suddenly, but left the thought unspoken.

Catherine sank to a crouch and prodded the earth with an expensively manicured finger. "The soil seems fine. I'm puzzled, to be honest."

In the few hours that Laura had known Catherine Charteris she'd come to like her enormously. First thing that morning the woman brought breakfast to her room on a large silver tray and then sat at the foot of the bed chatting while Laura sipped at her coffee and dipped bread soldiers into her perfectly boiled egg. She seemed keen to talk about the party the night before, delighting in ridiculing some of the more pompous guests and telling Laura about a couple who were engaged in extramarital activities. Laura soon realized that Catherine Charteris was very down-to-earth and had little time for the privileges her position afforded her. Before she left the bedroom to allow Laura to dress she said, "Richard tells me he's invited you to London with him."

"Yes, he has," Laura said noncommittaly.

"Are you accepting the invitation?"

"I'm still thinking about it."

Catherine laughed. "I can see he's going to have to work hard with you. The last girl he was with, Abigail or Annabel or something, wasn't the brightest button on the coat. She had all the right connections, but she was definitely short-changed when it came to intellect."

"Was he with her long?" Why should she feel a stab of jealousy?

"Three years, but he ended it six months ago," Catherine said, then laughed again. "I think he only stayed with her out of sympathy. No, you're much more his type." She paused for a moment as a thought occurred to her. "You *do* like him, don't you? I mean, I can tell he's fairly smitten with you. Ever since he visited your house earlier in the week he's never missed an opportunity to drop your name into the conversation."

Laura felt herself blushing at Catherine's candor, but she was very glad to hear it. "Yes," she said with a smile. "I like him very much. I just think it's moving a little fast. I mean, a weekend at his flat . . ."

"You haven't seen his flat. It's a three-bedroomed duplex overlooking the Thames at Richmond. Hardly a bed-sit. And I know my son. If nothing else he's the perfect gentleman. Too much so sometimes."

Laura relaxed slightly. "I could do with some time away from the site, and that damned caravan. You wouldn't believe how well I slept last night. To have a proper bed, as opposed to the apology for one I normally sleep on, was a real luxury."

"Think on it," Catherine said. "But if you refuse I know a young man who's going to be very disappointed."

Now, as she was standing in the dying garden, looking at the building site that was her temporary home, the prospect of a trip to London seemed very appealing. And if Richard did decide he wanted to rush things along, she didn't think she'd object too much. "Come inside," she said to Catherine. "I'll show you what I've got planned for the house."

Before they left the site Laura went back to the caravan and phoned Shaun to ask him to keep an eye on the site over the weekend. "I'm sorry to ask you this," she said. "I don't want to intrude into your weekend."

"It's no problem," Shaun said. "Two of the kids are having some friends round for a sleepover. It's an excuse to get me out of the house for a while."

"Siobhan won't mind?"

"Not at all. Going somewhere nice?"

"London. With a friend. I'll be back Sunday night."

There was a pause on the other end of the line. Finally Shaun said, "Have fun. You deserve a break."

She thanked him and hung up.

As she packed an overnight bag she glanced out through the window. Catherine was standing at the entrance to the cellar. She'd pulled the board to one side and was staring down into the blackness. As Laura watched she hugged herself tightly, shook her head, and turned away, walking quickly back to her car.

Laura locked up the caravan and went to join Catherine, who was sitting behind the wheel. As Laura slipped in beside her Catherine said, "Ready?" Her eyes were bright, glittery.

"Just about."

"So you're going to London with Richard?" Catherine said.

Laura smiled. "Yes, I think I am."

Shaun put down the phone and scratched his shoulder absently. Upstairs the children were playing noisily while Siobhan washed up the breakfast things in the kitchen. He stuck his head round the door. "I'm just popping over to the site," he said.

She glanced round at him and frowned. "But it's Saturday," she said.

"I know. I'll be back in time to ferry the kids around."

"On pain of death," Siobhan said. "I'm not coping with that lot on my own."

"Promise," he said, and kissed her good-bye.

He arrived at the site thirty minutes later. It was the opportunity he'd been waiting for. The last two days at work were busy and he hadn't had time to get back down in the cellar. Now he had a few hours to take a sledgehammer to the wall and satisfy his curiosity.

He lit the hurricane lamps and waited for their light to fill the room, then hefted the hammer and aimed it at the wall.

The first blow produced a crack in the blocks three feet long. The second blow shook the mortar out of the joints. He paused, drew a breath, and looked about him. The atmosphere in the cellar seemed to have altered slightly. It was nothing he could pin down, just a curious ambience, as if the room was holding its breath, waiting for the next hammer blow.

He raised the sledgehammer again and swung it at the wall. The impact made him stagger, but this time the result was more dramatic. Three of the blocks fell inward, leaving a gap two feet by one, and a blast of stale air hit him in the face. He blinked as mortar dust blew into his eyes, making them stream. He wiped the tears away from his face and reached for one of the lamps, swinging it into the hole he'd made.

Whatever he'd been expecting to find, it certainly wasn't this. There was a room on the other side of the wall, but unlike the cellar with its rusting bed and moldering bookcase, this one was pristine, untouched by the water that had filled this room.

The lamp offered scant illumination, but he could see the other room was furnished and decorated. A sense of growing excitement drove him on and several hammer blows later he was standing in a doorway. Holding the lamp in front of him like a beacon, he stepped through the gap.

There was a bed, fully made with sheets and pillows, a small bedside table piled with books and a travel alarm clock in a leather case. The walls were plastered and painted white, and hanging from them were three watercolor landscapes depicting desolate sandy expanses of land, purple mountains in the background, and clear blue skies above. Rugs with an intricate Persian pattern covered the floor, and against one wall was a large mahogany wardrobe. Against the other sat a large pine box, with brass straps, secured by a worn and rusting padlock.

There were no other doorways into the room and the ceiling was solid, concrete painted white like the walls.

His mouth was dry, his tongue sticking to the roof of his mouth. He swallowed several times to get his saliva glands working, and then he stepped forward and opened the wardrobe.

It was racked out neatly with clothes. Down one side shirts and jumpers were folded neatly on shelves, and from a chrome rail hung several suits, covered to keep them dust-free. He pulled out one of the suits. It was small; it certainly wouldn't have fitted him. The trousers barely came up to the top of his thigh and he couldn't fit his arm into the sleeve of the jacket. A child's suit, expensively made with hand stitching on the lapels and a Saville Row maker's label on the inside. Likewise the shirts were mostly silk, hand-made and expensive. He replaced the clothes carefully and shut the wardrobe door.

The rusting padlock on the chest succumbed to one blow from the hammer and he knelt down, set the lamp on the floor, and opened the lid.

On the drive back to Dunbar Court the conversation turned once again to Richard. Laura didn't mind. She enjoyed talking about him. She wanted to know everything there was to learn about him, and his mother provided that inside track.

"Richard was the apple of my father's eye," Catherine said. "Unfortunately I was a terrible mother. Looking back now I cringe at just how awful, how self-centered I was. I hit my teens and set off on some sort of hedonistic quest. I craved excitement, pleasure, away from the stuffy confinement of the Court. I think the key to it was David dying at such a young age."

"David?"

"My brother. I idolized him, even though he was only a few years older than me."

"I didn't know you had a brother," Laura said. Though of course Maggie had more than alluded to the same fact.

"Once he died I'm afraid my parents buried his memory along with his body. I don't know if that happens in families, but it certainly happened in mine. There were never any photographs of him, and his name was never mentioned. It was almost as if he hadn't existed at all. I suppose it was their way of dealing with it, but as an impressionable eight-year-old I found it very difficult to come to terms with, and I suppose it increased my resentment of my parents. So when I hit my teens I rebelled. I ran away from home when I was sixteen."

"How did he die?" Laura said, and then cursed herself for asking such a crass question. "I'm sorry," she said. "None of my business."

Catherine stared out through the windshield, but her mind was turned inward. "It's all right," she said. "It was a long time ago. I don't mind talking about it. But the truth is I'm not really sure. You see, after he died nobody spoke of him, not my mother, my father, or any of the staff. When I came back to Dunbar Court for the final time my father was very ill, very weak. A lot of the time he was incoherent and rambling, probably due to the cocktail of drugs he'd been prescribed. He'd talk about David as if he were still alive, and it took me a while to realize he wasn't talking about David at all, but Richard. In his mind the two boys had merged to become one, and he couldn't differentiate between them.

"But he did have periods of lucidity. Once, when he was having a particularly good day, I asked him what had happened to David, how he'd died. But even then he was guarded. He explained it away as some congenital defect, but the more I pressed him on it the more confused he became. So to this day I'm not really sure what happened to him. He was thirteen when he died. So young. And I'd never known him to have a day's illness. Even common colds seemed to pass him by. I remember having chicken pox, and his sitting at my bedside reading me *Thomas the Tank Engine* stories, but he never caught it himself. Looking back now, it seemed that one day he was there, lighting up my life with his laughter, his kindness, and the next he was gone. It was like someone had switched off a light in my life."

Laura took her eyes off the road. Tears were streaming down Catherine's cheeks and she was reaching into her bag for a tissue to wipe them away. "I really must apologize," she said to Laura. "Talking about him always gets to me like this. Perhaps that's why my parents carried on with their lives, pretending he'd never existed. Better than facing this pain on a daily basis."

Laura said nothing. There was nothing she could say to ease the pain of Catherine's loss, but she was both surprised and flattered that the woman had unburdened herself to her so early in their relationship.

"Anyway," Catherine said, sniffing back the tears. "We were talking about Richard. I shouldn't be raking over such ancient history. I'm sorry."

They reached the gates of Dunbar Court and Laura turned into the drive. As they reached the front door it opened and Richard stood there, grinning when he saw Laura's overnight bag.

Shaun sat on the bed in the subterranean room reading. The first thing he'd come across when lifting the lid of the pine box was a complete set of watercolor paints, together with paper and pencils, contained in a wooden tray that slotted snugly into the top of the box. He lifted the tray out and set it down on the floor beside him. Underneath the tray were a pile of adventure novels, several model airplanes, a crystal set, complete with headphones, a small wind-up gramophone, and a few ancient 78 rpm records, mostly classical. He lifted each of the items out of the box. It was like opening a time capsule.

There were comics, *The Hotspur*, *Lion*, and *Tiger*, tied neatly into bundles with string, and in a battered cardboard box in the bottom corner of the chest a green-and-red steam engine.

These were the possessions of a young boy.

Shaun took out his pocket knife and sliced through the string holding one of the bundles of comics. He flicked through the pile, checking the dates. They ran in sequence from 1956 through to the middle of '59, but there were no later issues. He checked the other bundles, but again the dates stopped before they reached the 1960s.

Had this room been closed up that long? And what had happened to the boy whose possessions were so pristinely preserved?

He reached into the box again, lifting out the steam engine. The box might have been showing signs of wear, but the engine itself had been lovingly cared for. The moving parts still had a thin coating of oil, and the brass and steel pistons gleamed in the lamp-light. The methylated spirit burner was empty, of course, the spirit having long since evaporated, but the wick was fresh, unused.

He put the engine back in its box and was about to replace it when he saw that the engine had been sitting on a small cloth-bound book, with a ring-bound spine. He took it out and flipped it open.

A diary, or a journal. Page after page filled with neat, orderly handwriting, the paper crisp and as fresh as the day it had been placed in the box. He car-

ried the book and the lamp across to the bed and
started to read.

*Six days now I've been down here and I'm bored. Fa-
ther says I must stay down here until the Transition
has passed, but I'm not sure when that will be. My
constant companion is Mary (note to self: try to
learn her proper, Arabic, name), and she tells me
wonderful stories about her past and about the Verani. She constantly tells me I'm special, and deserve special treatment, but I can't see that I'm any
different from other boys at school. I certainly don't
feel different and I certainly don't feel special.*

*She calls this place my shelter, though I have no
idea what it's supposed to be sheltering me from.*

*I know I must be patient, but I'm missing a lot of
things. Football, playing in the garden with Cathy. I
certainly miss Cathy and her funny little ways. I'm
even missing school! I hope this will be over soon
and I can go back to my normal life.*

*A week now and still no sign of the Transition. I
wish I knew more about it and what to expect. I
asked Muminah (Mary) earlier today but she was
cagey with me. I'm not sure she actually knows.*

*Father came to visit me last night. He seemed in
good spirits. He says he's missing me and that Cathy
keeps asking about me. He told me to be brave and to
be patient, but even he couldn't tell me when the
Transition would be, and when I asked him about it
he changed the subject. When he left I cried. Not for
long though. I can't stand crying; it makes me feel
like a baby. Before he went I asked him if Cathy could
come and visit me, but he said it wouldn't be safe. I*

think he was talking about the well in the other room. Perhaps he's worried she might fall down it. Mary tells me it's very deep. He didn't seem worried that I might fall down it though.

Southampton seems to be doing well in the FA Cup this year, so at least something's going right.

This is like being in prison. I'm not sure now if it's ten or eleven days I've been down here. I asked Muminah but she couldn't say. She doesn't speak to me much now, although she seemed delighted that I'm using her Arabic name. She said it means "pious believer," but then she started acting strangely, as if she'd said something she shouldn't have done. After that she shut up like a clam.

Now she just sits on the bed in the other room, sewing. I think I must be going mad, because I swear I can hear the needle puncturing the cloth, and the squeaky sound of the cotton being pulled through the material.

I'm thinking about trying to escape. I read a book yesterday by Major Pat Read and his escape attempts from Colditz and it got me thinking. The only thing stopping me from getting out of here is the trapdoor in the ceiling in the other room. I know it's locked. I tried it this morning when Mary had to empty the chemical toilet. It gave slightly when I pushed it, so I think it's only a bolt holding it in place. I might try again tomorrow.

Something seems to be happening to me. I noticed today that my hands look different. The skin looks darker, almost leathery. I checked my arms but they seem all right. It's just my hands. Very strange!

*Could this be the start of the Transition? It's quite
frightening really.*

Shaun stopped reading and rubbed the tiredness
from his eyes. He checked his watch and swore. He'd
told Siobhan he'd be back by four and it was already
half past. He closed the book and laid it on the bed,
then packed everything back into the pine box. There
was no need to try to fix the lock—he couldn't imagine anyone else but him coming down here.

He tucked the book into the waistband of his
trousers and climbed up into the daylight.

CHAPTER FOURTEEN

The office building was a bright, modern structure of smoked glass and stainless steel halfway along Cheapside. Richard drove his Mercedes down the ramp to the underground car park, showed his pass to the guard at the barrier, and parked in his reserved bay. "You're sure you don't mind coming here first?" he said.

"Not at all," Laura said. "It's quite interesting to see where you work."

They took the elevator up to the third floor. The doors opened onto a plush lobby with a deep-piled beige carpet and chrome and leather furniture. There was a mahogany desk with a computer, two telephones, and a small intercom. Behind it was a door.

Richard pointed to a large brown leather sofa. "Make yourself comfortable. This won't take too long," he said and went through the door to his office.

On a rack underneath a low coffee table was a pile of trade magazines and catalogues. Laura pulled out a Sotheby's catalogue, sat back in the sofa, and started leafing through it.

Richard shut the office door behind him and sat down at his desk, a larger partner to the secretary's desk in the lobby. He picked up the phone and punched in a number, then leaned back in his office chair. The phone was answered on the third ring. "Raymond Security."

"Jim, it's Richard. I've got a job for you."

There was a pause on the other end of the line and the sound of paper being shuffled. "Okay, Richard, shoot."

"Two names for you. The first is Brian Tanner, a property developer based in Dorchester. He was a partner in Tanner and Craig, but now works on his own."

"Tanner and Craig. Got that. What do you want?"

"Laura Craig is a friend of mine and she's recently ended the partnership with Tanner—acrimoniously, it appears. Only he seems reluctant to let it lie. He turned up at the Court on Friday. It upset Laura considerably."

"And the other one?"

"Simon Lawson. Works for . . ." Richard reached into his pocket for the name of the company Laura had mentioned and read it out. "The company specializes in accident claims."

"I've heard of them," Jim said.

"He's representing a family by the name of McMillan and he's causing a few problems for a friend of mine."

"Details?"

Richard told him briefly.

"And you want me to stop them making a nuisance of themselves?"

"Yes and no. Go to the McMillans direct and make them an offer to back off." He gave Raymond the address. "Use your discretion, but you can go up to five grand. If that doesn't work, then have a friendly word with the man himself."

"Okay. I'll see what I can do. What about Tanner?"

"Find out everything you can about him, but don't confront him directly. He could be trouble. Keep a watch on him and keep me posted on his movements. But call me here in London, not the house. I'm only here on a flyer, and I'm driving back down to Dorset tomorrow night, but I'll be back in town on Wednesday, so leave it until then. Is that enough time for you to get things moving?"

"Ample. I'll be in touch."

The line went dead. Richard replaced the handset and sat for a while, eyes closed. He knew from the moment he'd heard the old Hooper house was to be sold that his life was going to change.

It was his twenty-first birthday when his grandfather had called him into the study and told him to close the door behind him. The story Lord Dunbar told his grandson was so incredible that for a moment he thought the old man was playing a joke on him. But, when he looked into his grandfather's eyes, he realized that every word was true.

Since then the knowledge imparted to him that day hung like some huge invisible weight, and with the knowledge came responsibility, much increased since his grandfather's death. He wasn't sure now if he was up to the task of guarding the family's secrets, but he felt honor-bound to try.

He pushed himself out of the chair and went back out to the lobby.

Laura looked up from the catalogue and smiled uncertainly. Richard looked strained and pale, a tightness around his eyes that hadn't been there earlier. "Is everything all right?" she said.

He made a visible effort to relax, returning her smile. "Fine," he said. "Shall we go?"

She slid the catalogue back onto the pile and picked up her bag. "Yes," she said. "Let's."

The beginning of the end for Brian Tanner had begun as soon as he had dropped his torch into the cellar. It was some time later that his hand closed around the rusting metal rung of the ladder for the second time and he hauled himself upward. Arms and legs shook with effort as he climbed upward, pushing the board to one side. The sky was a sheet of black velvet, pierced with brilliant pinpoints of silver, the moon hanging like a pearlized orb to the east.

How long how had it been since it had seen a sky like this? Months? Years? It had no way of telling. Trapped in the darkness, alone in the well, time ceased to have any kind of meaning. Time passed inexorably, a constant vigil of waiting in the cold and damp, until somebody broke the seal and came close enough. Now the time had come, and as it pulled itself out of the cellar, taking in deep lungfuls of air, it gave a silent prayer of thanks that the waiting was over.

It had changed from the boy known as David, and that part of its life was already a distant memory. Traces might remain, locked in dark recesses of the brain, but once the Transition took place the Verani was paramount, all human reflexes, all instincts of humanity, disappeared.

Now Verani had escaped the watery tomb. For the present it would use the body it had inhabited, use the human body of Brian Tanner until it was no longer needed.

The part of him that was still Brian Tanner recognized where he was, recognized the cement mixers, the piles of bricks, the building site. The other part, the part that had waited patiently in the depths of the well for all that time, wondered what had happened to the place the boy he had once been had called home.

Its legs shook, as it stood upright, breathing in the night air, savoring its sweetness, feeling its touch as a cool breeze played on the skin of the face. With tentative fingers it reached up and traced the contours of the nose, the mouth, snaking through the hair in a voyage of self-discovery. Then it opened the mouth and cried out, a deep roar of exaltation. It was free at last.

The controls of the car were alien to it and it sat behind the wheel, letting its mind recede, allowing another to turn the key in the ignition, to press the accelerator, to ease the car forward. The man with whom it shared this body would have his uses, and this would be one of them. There was much to learn, much to see, and there was an insatiable hunger to satisfy.

There was an insatiable thirst as well, for revenge against those who had imprisoned the Verani all those years ago, the Charteris family.

Chapter Fifteen

Jenny McMillan stood in front of the bathroom mirror coating her eyelashes with mascara. Her husband stood in the doorway, his face pale, his features gaunt. He leaned against the doorjamb, as if he was having trouble supporting his own weight. "But you never work Saturday nights," he said.

With a sigh Jenny put down her mascara brush and took a lipstick from her makeup bag. "I told you, they're short-staffed tonight, and I told Vic I wouldn't mind helping out. It's no big deal. And God knows we could do with the money."

"So that was the phone call, was it? Vic asking you to work tonight?"

She flushed slightly. "Yes," she lied.

"I don't believe you."

She dropped the lipstick back into the bag and zipped it up. She was wearing nothing but a black silk slip, her ample body pressing at the thin fabric. She pushed past him and walked through to the bedroom to dress. "Why don't you come down to the Bell and see for yourself?" she said acidly.

He hobbled after her. He'd started to limp badly in the last few days. The lower part of his injured leg was swollen to twice its normal size and it was agony to put any weight on it. "How am I meant to go out like this? I can barely walk." He had managed to hide it from her, but his leg was entirely covered in a kind of black mold. It itched uncontrollably and when he scratched it the skin bled.

"And I told you, until you go to the doctor and get that leg sorted out you won't get any sympathy from me." She slid the black skirt over her hips and pulled on her blouse. "That Craig woman was right. It's probably infected."

McMillan sat heavily on the bed and reached out for his wife's hand. "You wouldn't leave me, would you?"

She pulled her hand away impatiently. "For God's sake, what's the matter with you? Ever since the accident you've been wallowing in self-pity. Would you blame me if I did pack my bags and go? Jamie gives me less trouble than you."

"But I need you, Jen," McMillan said.

She glanced around at him and saw the tears welling in his eyes. She sat down next to him and took his hand in hers. "For the last time," she said gently, "there's nothing to worry about. I'm just going in tonight to help out. Nothing more, nothing less. I'll be back by midnight. Now, let me finish getting ready. I'll be late if I don't get on."

He got up from the bed and hobbled to the door. He paused and looked back at her, opened his mouth to speak, shut it again, and shook his head slightly.

She waited until she heard his heavy, faltering tread on the stairs, then lay back on the bed and stared up at the ceiling. She couldn't carry on like this for much longer.

The telephone call earlier had filled her with an excitement she hadn't felt in years. She wasn't working tonight. In fact she wouldn't be going within miles of the Bell.

She drove just three streets before pulling up behind a dark blue BMW. She locked her own car behind her and walked quickly to where the other car was waiting. As she slid into the passenger seat she turned to the man she knew as Brian Tanner and smiled warmly. "Sorry I'm a bit late," she said. "But Dean decided it was time to discuss the state of our marriage. I didn't think I was ever going to get away."

Tanner leaned toward her and kissed her cheek. "No problem," he said. "No problem at all." Then he eased the car smoothly out into the traffic.

Dean McMillan watched from the window as Jenny's Ford Fiesta disappeared from sight, and then he went across to the phone.

"Vic, it's Dean, Jenny's husband. She asked me to ring to tell you she might be a little late tonight. Trouble with the kid, y'know?"

There was a long pause on the other end of the line as the mouthpiece was covered and a conversation exchanged. Finally Vic said, "You've got the wrong night, Dean. Jen's not on until Monday."

McMillan took a deep breath as a wave of sickness swept over him. "But I thought you phoned earlier. Something about being short-staffed?"

"Not me. I've only just got back from the cash-and-carry. Sounds like you've got your wires crossed." Another pause, another conversation. "I hope I haven't put my foot in it," Vic said, laughing.

Dean shook himself, trying to step back into reality. "No, no. It's all right. I must have misunderstood. Thanks, Vic." He cradled the receiver and took several deep breaths, trying to stem the anger that was threatening to engulf him. The lying bitch! She would pay for this. In one movement he swept the phone from the table and, lifting the table, threw it across the room.

Jamie ran into the lounge, attracted by the noise. "Something wrong, Dad?" he said, then saw the expression on his father's face and ran back to the garden.

As they pulled up on the gravel drive of Tanner's five-bedroomed Victorian house Jenny McMillan laughed nervously. "I thought you were taking me out for a drink," she said. She felt unsettled. Apart from the greeting when she'd first got into the car he'd been silent, not offering any kind of conversation, and answering her questions with shrugs and grunts. This was not the way she thought the evening would go. She'd imagined an intimate drink in some secluded wine bar, perhaps a meal. He'd been so persuasive over the phone, telling her that since meeting with her the other day he'd barely been able to get her out of his mind. She was flattered that he found her attractive, even more so that he wanted to pursue some kind of relationship with her.

How long had it been since a man had shown any interest at all in her? Apart from the lecherous drunks in the bar who pawed her and made lewd suggestions, Jenny's recent experience of the attentions of men was limited to her weekly fuck with Dean, usually after he'd had several lagers and a curry. If their lovemaking lasted ten minutes she considered herself lucky, and afterward he would sleep, ignoring the fact that for much of the night she'd lie there unfulfilled, until her restless fingers finished the job he'd started.

Now she found herself alone with a very attractive man, about to enter his house, with sex very much on the agenda, and she found herself as nervous as a schoolgirl out on her first date.

"I said, I thought we were going for a drink."

"I have drink inside," he said and got out of the car. He walked round and opened her door.

"I'm not sure this is such a great idea," Jenny said, not moving from her seat.

Instantly his manner changed. "I'm sorry," he said gently. "Have I done something to upset you? I thought you wanted this."

"I did . . . I do . . . oh, I don't know."

He smiled at her. "It's okay, really. I'll take you home."

"No!" she said vehemently. "I mean, no, it's all right. Only I told Dean I was working tonight. He'll find it bloody funny if I swan in an hour after leaving the house."

The man she knew as Brian Tanner folded his arms. "One drink," he said. "Where's the harm?"

"Oh, what am I like?" Jenny said, unbuckling her seat belt and slipping her legs from the car. "Whatever must you think of me? I'm not usually this stupid, honestly."

"I never thought you were." He closed the door behind her as she stepped out of the car, and wrapped an arm around her shoulder. Together they walked to the front door.

She trembled slightly as his fingers found the buttons of her blouse and started to undo them. They were in his bedroom and it was a little less than thirty minutes since they'd entered the house. Once inside he'd poured her a large vodka and topped up the glass with tonic. The drink had done its job quickly and she started to relax. They'd sat together on the couch and she'd talked as she drank; telling him about her childhood in the East End, about Dean and how they'd met, about how unsatisfying her life was now. And then they kissed.

For Jenny McMillan the moment was more than just a kiss. A whole cast of emotions battled inside her for dominance. Guilt—that was a major feeling. She'd never before been unfaithful to her husband. Of course she'd been tempted in the past, and there had been several opportunities to break her marriage vows, but for ten years she'd played the faithful wife and let the temptations pass her by. Along with the guilt came a tidal wave of excitement. Feeling another man's lips on hers, a stranger's hands caressing her breasts through the thin material of her blouse, sent sharp spasms of shock through her body, and she relished the sensations.

She responded enthusiastically, ignoring the slightly metallic taste of his mouth and the urgent, slightly painful dig of his fingernails as his hands snaked up her back to unhook her bra. As his fingers slid across the top of her nipple she pushed him away. "Not here," she whispered breathlessly. "Upstairs."

Without a word he took her hand and led her up the stairs.

She barely noticed the other furniture in the room. The bed was dominant, a symbol of her incipient adultery. Without more than a passing thought for her husband and son she allowed herself to be lowered backward onto the yielding mattress as his mouth again closed over hers.

Within minutes he had removed her blouse and her bra, and she folded her arms across her exposed breasts self-consciously, aware more than ever before of her body. Once she'd been slim, her flesh tight and toned, but childbirth and endless takeaway suppers had taken their toll and she was no longer as svelte as when she was a teenager.

He pulled her arms away gently and bent forward to kiss first one breast, then the other, while his fingers pulled down the zip of her skirt.

She lay there, responding to his touch, gasping slightly as a finger slid inside her, moving gently, bringing her to orgasm within minutes. As she climaxed she wrapped her arms around him, pulling his body down on hers, her mouth finding his, kissing hungrily.

When he pulled away she said, "Get undressed."

He looked deep into her eyes, a slight smile playing on his lips, and then he got up from the bed and started to unbutton his shirt.

She pushed herself upright, drawing her knees up to her chest and encircling them with her arms. There was so much she wanted to say to him, so much she wanted to ask him. What was it about her he found so attractive? What had happened between him and Laura Craig to make him feel so bitter toward her? But she said nothing, terrified she would spoil the moment. And she wanted nothing to spoil this moment. She felt more alive now than she had for years. Even the guilt had abated. All she wanted now was to feel him on top of her, to feel his skin against hers, to feel him inside her.

He stood in front of the window, his back to her. She imagined she could hear the buttons of his shirt popping open. She watched him shrug it off, letting it fall to the floor with a soft whisper, but still he didn't turn to face her.

When the trousers also fell and he stepped out of them she found herself gazing longingly at the taut flesh of his buttocks. She said, "Don't be shy." But he didn't turn, and she wanted him to turn. She wanted to see the toned muscles of his stomach, the smooth outline of his chest. Still he didn't move.

She eased off the bed and approached him from behind, sucking in her belly and throwing her shoulders back so her breasts lifted slightly and appeared firmer than they actually were. "I'm waiting," she said and slid her arms around his waist.

He seemed to shudder slightly. His skin was cold, clammy to the touch. She kissed his shoulder, her fingers creeping up his stomach, making small intimate circles around his navel.

And then with a cry she recoiled, as something sharp buried itself in her palm. She took a step backward and stared at the blood dripping from her hand. Her mouth formed the word "What . . ." as an echo to the questioning look in her eyes.

And then he turned to face her and the question died on her lips, to be replaced by a scream.

Laura nestled into Richard's embrace and stretched her legs out in the bed. "Silk sheets," she said. "I'm impressed. This sure beats the bed in the caravan."

"I should hope so. They cost a fortune," Richard said with an easy smile. Absently he stroked her hair, planting small kisses on her cheek.

"Thank you for a wonderful evening," she said. "That meal! I've never tasted food like it."

"It *was* pretty good. I know several other superb restaurants with food as good as that, if you're interested."

"I'm interested. I still can't believe how much London has changed since I last came up. Mind you, then I was a penniless student living in digs with three others. Our idea of a gourmet meal was pasta with tomato ketchup."

"What did you study?" His interest was earnest and quite genuine. She was flattered; but then she was also surprised to find herself here in his bed.

"Journalism at City University. I got my degree, but couldn't find a job up here, so I went home to work on the local rag. Even then hard news was pretty thin on the ground, so for much of the time I helped out in the advertising section. That's how I met Brian, and the rest is history." Mentioning Brian stirred up a hundred unpleasant memories. She tried to push them away. She didn't want anything to spoil this evening.

The drive back from the restaurant was wonderful; cruising along the embankment, staring across the Thames in wonder at the London Eye, the huge, futuristic-looking Ferris wheel erected to celebrate the millennium. Tonight it was illuminated with glowing blue light. She couldn't remember seeing anything so beautiful, but then the whole of London looked beautiful tonight.

Richard's flat was the top two floors of a newly built block, overlooking the river. Sitting on the balcony, drinking strong coffee, and watching the lights of the pleasure cruisers as they swept past on their way to Hammersmith Bridge filled her with a sense of wonder she hadn't felt since childhood. The transition from balcony to bedroom happened so smoothly she could barely recall the circumstances that led up to their lovemaking. One moment they were standing at the balcony rail watching a police launch on patrol, the next they were in each other's arms, kissing passionately, their tongues and hands exploring, with no words necessary to enhance the moment.

"So where do you call home?" Richard said.

Laura laughed. "You've seen it. It has two wheels and rocks about in the wind."

"The caravan? You're kidding."

" 'Fraid not. I used to have a tiny cottage in Abbotsbury, but I had to sell when the partnership broke up. I needed all my capital and more to continue working."

"I see. Do you miss it, the cottage?"

"Every single day. As I said it was tiny—a *bijou residence*, my friend Maggie would call it; she's an estate agent—compact and with clever use of space, but it was my first proper home. I loved it."

"Well, that explains one thing anyway."

"Oh?"

"When the Hooper place came on the market I

thought I might try to buy it myself, but someone had already beaten me to it."

She pulled away and turned to look at him. "You wanted to buy it? But why?"

He pulled her gently back into his arms. "Because I didn't want some property developer to get their hands on it and turn it into a holiday home."

"I hope you're joking," she said nervously. Surely he hadn't bedded her to persuade her to change her plans?

"Actually, no, I'm not. There are villages in Dorset that have been almost destroyed by that sort of thing. Cottages standing empty for the best part of the year, only filled on bank holidays, and the occasional couple of weeks in the summer. Local people are being deprived of places to live because rich yuppies want their country retreats."

"But when we first met and I told you my plans you said you applauded free enterprise." She was sitting up in bed now, the sheets pulled demurely across her breasts.

"And so I do, but entrepreneurs should have a conscience and realize there are some things best left alone. I'm sorry, but when we first met I wasn't exactly honest with you, I didn't want our relationship to get off on the wrong foot."

Laura was starting to feel uncomfortable, and it had nothing whatsoever to do with the silk sheets. "So you're saying you don't approve of what I'm doing?" She was starting to get angry, the memory of the lovemaking already altering in her mind from selfless pleasure to exploitation.

"Yes and no. I think you're the type to make sure the house will be full fifty-two weeks out of the year."

"It had better be or I'll be bankrupt."

"So at least you'll achieve continuity. Houses should be lived in, not left standing for most of the year like empty coffins." Richard was not a foolish man; he could see from her eyes she was having doubts about where she was and what they were doing, and had just done.

"But what about depriving the local populace of places to live?" Laura's face was flushed with annoyance now, the sheets tightly gripped in her fingers.

"Well, you're local, aren't you?"

"Bournemouth, born and bred."

"And I've got nothing against a local girl squeezing money out of grockles. It's almost a Dorset tradition."

"You're teasing me," she said, relief flooding through her. "You bastard!"

"Yes," he said. "Partly, though what I was saying about absentee landlords I feel with a passion. It's one of my hobbyhorses. Sorry." He kissed her cheek again. She twisted her head and met his lips with her own.

"I was beginning to think . . ."

"That I'd led you on? Used you to stop your house conversion?"

"Shut up and get busy."

Within seconds they were making love again.

Later they went through to the kitchen to make more coffee, and took it out to the balcony to look at the stars. Laura stood, her hands gripping the rail, staring up at the sky. It was only when she felt the wetness on her cheeks that she realized she was crying.

Richard noticed immediately and wrapped an arm around her, pulling her close. "What's the matter?" he said softly.

She sniffed back a tear. "I'm sorry. I'm not sure why I'm crying. It's stupid." She was angry with herself. The tears had come unbidden and she couldn't even say now what thoughts had prompted them. "It's been a shitty week," she said. "And tonight has been so wonderful. I'm not sure I want to go back to my life again."

He hugged her tightly. "Is your life really that bad?"

"Yes," she said. "At the moment it is. I had to sell my lovely little cottage. I'm living hand to mouth in a grotty caravan. The wolves are baying for my blood after that sodding accident, and bloody Brian turning up ruined even last night. I feel as if my entire life is hanging by a thread, and it's stretching thinner and thinner by the minute. I so want my business to succeed, but I seem dogged every step of the way by bloody bad luck." She yawned. Suddenly she felt tired, bone-achingly tired.

"Come to bed," he said.

"And sex isn't the answer either," she snapped.

"I wasn't suggesting it was. I'm tired, you're tired. Let's sleep." He led her inside.

At the door to the bedroom she hesitated. "I've ruined everything, haven't I?"

"You haven't ruined anything. Come on."

Lying once again in his arms she felt the tension ebb away. He switched out the light. "All the things you mentioned," he said, "are manageable. I don't think the McMillans will pursue their claim, and as for Brian Tanner, I shouldn't think he'll be featuring in your life for much longer. I'm sorting them out for you."

"Hmm?" Sleep was rushing in to claim her. She

could hear his words, but was having trouble making sense of them. He seemed to be saying that he would sort everything out, that he would fight her battles for her. Normally she would have railed against such interference in her life, but for now she was content to lie there, protected in his embrace. It had been a long time since she'd allowed herself to feel this secure.

By morning the comforting words were forgotten.

Jenny McMillan screamed until there was no air left in her lungs. Tanner stood before her, his eyes rolled up into his head so that only the whites showed. The flesh of his stomach was crisscrossed with small slits, dripping blood. Raw-edged, the slits opened and closed like the gills of a fish and, from inside the slits, thin, sharp, coral-pink spines emerged, pushing out through the skin, their tips wet and quivering.

Jenny screamed again. He took a step toward her, reached out, and grabbed her lower jaw, twisting it savagely, cracking bone and tearing muscle until Jenny's mouth hung slackly open. The scream stopped. He wrapped his arms around her and forced her backward onto the bed, pressing her down with the weight of his body. Before she could make another sound he brought his mouth down onto hers, his tongue snaking past her ruined jaw, probing deeper, sliding smoothly down her throat.

Her eyes stared wildly up at him, widening in pain as the coral spines burrowed under her skin, boring deeper and deeper, seeking out her organs.

She shook, her whole body going into spasms as the pain deepened. She knew with absolute clarity that she was going to die. No one could endure pain like this and survive. The knowledge brought with it an overwhelming calm.

She could no longer breathe. His tongue was blocking her windpipe. As the spines threaded through her, the gill-like mouths started to suck, drawing the blood and other fluids from her body, and she felt her life seeping away. All she could see was a handsome face above her, eyes closed, ecstatic, as he filled himself from her. Her body stopped shaking and she felt the pain ebb away, like the tide receding from beach. With a final shudder, Jenny McMillan died.

CHAPTER SIXTEEN

The Verani awoke early the next morning, climbed from the bed, and stared at its human form in the full-length wardrobe mirror. Across the stomach, spaced about two inches apart, were a series of diagonal scars, pink and slightly raised from the flesh around them. It probed with an index finger, tracing the rim of a scar. When it reached the center it smiled as the flesh parted wetly. Something sharp buried itself into the fingertip, drawing blood. It pulled the hand away and stuck the injured finger into its mouth, tasting the blood. Glancing down, it saw that a number of the other scars were opening, sharp pink spines pressing out and then drawing back, vanishing from sight, back inside the body. It glanced back at the bed. The desiccated husk of what had once been the plump body of Jenny McMillan still lay there. It would have to dispose of the remains. But that could wait.

It walked across to the window and looked out at the world. Now it had satisfied the immediate hunger it could take time to plan what the next move should be. If it searched the mind carefully it could still detect the memories of the man called Tanner. A whole host of memories for it to use. People, places, names, and faces. And it would use them ruthlessly in order to survive.

Having been trapped, shut away for so long, it had a desire for new experiences, and for the time being this body would serve, it would be used to experience as much as possible. There were old scores to settle; people who would pay for its incarceration. At Dunbar Court last night it had caught a glimpse of a life denied to it for so long. It had hoped to see the face of the man it had come to hate, but there were too many people there, and this body was too new, too unfamiliar to be used to its fullest extent. But that would change soon, and after all those wasted years it had learned patience.

The solution for getting rid of the body came quickly when it searched Tanner's memories. This house had a basement, a room that had only ever been used for storage, but the floor was flagstoned so it was an easy matter to lift several of the stones and dig out a few feet of the soft sandy earth. It would make a suitable grave.

Equally, carrying the body down to the basement was just as easy. It had no weight. It was nothing more than skin and bone, all fluids having been drained from it. The skin crackled like parchment as it lifted the body and threw it across its shoulder. Decomposition would not be a problem. Jenny McMillan's body had effectively been mummified.

It scraped the earth back over the body, replaced the slabs, and went back upstairs, where it showered. Its human body wasn't feeling particularly dirty or sweaty, but it had an overwhelming urge to feel the water on the skin.

After it dressed it made breakfast of toast and coffee, but everything tasted unpleasant, the coffee bitter and acrid, the toast like charred cardboard. It only took a couple of mouthfuls of each before the stomach heaved and it rushed to the sink to be violently sick. It vomited until the stomach was empty, but the spasms continued, and it dry-heaved for several minutes before the feeling passed.

Weak, it sat down at the kitchen table, pushed the remnants of the breakfast away. Its head pounded with intense pain. There was something within Tanner's mind that was fighting the Transition. It probed clumsily, still unused to using its powers and abilities. There it was, there, hatred. Inside Brian Tanner's trapped mind was hatred. The Verani let a low growl escape from its mouth. This was good. Hatred was something it could use to drive the human, to get closer to the family it wanted to destroy. *Laura.* That was the name Tanner kept repeating over and over in his brain.

Dean McMillan shifted uncomfortably in his seat. He'd spent a long, sleepless night waiting for Jenny to come home. When the sky outside his bedroom window altered subtly from a bluish black to a dull, metallic gray, and the first birds of the morning started their dawn chorus, he finally admitted to himself that she probably wouldn't be coming home. As he tossed and turned in bed, imagining his wife wrapped in the arms of another man, he cried, fat, wet tears that soaked his pillow and made him feel wretched.

He sent Jamie to his mother's house shortly after

breakfast. His mother only lived two streets away in a house very similar to his own. She loved the boy as if he were her own and was thrilled to think she'd have him for the day.

An argument with Jenny three years ago meant that she rarely got so see her grandson these days. The phone call from Dean was an unexpected delight and she immediately started to form a plan for the day. A trip to the park, maybe even a visit to Monkey World, the primate sanctuary just outside Wareham. For her it would be like old times. Her husband had walked out on her three years after the wedding when Dean was just two, and she'd built a close relationship with her son, always organizing trips they could take together, days out at the seaside—Weymouth or West Bay—visits to Hardy's Monument, sometimes something as simple as a walk through the nearby countryside.

Their special relationship lasted until Dean turned up one day with Jenny on his arm, and after that things were never quite the same again. Not that she didn't try to warm to her son's intended, but she found it difficult. Jenny's brash East London manner and her aggression grated, and soon the two women were at loggerheads, a situation that lasted to this day. As far as Marjorie McMillan was concerned, Jenny was common and nowhere near good enough for her son.

She'd hoped that with the birth of Jamie she could recapture some of the innocent pleasure of her past, but her daughter-in-law seemed to block her at every turn. Now she had a day with her grandson—just the two of them—and she could barely contain her excitement.

With the boy out of the house McMillan embarked on a long series of phone calls, telephoning each of Jenny's friends in turn, asking whether they'd seen her, trying to detect some hint, some clue as to where she might be. At eleven o'clock the doorbell rang and he hobbled to the door expectantly, disappointed when he saw a stranger standing on the doorstep.

Now the disappointment had turned to something like apprehension. Jim Raymond sat opposite him—cross-legged, totally relaxed—as he explained why McMillan should drop the claim he was making against Laura Craig.

Raymond was about Dean's age and about his size, but there was something in his manner that suggested immense power and latent violence. From the cropped brown hair to the muscular arms filling the sleeves of his jacket, stretching the leather, he looked every inch the professional thug.

"Who did you say sent you?" McMillan said.

Raymond allowed a brief smile to spread across his hard face. "I didn't, and that is information I'm not at liberty to divulge."

Since leaving the army in the early nineties Raymond had established himself as one of the foremost security experts in the country. The company he'd built from nothing provided bodyguarding duties for rock stars, advised on security for countless high-profile social events, and leased out doormen—bouncers—for many of the local pubs and clubs. But this was his favorite part of the job—acting as a negotiator on behalf of one of his many well-heeled clients. He'd worked for Richard Charteris many times in the past, liked him and respected him. This in itself was unusual, as there were few people he came into contact with that he respected without question. But Richard Charteris was different from many of the wealthy clients he worked for. Charteris's grandfather was an army man and had filled the young Richard's head with stories of his time in the forces. When he learned of Raymond's service background Charteris questioned him endlessly and enthusiastically about his time in the army. This common interest formed a bond between the two men and Raymond felt he would always go that extra mile to help Richard Charteris in any way he could.

At the moment he had five thousand pounds of his client's money in his pocket with which to persuade the shifty, nervous man sitting opposite him not to pursue the case against one of his friends, and he didn't intend to spend a penny of it.

He got up from the chair and went across to the fireplace. On a shelf above the outdated gas fire was a photograph in a cheap silver-plated frame. McMillan watched anxiously as Raymond spent several moments looking at the photograph of Jenny and Jamie taken last year on the beach at Bournemouth. His leg itched atrociously, but he tried to keep the scratching to a minimum; any more would have seemed a weakness in front of a man like Raymond.

"He looks like you," Raymond said. "Same eyes." He carried the photograph back to the seat and sat down, crossing his legs and resting the frame precariously on his knee. "You must be thankful that the accident happened to you and not your son. Young bodies break easily."

McMillan's mouth was dry. "What are you getting at?" he said.

"Nothing," Raymond said. "Nothing at all. I expect Jamie's having a whale of a time with his grandmother at the moment. So nothing to worry about there." With a flick of his hand he knocked the photo frame from his knee, sending it spinning into the hearth. The glass shattered on impact. "Sorry, clumsy of me. You see how easily accidents happen. Nobody's fault—but then that's the nature of accidents, isn't it, Dean? They just happen and nobody's to blame. Like *your* accident. There you are, knocking down a building, and suddenly, pow!" He slapped his leg with his hand. McMillan jumped in his seat.

"How did you know Jamie was with his grandmother?" McMillan said, staring down at the broken photo frame.

Raymond smiled. "Oh, I know an awful lot of things. Comes in handy in my line of work."

McMillan reached down and scratched at his leg savagely. He just wanted the man to go. He wanted to be left alone with his misery. "You're threatening me," he said.

Raymond gave a low whistle. "Harsh words, Dean. I was just trying to explain to you that this claim you're making against Laura Craig is ill-conceived, wrong-headed, and I feel it would be very unwise to pursue it, don't you?"

Oh, what the hell did it matter? McMillan thought. He had enough on his plate with Jenny gone and having to look after Jamie. He didn't need this thug in his house making veiled threats and scaring the life out of him. The claim was Jenny's idea anyway, and now she was gone and he didn't have the energy to pursue it further. "I suppose you're right," he said, avoiding the man's eyes.

Raymond nodded. "I usually am." He reached

into his pocket and took out a card with Simon Lawson's telephone number on it and handed it across to Dean, who took it without even looking at it. "That's Lawson's mobile, so you should be able to reach him, even on a Sunday. I'll just wait until you've made the call, and then I'll be gone. I don't want to take up any more of your time."

With a sigh Dean McMillan got to his feet and limped to the phone.

The phone call was brief and acidic. Lawson was furious to be pulled off the case and let his feelings be known. McMillan put the phone down. "Satisfied?" he said.

"Very," Jim Raymond said. "Well then, I'll leave you in peace. Alone with your thoughts. And take good care of the boy."

"Fuck off!" McMillan said bitterly, slamming the door behind Raymond's departing back. He hobbled back to the living room and bent to pick up the remnants of the smashed photo frame from the hearth. As he lifted a shard of glass his hand was shaking so much his fingers slipped and the glass sliced into the heel of his hand. He swore savagely, glaring down at Jenny's smiling face in the photograph. "Bitch!" he said. Well, he'd show her. Once and for all he'd show her.

He picked up the sliver of glass again and flopped down into his armchair. The pain in his leg was unbearable now, the inflammation, or whatever it was, was burning through his senses, making it the only thing on which he could concentrate. He laid his hand down on the arm of the chair, palm up, and drew the sliver of glass across his wrist. He hissed with the pain but grinned with satisfaction as blood spurted from the wound. It was not deep enough to cut into the vein, but the pain distracted his attention from the leg for a moment. But it was only a fleeting relief.

As quickly as he could, wincing throughout, he undid his trousers and pushed them with a combination of his hands and his feet. As they pooled at his feet on the sofa the state of his leg shocked him into a shivering fear. The leg was swollen as though it was filled with water. The skin was inflamed, the wound open and raw. The rash—it was too mild a word for the purple lesions on the flesh—had spread to his groin and was creeping down the other leg, and across his stomach.

The rash was covered with fine hair like a downy coating. It was like a growth, the hair was spreading, like fur growing into his skin. He could feel it probing under the skin, almost believed he could feel it tickling the underside of his flesh, feel it pulling at the veins, scraping the actual bones of his legs.

As he watched, horrified, the skin began to move. It rippled from inside as though something was burrowing underneath. Eventually his whole lower body was undulating, an obscene movement of flickering motion. With each movement the pain ricocheted through his body, causing his heart to stammer, his brain to explode with surges of energy, his lungs to contract.

Suddenly the skin on both legs peeled open, followed by the groin and stomach. The wound dripped pus and blood as the flesh drooped onto the furniture. Dean screamed as the pain became too much to bear. The skin continued peeling away until it fell to the floor, where it twitched like a dying snake. The legs were eaten away; there was almost nothing of them left once the outer skin was gone. A pain in the chest told Dean that his life was ending. The pain in his legs was as nothing compared to the hammer that hit him directly in his chest.

His dying thought was as inelegant as much of his life had been. Fuck you, Jenny.

Later that afternoon Raymond sat in his car across the street from Brian Tanner's large Victorian house. He'd been waiting for an hour, waiting for Tanner to go out. Housebreaking wasn't in his brief, but he prided himself that he was always prepared. He'd spent much of his waiting time with his laptop, checking Tanner out on the Companies House Web site. It told him little, but every scrap of knowledge was useful in its own way. And it *had* killed some time, but the minutes were ticking by and it looked as though Tanner was settled in for the rest of the day. He'd give it another half an hour, and then he'd call it quits and try again tomorrow. Surveillance was almost second nature to him. In the Gulf he'd spent many hours holed up in cramped positions, trying to flush out Iraqi snipers. Sitting in his comfortable car with his packet of foil-wrapped sandwiches, a Thermos flask of hot sweet tea, and a day's supply of chocolate bars was a much more luxurious stakeout situation.

Earlier he'd telephoned Richard's London flat to update him and tell him of Dean McMillan's decision to drop the claim against Laura Craig. He'd been mildly disappointed when the phone at the other end rang and rang, but when the answer machine kicked in he left a message. Hopefully Richard would hear it before he left for Dorset.

Although he had infinite patience for surveillance he liked quick results in every other aspect of his work, and he'd been pleasantly surprised how rapidly McMillan had crumbled. He had a fair grasp of psychology and the army taught him to identify his enemy's weaknesses and play on them. Of course he would never have hurt McMillan's son, never in a million years. He loved kids, especially his sister's two, who called him Uncle Jimmy and played with him endlessly whenever he went to visit. But McMillan wasn't to know that. Jim Raymond had saved his client five thousand pounds, defused a nuisance situation, and the only casualty was a cheap photo frame. It had been a satisfying morning's work.

He poured himself another cup of tea from the Thermos, bit into a Snickers bar, and watched the house. A short while later the front door opened and Tanner walked out into the late afternoon sunshine. Raymond slid down in his seat, watched, and waited. Tanner climbed into his BMW, started the engine, and drove out through the front gates without even a glance in Raymond's direction.

He watched as the car traveled the short distance to the end of the road, indicated right, and turned.

"Bingo," Raymond said under his breath, took another bite of his chocolate bar and washed it down with a mouthful of tea, and screwed the cap onto his Thermos flask. Now the game could begin.

CHAPTER SEVENTEEN

The red light on the answer machine was flashing as Richard hung his jacket up on a hook on the wall. He was about to press the *retrieve message* button when Laura called from the kitchen. "The kettle's on, tea or coffee?" The message would wait. It was probably work, and he was having too good a time at the moment to be bothered by the more mundane aspects of his life.

"Coffee," he called back and went through to the kitchen.

Laura was crouching down, examining the contents of his fridge critically. "What do you do for food when you're in town?"

"I normally eat out."

She stood upright and made an equally critical survey of his cupboards.

"We could always order a takeaway," he said. "There's a pretty decent Chinese up the road, or there's always pizza."

She turned to him, frowning. "I want to cook for you," she said. A packet of pasta caught her eye. Within moments she had the makings of a reasonable meal. Pasta, tuna, sweet corn, an unopened tube of sun-dried tomato paste, and a jar of sweet peppers. "Presto!" she said. "Pity there's no garlic, but I think I'll manage. Do you have any wine?"

"Merlot? I'm out of white."

"It'll have to do." She grinned at him.

Thirty minutes later they sat down to eat. Richard took a mouthful of the pasta bake she'd concocted and pulled a face. "Bloody awful," he said.

Laura smiled sweetly. "Just shut up and eat. It may not be up to Maison Novelli standards, but it's tasty enough."

He smiled at her. "Actually, it's quite delicious. Okay, you're great company, terrific in bed, and a resourceful and inventive chef. Marry me."

"Just like that? What happened to the noble tradition of getting down on one knee? And then there's the matter of the ring. An oversight maybe, but I'm a traditional girl. I like things to be done properly."

"And there was I thinking you were a maverick, a bit of a rebel. I'll bet your cottage had roses around the door."

"And a wishing well in the front garden."

"All you'd need is a dog, perhaps, to welcome you home after a hard day at the building site."

"There's always Socrates."

"Ah, a point in my favor. Tell me, when we first met, were you attracted to me, or was it really my dog that captured your heart?"

"Oh, the dog. No doubt about it. But then I got to

thinking. Owning a dog like that meant you had to be just the tiniest bit interesting."

"And did I live up to expectations?"

"Yes," she said. "You did."

He raised his glass to her. "Then here's to you and your expectations. Let's hope I never fall short of them."

Later, as she loaded the dishwasher, Laura said, "I had an interesting conversation with your mother on Friday. I had no idea her brother died, and at such a young age."

He said nothing. Laura glanced up at him. He was no longer smiling. There was a faraway look in his eyes.

"Sorry," she said. "Perhaps I shouldn't have mentioned it."

He seemed to shake himself. "No, it's all right. I didn't realize she'd spoken to you about it. What did she say exactly?"

"I'm afraid she got quite emotional. I think she still finds it hard to deal with, not knowing how he died. And the fact that once he died his memory was buried along with him."

"The old-fashioned British stiff upper lip, I'm afraid. I think my grandparents felt that if they didn't speak of it, then it never happened. I never knew my grandmother that well, but I know my grandfather was in denial until the day he died. Mother once said to me that I, in some way, had taken Uncle David's place, but I feel that's oversimplifying things. I can't begin to imagine what it must be like to outlive your children, and hopefully I shall never experience it myself." He closed the door to the dishwasher. "Would you mind if we changed the subject? I find this one quite depressing."

"Of course," she said, flushing slightly. "I shouldn't have brought it up. Thoughtless of me."

"I think we should make a move soon—head on back to Dorset."

"Oh, right, yes, I suppose we should."

"I'll go and pack my bag." He walked from the kitchen, leaving Laura floundering. Suddenly the carefree, happy mood of the weekend had changed, become darker, melancholy. Me and my big bloody mouth, she thought. But it was too late now to do anything about it. If she could turn the clock back five minutes she would. She realized then that there was an awful lot more to Richard Charteris than his happy-go-lucky, charming personality revealed. She just hoped she hadn't blown her chance of getting to know him better, because one thing had become more and more apparent to her over the course of the weekend. She was starting to fall hopelessly in love with him.

The drive back to Dorset was painful—a long, drawn-out journey interspersed with sporadic conversation and pregnant silences. Richard's mood had deepened to a surly moroseness, and Laura's attempts to lighten it grew more and more desperate. By the time they reached the M27 she gave up trying to repair the damage done by the conversation in the kitchen. She leaned back against the headrest and closed her eyes. If she pretended to be asleep it would at least spare her the trouble of proffering olive branches only to see them dashed from her grasp.

GET UP TO 4 FREE BOOKS!

You can have the best fiction delivered to your door for less than what you'd pay in a bookstore or online—only $4.25 a book! Sign up for our book clubs today, and we'll send you FREE* BOOKS just for trying it out...with no obligation to buy, ever!

LEISURE HORROR BOOK CLUB

With more award-winning horror authors than any other publisher, it's easy to see why CNN.com says "Leisure Books has been leading the way in paperback horror novels." Your shipments will include authors such as RICHARD LAYMON, DOUGLAS CLEGG, JACK KETCHUM, MARY ANN MITCHELL, and many more.

LEISURE THRILLER BOOK CLUB

If you love fast-paced page-turners, you won't want to miss any of the books in Leisure's thriller line. Filled with gripping tension and edge-of-your-seat excitement, these titles feature everything from psychological suspense to legal thrillers to police procedurals and more!

As a book club member you also receive the following special benefits:

- 30% OFF all orders through our website & telecenter!
- Exclusive access to special discounts!
- Convenient home delivery and 10 days to return any books you don't want to keep.

There is no minimum number of books to buy, and you may cancel membership at any time. See back to sign up!

*Please include $2.00 for shipping and handling.

YES! ☐

Sign me up for the Leisure Horror Book Club and send my TWO FREE BOOKS! If I choose to stay in the club, I will pay only $8.50* each month, a savings of $5.48!

YES! ☐

Sign me up for the Leisure Thriller Book Club and send my TWO FREE BOOKS! If I choose to stay in the club, I will pay only $8.50* each month, a savings of $5.48!

NAME: _____

ADDRESS: _____

_____

TELEPHONE: _____

E-MAIL: _____

☐ **I WANT TO PAY BY CREDIT CARD.**

☐ VISA   ☐ MasterCard.   ☐ DISCOVER

ACCOUNT #: _____

EXPIRATION DATE: _____

SIGNATURE: _____

Send this card along with $2.00 shipping & handling for each club you wish to join, to:

Horror/Thriller Book Clubs
20 Academy Street
Norwalk, CT 06850-4032

Or fax (must include credit card information!) to: 610.995.9274.
You can also sign up online at www.dorchesterpub.com.

*Plus $2.00 for shipping. Offer open to residents of the U.S. and Canada only.
Canadian residents please call 1.800.481.9191 for pricing information.

If under 18, a parent or guardian must sign. Terms, prices and conditions subject to change. Subscription subject
to acceptance. Dorchester Publishing reserves the right to reject any order or cancel any subscription.

JOIN NOW!

He took her directly to the site, got out to take her overnight bag from the trunk of the car, and handed it to her.

"I'm sorry," she said, not really sure why she was apologizing.

"There's no need to be," he said, but his tone was somber and there was no longer a smile in his eyes. "I'll call you," he said, pecked her on the cheek, and got back in the car. Seconds later she was staring at his taillights as he drove out into the lane.

"Yeah," she said, running her fingers through her hair. "Sure you will." With a sigh she hefted her bag onto her arm and let herself into the caravan. She dropped the bag onto the bed and followed it down, kicking off her shoes and lying full length. "Fuck it!" she said.

Richard drove with his headlights on high beams, illuminating the eyes of rabbits in the hedgerow and drawing countless moths into suicide collisions with the car. He was angry with himself. His behavior was inexcusable and unforgivable. He'd had no idea his mother had spoken to Laura about Uncle David until Laura dropped it into the conversation like a bombshell. His reaction had shocked him, and he was furious with himself now that he'd let himself be lulled into a false sense of security. It was naive to think that just because he was having a good time his responsibilities could be ignored. But that was exactly what he'd done.

For a few short hours he'd allowed himself to believe that he could act and react like a normal person, that he could enter into a relationship without heed of the past and its legacy. He'd learned from an early age that was not the case. A relationship could not be founded on half-truths and lies, and that was exactly what he'd have to do if he ever wanted to see Laura as anything other than a friend. The alternative was unthinkable. There was no possible way he could tell Laura the truth about David.

He realized he'd probably damaged their relationship beyond repair, but perhaps that was for the best.

Jim Raymond laid the Thermos down on the passenger seat. He got out of the car, locking the door behind him, walked across to the drive, and approached the front door. From his wallet he took out a thin strip of plastic and used it to open the lock of the front door. If only people realized how easy these locks were to open, they'd never sleep soundly in their beds, he thought as he pushed the door open and slipped inside the house.

The hallway was dark and cool and the house silent. Moving silently from room to room, he checked out the ground floor. The lounge was neatly furnished with a modern, comfortable-looking three-piece suite in white leather. There was a television flanked by a video recorder and DVD player. Set into an alcove in one wall was an illuminated fish tank, the brilliantly colored tropicals flitting backward and forward through the warm water while bubbles from an air pump eddied upward through a plastic model of an undersea wreck. A glass-topped coffee table occupied space in the center of the room, a large illustrated book on Spanish architecture lying open on it, a pile of music magazines beneath.

The dining room was similarly neat with a long

walnut dining table and six matching chairs, a low sideboard, and an expensive-looking music center. On the sideboard was a collection of framed photographs, mostly showing Brian Tanner at various stages in his life. Tanner the boy, dressed in football kit, crouching with a ball in front of a sports pavilion; Tanner the university graduate in ceremonial robe and mortarboard; Tanner the man, standing at the rail of a small motor launch in a marina surrounded by much grander craft.

Raymond moved through to the kitchen, but there was nothing here to engage his interest. The granite work tops were free of clutter, cupboards closed, the sink empty. Set in one wall was a door, which Raymond guessed led down to the basement. He tried it. Locked. He opened one of the cupboards. Packets and tins were stacked neatly, no half-used bags, plastic containers for flour and sugar.

A neat man, Raymond thought. A place for everything and everything in its place.

He went back out into the hallway and stood at the bottom of the stairs listening. Silence; as expected. All his research so far told him that Tanner was a bachelor and lived alone. But one could never be too careful. A girlfriend might have stayed over, and he moved through the house cautiously.

The bedroom door was open, the bed littered with discarded clothes. He walked past, stopping next outside a door he presumed to be the bathroom. He pressed his ear to the door. He could hear the spray from the shower hitting the tiles. He swore softly. Perhaps he'd been right about the girlfriend. He eased the handle down and opened the door a crack.

The room was filled with steam. It condensed on

the mirror above the sink and on the large frosted-glass window set in one wall. He stepped quietly into the room. The shower curtain was pulled around the stall, but there didn't seem to be any movement beyond it, not even the shadow of someone using the shower. Puzzled, he closed his fingers around the edge of the curtain and with one movement drew it back, making the curtain rings hiss on the rail.

Empty.

The water streamed out of the showerhead to splash uselessly on the pristine white tiles.

He heard a small cough behind him, and instantly realized his mistake. He really should have locked the front door behind him. He barely had time to turn before something hard and heavy crashed down on the back of his skull. His legs buckled as he lost consciousness and pitched forward into the shower stall.

A bee was buzzing around her head. Sleepily she waved it away. The caravan was in darkness and the bee continued to buzz. Gradually she came to, rubbing the sleep from her eyes. Her mobile phone rang persistently—not a bee at all. She yawned and stretched out her hand, picked up the phone, and switched it on. "Yes?"

"Ah, the wanderer returns," Maggie said. "Where the hell have you been? I've been worried sick."

"London," Laura mumbled. "Been to London. What time is it?"

"Ten o'clock. Were you asleep?"

"Must have been," Laura said, gathering herself and shaking off the last vestiges of sleep.

"Sorry. Didn't mean to wake you. So what were

you doing in London, and whom were you doing it with? As if I need ask. The lovely Richard?"

Memories of the drive home from London came crashing in on her. At least while she was sleeping she didn't have to torture herself, but now she was awake and the pain was like a sharp knife cutting slices from her. "Yes, he was there too," she said.

"Well, you don't seem very happy about it."

"No, I'm not. I think I've blown what could have been a wonderful relationship."

There was an element of sadness in Laura's voice that Maggie had rarely heard. "Tell Auntie Maggie all about it," she said gently.

Laura hesitated. She wasn't sure she really wanted to talk about it. The wound was too new, too raw. But at the same time she needed to go through, to see if she'd made such a terrible mistake. Maggie could provide a fresh perspective. She took a deep breath and began.

"So, do you think I've blown it?" Laura said.

"I agree it doesn't sound good," Maggie said. "But I don't think you should blame yourself. It sounds as if Richard has some issues that need to be dealt with. I *did* tell you they were rather an odd family. Mind you, losing her brother like that, it's not surprising that Catherine went off the rails. I think you should give it a few days, then call him. He'll have probably come round by then, realized he let a terrific catch like you slip through his fingers."

"I'm not chasing him, Mags. If he wants the relationship to continue, then it's up to him to make the first move."

"And we all know what pride comes before, don't we?"

"It's not pride, Maggie, honestly it's not. If you'd been in the car with us coming back from London you'd understand. I tried and tried to make it up with him. In the end I was making conversation just to break the awful silences. As you say, he's got issues. The first approach has got to come from him."

"So what are you going to do while you wait for him to come to his senses?"

"I have enough to do here to keep me occupied. I've got a stack of wallpaper catalogues and paint charts to go through. I'll keep busy. But . . ."

"But what?"

"I just hope I *haven't* blown it!"

Shaun slouched on the sofa aware of but not really watching the television. Siobhan stood in the doorway. "Are you going to be much longer?" she said. "Only I'd like to go to bed."

Shaun didn't look round from the screen. "You go on up. I'll be a while yet."

"What are you watching?" she said, taking a step into the room.

So far as he could make out it was some kind of American made-for-cable drama. The women were always impeccably made up, the men had hair that never moved, and the action took place in attention-deficit sound bites. Ideal for someone like him who was thinking entirely of something else. "A film. Not very interesting, but I've got into it now, you know. . . ."

"I thought you might have found a porn channel," she teased. "Come to bed. I'm feeling . . ." She came up behind him and wrapped her arms around his neck, nuzzling the soft skin beneath his ear with her lips.

Inside he tensed but he tried hard not to let that translate to his body. He didn't want to upset her. The last thing he wanted to do was upset her, but he was more afraid of what else he might do to her. "Another hour. Go and pour yourself a glass of wine, run the bath, light some candles. I'll be finished by the time you're ready for bed. Promise."

She disengaged herself. "Okay," she said. "Sounds good. Do you want a glass?"

"Yeah," he said. "Why not?"

He waited until she'd brought the wine and he could hear the bathwater running; then he turned the sound down and slipped his fingers beneath the thin material of his T-shirt, feeling the hairy, slimy growth that was covering his shoulder.

He would wait until he was sure Siobhan was asleep before getting into bed. He wanted to make love with his wife—they hadn't yet reached the stage where he was avoiding it, and hoped they never would—but he couldn't, not tonight, and maybe not again. The growth on his skin was spreading. It was getting deeper, the original patch denser, a coarser feel to it. He didn't want to risk spreading it to Siobhan.

He imagined he could feel tiny roots from the hairs burrowing under his skin, felt a tightness in the area beneath it that made it easy to believe the growth was eating his flesh.

For the first time since childhood he began to feel afraid. Very afraid.

Raymond's head felt like a mule had kicked it. He was lying naked on a stone floor, his wrists and ankles bound by what felt like duct tape. He struggled with the bonds briefly but soon realized that the more he strained against them the tighter they became. Eventually he stopped struggling and lay there, conserving his energy.

The room was dark, the only light entering the room seeping in from a dusty window set high in one wall. It seemed to be some kind of storeroom. There were the shadowed shapes of old furniture, piles of cardboard boxes, shelves on one wall stacked with tins of paint and rolls of browning wallpaper. Set in the wall to one side of the shelves was a steep wooden staircase. Leading to where?

The floor on which he was lying was rough and cold, concrete or stone. Its coldness seeped into his body, making his joints ache. Probably the basement, he realized. These old houses always had a basement. He wondered how he'd got down here. He weighed 220 pounds and it would have taken a feat of considerable strength to carry him down that narrow, almost vertical staircase, but apart from the crushing pain in his head, his body seemed undamaged.

He couldn't believe he'd been ambushed so easily. All those years of training counting for nothing. He was used to commanding situations, used to being in control. Now that control had been taken away from him and he felt foolish and vaguely frightened.

A noise to his left made him turn sharply—a furtive, skittering sound of something moving through the bundles of old magazines in the corner. Probably a mouse, he thought, and dismissed it. The noise above his head was not so easy to ignore. The ceiling was creaking as someone walked across the floor of the room above him, steady measured footsteps, unhurried. There was a small click and a creak as a door was opened. More light spilled into the room from the staircase. Feet appeared at the top of the stairs and then a light was switched on.

Raymond screwed his eyes up against the glare from the bright bulb hanging down from the ceiling.

"Is the light bothering you?" Brian Tanner said. He stood with the light behind him, throwing his face into shadow. Raymond said nothing. *Assess your enemy. Find out what he wants, what his motivations are.*

"You don't look very comfortable down there," Tanner said and moved around behind him. He slid his hands under Raymond's arms and dragged him backward across the floor, raking the skin from his buttocks. He propped him in a sitting position against a wooden tea chest. "There, that's better." Tanner took an old wheel-backed chair from a pile of furniture in the corner and set it down in front of Raymond, then sat down, leaning forward with his elbows on his knees, staring hard into Raymond's eyes.

Jim Raymond returned the gaze defiantly, his chin raised pugnaciously.

"So," Tanner said easily. "Who are you exactly . . . ? Oh, nearly forgot." He stood and took Raymond's wallet from the back pocket of his jeans. He flipped it open and produced a small white business card. "James Raymond—Raymond Security. Is this you? Yes, I suspect it is."

Raymond watched him cautiously. The ease in which Tanner had dragged him across the floor was alarming. He could have been dragging a bag of feathers, yet there was nothing about the other man's appearance to suggest such strength. He was big enough, but there was no obvious muscle development, no signs that he was anything other than a man that worked in an office. There was no strength in his demeanour either; despite his present advantage he seemed uncertain, almost nervous. Looks in this case, however, were deceptive. Raymond moved his position slightly, trying to ease the pain that was coming from his raw skin. A thin film of perspiration polished his brow and slowly dribbled down into his eyes. He blinked to clear them.

The Verani used Tanner's face to smile. It was enjoying this. It had ambushed Raymond so easily. It had been aware of Raymond's car across the road for much of the afternoon, and it was obvious the man was watching the house. Tanner had driven out of the road and parked around the corner, returning to the house on foot, almost at the same time that Raymond pulled the plastic strip from his wallet. From then on, the Verani had been behind him as soon as Raymond stepped through the door, but the other man was completely oblivious. He hadn't heard it walking but a yard behind, hadn't even sensed its presence there. In the bathroom Tanner deliberately coughed, just to let his intruder know he'd been caught. It was an immensely satisfying moment.

Tanner sat down again, flicking through the contents of the wallet. There was a surprising amount of money—four or five thousand in crisp fifty-pound notes. He removed them, folded the notes in half, and slipped them into his pocket. They could come in useful later. He watched Raymond's eyes widen furiously, but still the man didn't speak.

"I suppose you're wondering what I'm going to do

with you," Tanner said. "I certainly would if I were in your position."

"You can't keep me here," Raymond said, his voice thick with the dust from the room.

"Ah, it speaks. I was beginning to wonder if you were mute. Well, as you've started you might as well continue. Who employed you to come snooping about here, snooping on me?"

"I said you can't keep me here. I'll be missed."

"Really? Who by?"

"My secretary. I keep a log of my movements at the office," Raymond lied. "She's only got to check my diary to see where I am."

Tanner smiled. "And what entry did you put in your diary? Breaking and entering at Brian Tanner's house perhaps? No, I think not. Anyway, I'm prepared to take that chance. Should anyone come knocking on my door tomorrow looking for you I shall simply tell them you popped in for a chat, stayed ten minutes or so, and then left again."

Raymond glared at him.

"Oh, of course, there's your car, parked conveniently outside my house. Well, at least it was. I've moved it, quite far away actually. So, you're here, bound like a Christmas turkey, in the basement of my house. Chances of escape? Nil. Chances of leaving here alive? Slightly less. Unless, of course, you tell me what I want to know."

As Tanner spoke the Verani felt such immense excitement that for the first time since leaving the shelter it could imagine blue skies and warm sun. For the first time, even after the killing of the woman, it felt its heritage and all the power and strength that came with it.

"Go to hell," Jim Raymond said.

"I've been there, James . . . or is it Jim? Yes, Jim, I think. Well, Jim, you *will* tell me what I want to know." Tanner started to unbutton his shirt. "Indeed you will."

CHAPTER EIGHTEEN

Maggie Kennedy took a file from the cabinet and opened it on her desk, rifling through the papers until she found the one she wanted, and then she kicked her shoes off, lit her tenth cigarette of the day, and washed down the smoke with a mouthful of strong Colombian coffee. She felt awful this morning. Influenza had swept through the office like an invasion and two of the regular staff were laid up in bed, with doctors' sick notes guaranteeing them a week off. Only Paul Foster and Barry Hayes had turned up for work today, and the way she felt now it wouldn't be long before they were holding the fort by themselves. Usually most of the coughs and sniffles that laid her colleagues low passed her by and she'd always maintained that her diet of coffee and cigarettes gave her an immunity her abstemious staff lacked. But now she was forced to eat her words. Her head was pounding and her throat was raw. Soon would come the shivers and she would be incapable of working.

She brightened immediately when she saw Laura

step in from the street. She greeted her friend with a hug and a peck on the cheek. "Feeling better this morning?" Maggie said, her voice hoarse.

"God, you sound awful," Laura said. "When did you go down with this? You were fine last night when we spoke."

"I woke up with it. Bloody flu, I think. Coffee?"

"Yeah, I'd love one. Yes, I do feel better today. The restorative powers of sleep and all that." She sat down at Maggie's desk. It was the usual untidy clutter, property details sharing space with a computer terminal, telephone, half-full ashtray, and piles of leaflets for a couple of the local building societies. Maggie pushed some of the papers to one side and set the steaming mugs down.

"I was quite concerned about you last night," Maggie said. "I can't remember when I've ever heard you so down."

"I was tired," Laura said. "And thoroughly pissed off. Today I feel differently. I think it's about being proactive. Actually doing something, rather than just sitting in that bloody caravan moping."

"So what brings you into town?" Maggie said, lighting yet another cigarette.

Laura sipped her coffee. It was hot and strong, and gave an intense caffeine hit. She shuddered slightly. "Well, that certainly blows the cobwebs away. To answer your question, I'm trying to dig into the family history."

"No need to ask which family. So what will you be asking Richard, should you happen to locate him?"

"That's the problem. I'm not really sure. I still can't fathom why Richard reacted so badly to my question about his uncle. I've got to dig deeper if I'm to make any sense of it. Still, it's not all doom and gloom today. I got a phone call this morning from that odious Simon Lawson from the claims company. It seems the McMillans have withdrawn their claim."

"I'll bet that upset him."

"He seemed a bit annoyed, but then he had the gall to recommend his company to me, if ever I should need that kind of service."

"Cheek!"

"That's what I told him. But I must say, it's a weight off my mind."

"Did he say why they'd withdrawn?"

"No, and I couldn't get the reason out of him. Either way it's a relief."

"Hey, I've just had a thought." Maggie was grinning. "Do you remember that bloke I went out with a couple of years ago? Mark Jameson?"

Laura made a face that showed her disapproval. "Real pig as I recall."

"True, but he did have one saving grace. He used to be the chauffer for the Charterises."

"You're kidding?"

"They sacked him, about the same time as I dumped him. Shit happens even to pigs."

"Got his number? He might have something for me."

"I don't have it. I never bother to keep the telephone numbers of my exes. It would be too easy then to get in touch with them when I go through one of my periodic desperate phases. I realized a long time ago that ex-boyfriends are ex for a reason, so I never go back. All I can tell you about Mark is that when he gave up being a chauffer he took a job with a courier company in Dorchester, A to Z Express. I saw him a couple of months ago whizzing around town on his motorbike, so the chances are he's still working for them."

"A to Z Express," Laura said. "I'll check it out."

"It's run by a bloke called Harry Sharples. Greasy little small-time crook. Thinks he's Dorset Mafia, but really he's just a middle-aged loser."

The door to the agency opened and a middle-aged couple entered. Maggie got to her feet. "John, Eleanor, have you made a decision on Larksfield?"

The couple glanced at each other and exchanged smiles.

"I'll let you get on," Laura said, looking at her watch.

Maggie squeezed her hand. "Call me later," she said.

"Okay," Laura said. "And you really should think about calling it a day here and going home to bed."

"Yes, Doctor," Maggie said with a rueful grin. "I might just do that."

Richard had risen early, called Socrates from his basket in front of the range in the kitchen, and left the house. Socrates was a loyal and trusting companion. Richard had bought him as a puppy from a local dog breeder and the two had become almost inseparable ever since. Three hours of hacking across the countryside with the dog at his heels had done little to dispel his anger and done nothing at all to help him reach a decision about Laura Craig.

Dogs were far less complicated than people, their needs simple, their devotion unquestioning. Together they'd walked almost as far as the Hooper house, but Richard balked at calling in to see Laura. He had no idea how to approach her after the debacle of the weekend. He couldn't believe now that he'd acted so badly, but it was an instinctive reaction, born out of panic. He'd always avoided questions about his family, preferring to live in the here and now, rather than to think too deeply about the past, but Laura's question about his uncle David brought him face-to-face with issues he sought desperately to avoid.

He returned home, legs aching, shoes muddy, ready to confront his mother.

Catherine was arranging flowers in one of the vases that lined the walls of the hallway. "Where have you been?" she said. "I missed you at breakfast." Then, seeing the thunderous look on her son's face, she said, "What's the matter?"

Richard glared at her. "We need to talk."

She looked at him uncertainly. "Come through to the library."

"You told Laura about David," he said without preamble as Catherine settled herself in a club chair in front of the still smouldering fire.

"I didn't see any harm," Catherine said.

"That's because you don't think before you open your mouth." He was pacing backward and forward in front of the fireplace, clenching and unclenching his fists.

"Oh, for God's sake! You're starting to sound like your grandfather. That's just the way he used to speak to Mother."

Richard looked at her steadily, and then his shoulders sagged. "I need a drink." He went across to a small cabinet in the corner, took out two glasses, and poured stiff measures of scotch into each. He handed one to his mother and took a mouthful of his own. Then he flopped down into the chair opposite Catherine's and ran a hand through his hair.

"So where's Laura? I thought she'd be staying over," Catherine said, sipping her drink economically.

"I dropped her off at her place last night."

"And are you going to see her again?"

"I doubt it . . . I don't know."

She reached across and squeezed his hand. "You should. I think she's good for you."

He snatched his hand away. "So do I, but how can I possibly get involved with her? Bringing her into this family would mean telling her the truth about David, about Grandfather, everything."

"What are you talking about?" Catherine said.

"You told her David died."

"David *did* die."

"He didn't," Richard said softly. He drained his glass and poured himself another. It was no use. He'd kept silent for too long. The burden of truth was weighing too heavily to be carried by one man. "Mother, David didn't die when he was thirteen. I know that's what you were told, and what you've told yourself all these years. But I know the truth, Grandfather told me on my twenty-first birthday. He made me swear I'd keep it to myself, not tell anyone— especially not you—but with what's happened over the past few days, I can't keep it to myself any longer."

Catherine took another sip of her scotch. He noticed her hand shook as she raised the glass to her lips. She said nothing.

"You must try to understand how this has affected me," Richard continued. "I've had to carry this burden all my life. If you had any idea—"

Catherine slammed her hand down on the arm of

her chair, slopping her whiskey over the edge of the glass. "For God's sake, Richard, stop being so bloody sanctimonious. You really think you're the only one to be touched by this? That you're the only one who knows the truth? If so, then you're being bloody naive."

He stared at her openmouthed.

"For as long as I can remember I've known that there was something very wrong in this family," she said. "Why do you think I ran away from this place as soon as I could? My life up until then had been layer upon layer of lies and deceit. Only getting away from it could I find myself, find the truth. David was my brother—at least I regarded him as such—we had different mothers, different genes, different blood running through our veins, but that didn't matter. I loved him more than I've ever loved anyone in my entire life."

"Grandfather told me you didn't know anything about him."

"Your grandfather said many things. Some true, some downright lies. What did he tell you about David?"

"He told me the most important thing. About his time in Africa. About the native girl he got pregnant and the thing she gave birth to."

Catherine glared at him hotly. "Don't talk about David like that. He wasn't a thing. He was a person. A kind, sweet, caring person."

"He fathered a monster! A monster so dangerous it had to be locked up, incarcerated."

Catherine laughed bitterly. "So that's what your grandfather told you. That's what you've believed all these years? And you thought I was the one deluding myself. Bloody hell! Why on earth have you never spoken to me about this before now?"

"With all due respect, Mother, you weren't here. You were never here. You were always off, indulging your whims like the true selfish bitch you are."

Catherine's eyes filled with tears. "Don't you dare judge me. You haven't the right. You understand nothing, Richard. I've never told you about what my life was like here, both before and after you were born. I've never wanted to burden you with it. But can you imagine what it's like to grow up, unloved, ignored by your own parents?"

"I've a pretty good idea," he said acidly. "Had it not been for Grandfather, that's exactly what my life would have been like. Let's face it; you were hardly the doting mother, were you? Christ Almighty, you were away for so long I actually forgot what you looked like!"

Catherine shifted uncomfortably in her seat. Richard's barb had hit home and she had no answer to it.

He continued. "When you came back here to live it disrupted everything. You expected me to treat you like a mother, but I didn't even know you."

Catherine stared down at the floor, avoiding the accusation in her son's eyes. "I'm sorry. I had no idea you felt like this."

"I've never told you, because I've never thought our relationship was strong enough to stand it. So many things we've never spoken about. We live in this house together, but in actual fact we're total strangers. All this time you knew what your brother was and not once, *not bloody once*, did you think to discuss it with me." He finished his drink and poured another.

She shook her head. "I didn't know your grandfather had told you about him. It seems we've been suffering from the same delusion."

"Grandfather was trying to protect you."

"No!" Catherine said hotly. "Your grandfather wouldn't have cared if I'd been hit by a bus. I didn't exist as far as he was concerned. David was all he cared about, and when you came along you took David's place in your grandfather's eyes. But please don't try to tell me he cared about me, because I know the truth. Did you know for instance that my conception came about when your grandfather raped my mother?"

Richard's eyes widened and he made a half-choking sound in his throat. "I don't believe—"

"Shut up and listen. I've listened to you; now grant me the same courtesy. Their marriage had ended a few years before, when he came back from Africa. When he and Tom Hooper were stationed in Aden your grandfather got a local girl pregnant. He returned home with the child she'd borne him. David—the monster, as you like to call him. For years they played out this ridiculous charade, pretending Tom was the father of the child, but my mother was so bitter she finally revealed the truth, and he was forced to accept David as his own. It became very clear to me then that I was unwanted and unloved. Not that I held it against David. He was a wonderful person and I worshipped him, but your grandfather did everything he could to discourage us from forming a proper brother-sister relationship.

"I was shut out, isolated. As soon as I was old enough I ran away. I'd met a local boy and he played in a pop group—Christ, that sounds so prosaic now—

and they'd been offered a residency in a club in Hamburg. I went with them, traveling to Europe in a beaten-up old Bedford van. Once there we stayed in a room in the basement of the club. Four boys and me. A romantic adventure it was not. We eventually split up and I hitched to Holland and then back to Belgium. It was there I met your father."

Richard's eyes narrowed. "I don't want to hear any more."

"Tough!" Catherine said sharply. "You can't sit there in judgment without hearing my side of the story. I wanted to tell you all this years ago; but, like you, I didn't think our relationship would stand it. I'm not blind, Richard, or stupid. I recognized your resentment years ago. I just hoped that as time went by the wounds would heal and we could at least learn to like, if not love, each other.

"Your father was a wealthy businessman from Bruges. We met while I was hitching. He gave me a lift and by the end of the journey he'd invited me to stay at his flat in the city. I was young, naive, and he was handsome and spoiled me, indulging my every whim. It was three months before I realized he was married with a young family, living in a small town just outside the capital. I was his piece on the side, a diversion from his otherwise mundane life. Of course by the time I discovered this I was carrying you.

"To be fair to Fabrice he didn't turn me out on the streets. He let me stay at the flat for the length of my confinement, and paid for a room at a private clinic when you were due to be born. Afterward he paid my airfare home. I never saw him again."

Richard was avoiding her eyes, sipping his drink and staring morosely at the floor.

"It's a measure of my naivety that I imagined things would be different when I returned home, but if anything they were worse. Your grandmother was drinking heavily by this time and was living in virtual seclusion in the east wing of the house. I rarely saw her, though she did go out from time to time. She had thrown herself into charity work with a vengeance, though how the people she worked with didn't realize she was an alcoholic I'll never know, but then they say that addicts are very adept at hiding their addiction."

"And there speaks the voice of experience," Richard said flatly.

She glared at him, but continued. "Once I was back here I was desperate to get away again. This place can be so stifling, like a prison. I tried all sorts of diversions, parties, inviting friends for long weekends, but I knew before long I'd have to leave here. Your grandfather had made you his personal responsibility and he more or less denied me access to you. He saw me as a disruptive and corrupting influence. Unfortunately I gave him the opportunity to send me away. He had friends in Switzerland and he paid them to find me somewhere to live out there. And there I stayed until I found out he was dying. You know the rest."

"I know you didn't waste any time getting back here once you realized you might inherit the Court."

"That's maybe how it seemed to you, but the truth was a little more involved than that. When I was away I spent a lot of time in libraries, researching. I had to find out the truth about David. Unfortunately I did, and then wished with all my heart I hadn't. I told Laura David died, because to me he did. He died when he was thirteen years old and by telling myself that over and over again all these years I've managed to stay sane. I knew what he was, Richard. God, I saw it with my own eyes."

Richard looked at her steadily. "Explain," he said.

"I will," she said. "I will."

Dunbar Court—July 1959

Catherine watched as Tom Hooper stuck a garden fork into the compost heap and hefted the forkful of rotted vegetation into a nearby wheelbarrow. She'd been playing in the garden for over an hour and he'd barely said two words to her. Normally he was chatty, ruffling her hair, telling her slightly rude jokes, but for the past few days he'd been withdrawn and moody, barely raising a smile. It made her isolation in the house nearly complete. Now there was only Elizabeth Ryder who had any time for her. She loved Elizabeth deeply. She was a wonderful, kind person who, no matter how busy she was, always had time for a friendly word. But today Elizabeth had gone into town with Catherine's mother and the responsibility of looking after the eight-year-old fell to Nanny Pyper. If Catherine loved Elizabeth, then she hated Nanny Pyper, an elderly woman with stiff gray hair and a ramrod-straight spine, who rarely smiled and always smelled of lavender water. Nanny Pyper's idea of fun was to stand over Catherine while she did her school homework, pointing out errors of grammar and math with a sharp fingernail and even sharper words. The only reason Catherine was in the garden now was that Nanny Pyper had drunk a glass of sherry with her lunch and was now asleep in her room, snoring loudly.

Her mother she rarely saw. Lady Helen occupied most of her time with charitable works, heading this committee and that women's group. She rarely acknowledged Catherine's existence, and when she did it was usually a criticism. Catherine could never remember her mother taking her on her knee, kissing her good night, brushing her long golden hair; the things she was sure other mothers did. At least they did in the books she submerged herself in. Little Women, Black Beauty, Peter Pan. Where would she be without her books? Her escape into fantasy worlds was so much more exciting than the life she lived.

Her father spent much of his time away from the Court. She knew he was fairly important, but the job he did was a mystery to her. She knew it involved dressing up in robes and talking a lot at the Houses of Parliament, but more than that eluded her. She saw him even less than she saw her mother and he hardly ever spoke to her, not even unkindly. Whenever she was in the same room as him it was as if she was invisible. Nanny Pyper was fond of saying, "Children should be seen and not heard," but in Catherine's case with her father she was neither seen nor heard.

She missed her brother terribly. David had been gone for weeks now and no one would tell her where he was. He didn't even say good-bye to her. The first time she realized he was no longer at the Court was one breakfast time when the table in the nursery was set for one instead of two. She sat eating her cornflakes in silence, wondering where he was, until at the third solitary breakfast she plucked up the courage to ask Nanny Pyper where he'd gone. She was *told to mind her business and eat her breakfast, and earned a slap on the leg when she refused to let the subject drop.*

After that she'd kept her distance from Nanny Pyper, turning instead to Elizabeth, hoping she might tell her where David was. Elizabeth was unusually reticent, telling her that the only person who could answer her questions was her father. She did, however, wrap her arms around her and gave her a hug. "I can't tell you, sweetheart, because I don't know," the maid whispered in Catherine's ear. "None of us do."

But Catherine was not to be easily dissuaded from her quest to find her brother.

A little over a week ago, when Tom Hooper was more his old self, he took her back to his house and they spent a warm summer's afternoon in Tom's potting shed as he showed her how to take softwood cuttings from the many shrubs that grew in his garden. As she filled pots with compost and watched as Tom stripped leaves from the short stems with his old army knife she looked out through the grimy shed window and was surprised to see Mary, her brother's almost constant companion, emerge from one of the outbuildings to the left of the house. The woman carried a bucket covered by a towel and made her way to the house, where she disappeared inside.

It was some time later when Mary reappeared, walking quickly, almost furtively, back to the outbuilding. With one quick look about her to check that she hadn't been seen, she pulled open the door and stepped out of the sunlight into the gloomy interior.

Catherine said nothing to Tom about what she'd seen, but when she got back to the Court she thought about it endlessly, her mind conjuring up all sorts of possible explanations. A steady diet of Enid Blyton mysteries to supplement the classic books she read had given her a vivid *imagination, and she finally convinced herself that David was being held prisoner at Tom Hooper's place. Why, she couldn't imagine, but a number of dark scenarios played over and over in her mind until she came to one firm decision. She would take it upon herself to rescue him.*

She waited patiently for an opportunity. Waited until the eagle-eyed Nanny Pyper was distracted and unable to check her whereabouts. As she watched Tom fork the compost into the wheelbarrow she realized she probably wouldn't get a better chance.

She edged slowly toward the gate at the bottom of the garden that led to the woods surrounding the Court. There was a path in the wood that would take her to Tom Hooper's cottage. She'd only taken it once before, with Tom as her guide, but was fairly confident she could find her way.

As Tom turned back to the compost heap she slipped through the gate and closed it silently behind her.

As the gate closed she felt she had stepped into another world—a world of dappled shade and flickering sunlight, of eerie birdcalls and mysterious scrabblings of woodland animals.

The path was a well-worn track of dried mud and flattened bracken. She walked quickly, brushing away clouds of midges that swarmed in small clouds, flitting pointlessly about her head. She glanced back at the gate, half expecting it to open and for Tom to emerge, angry words on his lips, calling her back to the house. But the gate stayed shut and after five minutes she'd lost sight of it altogether.

It was much cooler in the wood, cooler than she'd expected, and she shivered slightly in her crisp, thin cotton blouse. Her socks, as usual, were around her ankles, but she pulled them up her legs as far as they would go as some protection from the vicious bushes of stinging nettles that lined the path together with great clumps of dock and thistle.

As she walked deeper into the wood it grew even darker, the canopies of the trees above her growing closer together and shutting out the sunlight almost completely. Here the undergrowth changed slightly. Wild foxgloves grew in profusion, their stately spikes of purple flowers moving gently in a breeze only they could feel. Toadstools grew in fairy rings by the side of the path, and ferns replaced the stinging nettles, their lacy fronds catching what little light slipped through the crowns of the trees above.

Birdsong seemed more muted here, as if the magpies, thrushes, and jays were sitting on branches high above her watching her hesitant progress below. Occasionally she'd catch a glimpse of a squirrel scampering up the trunk of a tree or a wood pigeon gliding from one branch to another. Farther on she was startled when the undergrowth parted and a small deer stepped out onto the path in front of her. It only lingered for a second before it sensed her presence, its innocent round eyes swiveling to meet hers for an instant. Then it turned tail and darted off into the shelter of the thick swathes of rhododendrons that filled great areas of the wood.

She was beginning to feel frightened, and a nagging little voice whispered in her ear that she should never have come into the woods alone. Visions of the witch's gingerbread cottage from Hansel And Gretl popped into her mind, unwelcome visitors in her thoughts, joined by the wolf from Little Red Riding Hood. She quickened her pace, almost running along the path, not daring to look anywhere but straight ahead in case she saw a pair of evil eyes staring back at her from out of the undergrowth.

She'd been walking for an hour and the light in the wood was gradually changing, becoming brighter as the trees *thinned. Seconds later she emerged from the wood and found herself just yards away from Tom Hooper's cottage. The potting shed and the outbuildings were at the side of the house, and from where she stood, in the shadow of a tall elm, she had a clear view of them.*

All she needed now was for Mary to leave the outbuilding as she had the other day. It didn't occur to her that Mary, and indeed David, might not be there; neither had she prepared herself for a long wait on the woodland edge.

Thirty minutes later her stomach rumbled and she realized she hadn't eaten since breakfast. She should have prepared better for this. She should have made some sandwiches, or at least taken an apple to eat to stave off the hunger pangs that were starting to gnaw at her stomach.

She had no wristwatch, no way of knowing how long she'd waited, except for watching the passage of the sun across the sky. Tom Hooper once showed her the sundial in his garden and told her how to tell the time using the shadow. He'd said she could do the same with a stick planted in the earth, but she didn't really know how to mark out the increments for the hours. Instead she started counting. First the seconds, and then, using her fingers to keep track, the minutes.

She'd counted ten minutes thirty seconds when the door to the outbuilding opened and Mary stepped out, shielding her eyes against the sun. No bucket this time, but that didn't seem to matter. As before she walked up the flattened earth path to the house and let herself inside.

It was now or never, Catherine thought. Running on tiptoe she covered the hundred yards to the brick-built outbuilding in seconds. A Suffolk latch secured the door and she pulled the lever down and slipped inside.

For a moment she was disappointed. There was nothing here apart from a collection of garden tools, an ancient lawn mower, and a rack of lichened terra-cotta flowerpots. And then she saw the trapdoor. Set into the floor and constructed from stout boards, the trapdoor was secured by a heavy cast-iron bolt.

David was down there. He had to be. She sank to her knees and slid back the bolt. Using two hands she lifted the door, resting it against the wall of the building. She was expecting a dark and gloomy pit, but instead the room below was lit by the flickering light of an oil lamp. There was a metal ladder set into the wall below. Gripping it tightly she descended. She didn't dare try to pull the door closed behind her. It was far too heavy to support and she needed both hands to hold on to the ladder. When Mary returned and found her there she'd be furious. She'd tell Father and Catherine would probably get a spanking, but the imperative was to find David. Nothing else mattered.

She reached the bottom of the ladder and looked about her. She was in a large room, lined with brick. Against one wall was a single bed, neatly made. Resting on the counterpane was an embroidery ring, the work—a picture of a rose picked out in red, gold, and green silk—half completed. Against the other wall was a bookcase packed with Barbara Cartland romances and Louis L'Amour westerns. A suitcase stood open on a small trestle table in the corner, and next to the bed a nightstand with a clock and the oil lamp.

The most curious feature of the room was a circular hole in the floor, beyond it a doorway set into the wall covered by a thick brocade curtain. She approached the hole cautiously and peered over the edge. It was a well, the surface of the water just inches from the brick surround. She stepped around it and stood before the curtain.

"Who's there?"

The voice that came from behind the curtain sounded like David, but different somehow. Deeper, more guttural.

"David?" she said. "It's me, Cathy."

There was a thump on the other side of the curtain that sounded like a wet sack had been dropped onto the floor. This was followed by a slithering sound that made the hairs on her arms start to prickle.

"You shouldn't be here," the voice said.

"I want to see you," Cathy said, but stood stock-still, not venturing closer to the curtain.

"No!" The voice was vehement. "You mustn't see me. Not like this."

Cathy shifted from foot to foot uncertainly. She wanted to see her brother, but there was something about that voice, and that slithering sound, that stopped her moving forward. She glanced back at the ladder, at the opening made by the trapdoor. Perhaps she should just go. Go before Mary came back and discovered her here. Go before the curtain was pulled back and she saw what was on the other side.

No! She'd come here to see David and she wouldn't go until she had.

"David, please let me see you. Come back to the house with me. I miss you."

The slithering again, and the curtain twitched. Cathy took a step backward.

"Go away from here, Cathy. Go away before I hurt you."

"Hurt me? Why should you want to hurt me?"

A pause. Silence. The curtain twitched again. "Can't . . . Can't help myself . . . Go! Go now!"

The anger and anguish in her brother's voice terrified her. She took another step backward, then another, but her foot connected with empty air and she tumbled back into the well. She screamed as stale, brackish water poured into her mouth and down her throat as she sank beneath the surface. She flailed with her arms, trying to swim, but her

216

hands hit the slimy brick of the walls. Her clothes soaked up the water, growing heavier, dragging her down. "David!" her mind screamed. "David, please help me!" But a suffocating blackness was already beginning to envelop her, and her thoughts were starting to drift, buoyed on the inky black water. Gradually consciousness began to slip away.

Just as she closed her eyes and prepared to accept the cold, black embrace, strong hands grabbed her under her arms and hauled her out of the water.

She lay on her back on the cold hard stone at the edge of the well.

"Is she . . . ?" Mary's voice drifting through her hazy thoughts.

"Stand back. Give her air."

Cathy coughed, expelling a lungful of filthy water. She opened her eyes and stared up into the concerned and kindly face of Tom Hooper.

"Why she down here?" Mary's fractured English again.

When Hooper was sure Cathy was breathing normally he scooped her up in his muscular arms and carried her across to the ladder. "Not a word about this," he snapped at Mary.

"But I want to see David," Cathy said, struggling in Tom Hooper's arms, then looked back at the now open curtain. And she screamed.

Laid out on the floor, much like a discarded rug might be or a blanket slung over a bed, was a small uneven shape. In the few seconds she had to look she realized what the shape was. Shriveled with nothing left inside it, torn slightly where attack had taken place, it was the empty skin of David. The arms were thrust forward as if ready to dive into water, while the legs were spread out behind. The head was wrinkled with threads of hair curled across. The torso was split across the back, the pink raw skin already turning gray.

Suddenly the curtain billowed as something pressed against it.

"Get back!" Tom Hooper said, the distaste evident on his face. Mary moved forward, speaking quickly in Arabic, blocking Catherine's view.

Then a dark movement pushed past Mary; there were no legs, just a fleshy pad of tissue that rippled across the floor with wet, sucking sounds. Catherine screamed again and buried her face in Tom Hooper's shoulder.

"I said, get back!" Tom Hooper said again and moved purposefully toward the ladder and started to climb.

Hooper carried the sobbing girl up the ladder. Once at the top he kicked the trapdoor shut with his work boot and carried Cathy out into the daylight.

Cathy lifted her face from his shoulder. "But David—" she said.

"David's dead," Hooper said sharply. "What you saw down there doesn't exist, y'hear? Doesn't exist at all." He stared hard into Catherine's eyes, daring her to disagree. Eventually she nodded her head slowly as hot tears dribbled down her flushed cheeks.

CHAPTER NINETEEN

"You see? To me David died when I was eight years old," Catherine said. "For a long time I blocked that day out of my mind—children have the ability to do that. It was only when I reached my teens that I started to think about it again. I'd have nightmares where I was back in that room, just standing there in front of the curtain, watching it slowly being pulled back. I ran away to get away from my life here, but I think I was also running from the memory of that day. The drugs helped, and have helped ever since. They help me sleep dream-free, which is a small blessing."

Richard said nothing for a moment. He sat, cross-legged, picking at an imaginary thread on the knee of his chinos. Finally he said, "All these years and you never told me." It wasn't an accusation. He was beyond recriminations now. His mind struggled to digest what he had just been told. "I'm sorry," he said. "I had no idea."

"It's not your fault. Hell, it's not anybody's fault,

except maybe your grandfather's. He started all this because he couldn't control his libido. Couldn't keep it in his trousers long enough to think of anyone else. They say the sins of the fathers are visited upon their children. I think we, as a family, have been reaping the whirlwind ever since." Catherine got to her feet. "Come with me. I want to show you something."

She led him up the stairs to her bedroom. She reached under the bed and dragged out an old suitcase, battered, rubbed, and secured with a strap. A thick coating of dust covered the lid. She unbuckled the strap and released the catches. Inside was a collection of books and envelope folders.

"This is the result of all the research I did. The real breakthrough came when I went to Morocco. I found people there who were willing to talk about their myths and legends. To them, you see, they were very real, almost commonplace." She handed Richard a folder.

He sat on the bed and opened it, taking out a sheaf of paper covered with his mother's neat script.

"It took me five years to compile all this. The girl your grandfather got pregnant was a Verani—an ancient race of people from the area he was stationed in just after the war—but then he probably told you that. I have documents here, eyewitness accounts of this sort of thing happening time and time again throughout the centuries. Take your time, read through the papers. I think you'll come to the same conclusion as me that whatever David was, it wasn't his fault, and he certainly wasn't a monster.

"The typed sheets contain the information I managed to get from various libraries and from people I interviewed. The handwritten ones fill in some of the gaps. Most of that came from Tom. After Father died he saw no reason not to tell me what he knew. He was there when the Verani girl gave birth. He and your grandfather were summoned to witness it by the local chieftain. The Arabs killed the mother, you know. Slit her throat. Seems that's just another of the traditions."

Richard was listening without really hearing what was being said to him. His mind was reeling from these new revelations and he was beginning to feel slightly sick.

There were so many questions now, so much he needed to learn. If he had any future at all with Laura he had to deal with the question of his heritage once and for all. He had to get used to the fact that his grandfather had probably lied to him. He shuffled the papers, leaned back against the headboard of the bed, and started to read.

"I'll get us another drink," Catherine said, returning several minutes later with two more whiskies. Richard was engrossed. She sat on the chair by the dressing table and stared at her reflection in the mirror. Perhaps now was time to make a fresh start. It would be hard work. She would have to confront her own personal demons and nullify them. She would have to kick the drugs she had come to rely on so heavily. But today marked a new chapter in her relationship with her son, and with Richard at her side, she knew she could find the strength to change her life forever.

Richard's eyes flicked over the pages. The story that unfolded was in turn fascinating and frightening.

The Verani are believed to have come about in the ninth century when Prince Veran was ruling a small part of the Sudan. Legend has it that he travelled to Morocco with his family to trade and while they were there a Hurana, a Moroccan water demon, seduced his daughter. The result of this coupling was a race of people who took their name from the family. Verani were born with the ability to breathe on land or in water. They were feared and respected, treated like gods in some parts of North Africa. The legend has it that all the males of the race lived as humans until puberty, but once that time arrived they changed, the part of them that was Hurana became more dominant, turning them back into water demons.

Of course, water demons aren't limited to Arab culture. There are references to them in many cultures, all under different names. India has its Vrita; in Japan they fear the Kappa; in Tanzania they tell stories of the Katavi. And then, of course, there's the Scottish Kelpie. I believe there's even references to them in early Christian documents, though the collective churches of the West tend to sit on details like that, and I don't believe much has been heard about them.

Verani are particularly violent. Docile until puberty, they can live as normal humans for the first thirteen years of their life. After the Transition they can only exist out of water by infusing themselves into a human body. Effectively trapped like that until they can re-immerse in water, they also need to feed by killing other humans, and the feeding pattern seems to vary depending on the age of the Verani.

As they are capable of hibernating for years at a time, there is no record of how long an adult Verani lives. The other reason they appear to need human form is so that they can mate. Female Verani mate with human males and male Verani seek out human women to impregnate.

I first came across them in a work about the life of Pêro Da Covilhã, the Portuguese explorer. Da Covilhã was in the service of Alfonso V and when he died, he served his son, James II. James sent Da Covilhã on two missions to North Africa. In 1493 Da Covilhã sent a communiqué to James telling of his experiences in the area. It seems that while in Cairo he hooked up with a group of Arab merchants and travelled with them to Aden. In the communiqué he mentions that traveling with them were two women and a young boy. Both the women and the boy seemed to be held in extraordinarily high regard by the merchants—almost deference. He was told this trio were Verani, an ancient race of people from Morocco, and it was their job to see they had safe passage to the north. Da Covilhã didn't go into too much detail, but made a point of mentioning a rather strange occurrence at an oasis midway through their journey.

It transpired that upon reaching the oasis the young boy walked out into the middle of the water hole and simply disappeared beneath the surface. The women he was with seemed completely unconcerned, but the men threw themselves to the ground in supplication. Unfortunately Da Covilhã never elaborated further, but his account ties in with what I've learned since.

Slowly a picture began to form in Richard's mind and the more he read the more his stomach began to heave with apprehension. "One question," he said heavily.

"Go ahead."

"Where did Grandfather lock David away?"

"At Tom Hooper's. There are cellars underneath the grounds that used to belong to the Dunbar Court chapel. When they knocked the chapel down they built the house on the same site."

He threw the papers down on the bed. "But you were there the other day. Surely you saw the cellar was open?"

Catherine looked away.

"You saw and you said nothing? Why?"

"I told you before. David's dead."

"Oh, you stupid, stupid woman. You did all this research, you wrote ream after ream about the Verani, and you still cling on to your vision of your precious David."

"It's nearly fifty years, Richard."

"And the Verani *hibernate!* You knew that and still you said nothing. I've got to go and see Laura," he said, swinging his feet to the floor. "I need to get her away from there."

"Why? She accepted my story at face value. Richard, it's ancient history. Leave it buried."

"If the Verani is free, who knows what it can do or where it might go?"

"It's dead; nothing could survive so long without food. David is dead."

Richard looked at her and a wave of sadness washed over him. All these years they had lived together and neither had had the courage to tell the other what they knew. All those wasted years, each keeping their own part of the legend locked away and safe.

Now, now when it was too late, they chose to speak to one another.

He realized that his mother was clinging to her false hope that David had died at thirteen. It was the only way she could live with the curse that had been foisted onto her family, the only way she could cope.

"David didn't die, he changed into Verani. It says so here in your own notes."

Catherine shook her head. "Even if David remained alive—"

Richard interrupted her fiercely. "The human that turns into the Verani ceases to exist once the change has taken place. From that moment on all the Verani craves is food and reproduction. It says so here. . . ." Richard picked up a sheaf of paper and thrust it into his mother's hands.

"Dead," she repeated as if was a mantra. "He has to be dead. I saw his body."

Richard tried to speak gently but he was overcome with fear. If the Verani had escaped, Laura and anyone at the Hooper site was in grave danger. There was the physical danger of being attacked, but there was more to it than that alone.

"It says in your papers that the Verani can parasitize a human body in order for them to mate. What if it has already done that to some poor soul?"

"Impossible! You're letting your imagination run away with you," Catherine said. "How many more times? It's been nearly *fifty* years, Richard. Nothing could survive that long without sustenance. David died!" Catherine said vehemently. "If he was alive I'd know. I'd feel him, here!" She thumped her chest.

"But what if you're wrong?" Richard said hotly. "Anyone going near that cellar is in danger. I must

warn Laura, not just for her sake but the men working on the Hooper place."

Richard thought about Laura. He would never forgive himself if anything happened to her. As if being
stalked by her ex-business partner wasn't bad enough.

Suddenly his mobile rang, the bright ring tone at
odds with the atmosphere in the room.

"Richard? Is Jim there?"

"No, sorry, he's not. Is that Karen?" Karen was
Jim's personal assistant.

"I've been chasing after him all day. He didn't
come in this morning. I was expecting him hours
ago. I've got no idea where he is." Richard could hear
the combination of worry and annoyance in her
voice.

"Have you checked his diary?"

"Yes, and he should be here. He's got a very important meeting in half an hour. I've tried ringing at
home and on his mobile, but he's not answering."

Richard remembered the instructions he had given
Raymond. "Look, Karen, can you get him to phone
me as soon as he gets in? It's important."

"Will do. And if he gets in touch with you, tell him
he has a PA here who's slowly getting very, very
angry."

Richard hung up and dialed his flat in London to
retrieve his messages from the answering machine.

"Richard. It's Jim. It's Sunday. I've been to see
McMillan and he's seen sense and agreed to drop the
claim. I'm going to pay a visit on our other friend
now. I'll call you when I've got some news."

He listened to the message and waited to hear any
follow-ups.

"You have no further messages," the computerized voice of the machine said.

An irrational but sick feeling of dread twisting in his stomach, he slammed the phone down, then picked it up and dialed the number for Laura's mobile. The phone on the other end of the line rang and rang, but there was no reply. "Shit!" he said, grabbed his jacket, and ran out of the house to his car.

The site was busy. New windows were being put in and the cement mixer chugged monotonously as one of the laborers—a boy still in his teens—shoveled sand into the rotating drum. Richard knocked on the door of the caravan and waited. When there was no reply he pressed his face against the window. The caravan was empty. He walked over to the boy shoveling sand.

"Is Laura about?"

The boy shrugged, not breaking his rhythm. "Haven't seen her this morning," he said.

"What about Shaun?"

"Haven't seen him either."

"Any idea where they might be?"

The boy shrugged again, this time leaning on his shovel. "You should ask Pat Donnelly. He's the foreman. He might know."

"And which one's Donnelly?"

The boy glanced over at the house. "The one up the ladder, fitting the window."

"Thanks," Richard said and walked toward the house.

Donnelly was struggling with a heavy double-glazing unit, perched precariously at the top of the ladder. Another workman was inside the house, guiding the unit into place.

"Mr. Donnelly," Richard called.

Donnelly looked down. "Give me a moment," he said. "This is the tricky part." With a grunt of effort he slid the window unit into the recess and then, taking an electric screwdriver from the pouch on his belt, fixed it into place.

Richard waited patiently, but patience was a luxury he couldn't afford. He was getting a bad feeling about Jim Raymond, and it concerned his visit to Brian Tanner; and anything that concerned Tanner meant Laura was in trouble. Eventually Donnelly climbed down the ladder, holstering the screwdriver. "Right, what can I do for you?"

"I was looking for Laura Craig?"

"She went into town this morning, just after I arrived," Donnelly said.

"Did she say when she'd be back?"

"No, she didn't. But I wouldn't expect her to be long. She has a meeting scheduled for this morning with the borough surveyor. At least that's what I was told, but then it was Shaun who told me, and he's not here either, and as site manager he really should be."

"Well, when she gets back could you tell her I've been, and ask her to phone me?" He gave Donnelly his mobile phone number.

Pat Donnelly scribbled it down on the back of his hand. "Will do. And who shall I say wants her? It's Richard Charteris, isn't it?"

Richard nodded.

"Ah, from the big house. I thought I recognized you the other day. I did some work there a couple of years back. Only laboring, and only for a few days, but I rarely forget a face."

"You won't forget to tell Laura?"

"You can rely on me."

Richard smiled. "I'm sure I can," he said and walked back to his car.

Before starting the engine he tried Laura's number again but with the same result as before. He had no alternative now but to wait for her to contact him. He just hoped Donnelly would be as good as his word. He twisted the key in the ignition and started the engine, driving slowly out through the gates of the site and out into the lane.

CHAPTER TWENTY

The office of A to Z Express Couriers was set in a gloomy Dorchester side street sandwiched between a dry cleaner's and a junk shop. Laura pushed open the door and stepped into the even gloomier interior. The office was a basic box shape with a high desk made from plywood and angle iron bisecting it. The walls were plastered with posters of semiclad girls, menus for the local Indian and Chinese takeaways, and incongruously, a small, delicately wrought water-color painting of Weymouth Harbour.

A portly man with a greasy complexion and a stained beige shirt sat behind the desk reading a news-paper. On a shelf above his head a CB radio crackled with distorted voices, relaying messages from the various couriers going about their business, in front of him a large chrome-plated microphone, which he used to reply to them. He looked up as Laura entered and smoothed the thinning brilliantined hair across his pink scalp. "Can I help you?" he said, his voice thick with a Dorset accent. This was Maggie's Harry Sharples.

Laura smiled. "I'm looking for Mark, Mark Jameson."

The man's eyes narrowed suspiciously. "Why?" he said. It sounded as though it wasn't the first time Jameson had been asked after.

Laura's smile slipped at the faintly aggressive tone. "It's a private matter," she said formally. There was enough steel in her tone to dispel any thoughts the man might have had about her being a pushover.

He regarded her through the narrowed eyes, as if trying to assess whether or not she was trouble. "He's out on a call." He looked away dismissively.

"And he'll be back, when?" she asked, trying and failing to force the smile back to her lips.

He didn't reply but picked up a clipboard holding a ream of dog-eared papers. He flicked over the pages, found what he was looking for, and dropped the clipboard back on the desk. "He has a delivery in Poundbury, and then he's on to Blandford Forum. An hour, possibly longer depending on the traffic."

"And then he'll be back here." She framed it as a statement.

The man shrugged. "Depends on what else comes in," he said unhelpfully.

"So it may be worth me coming back later?" She looked at him directly and this time the smile came to her lips and almost reached her eyes.

"You can try. I make no promises."

"Well, thank you very much. You've been most helpful," Laura said, but the irony was lost on the man. He gave her one more suspicious look, then reached for his newspaper and started to read.

She had an hour to kill, so she walked across town to eat.

Harry Sharples hadn't changed position since her last visit. Only the reading matter had changed. The newspaper had been discarded in favor of an old paperback novel with a lurid cover.

"He's not back yet," he said to her as she walked in through the door.

"Is he on his way?"

Sharples shrugged his fat shoulders, barely taking his eyes from the pages of the book.

"Do you mind if I wait?" She phrased it to give him no choice.

"Please yourself."

Crammed into the corner of the office was a small wooden table piled with battered magazines. Next to it was a tubular steel chair with a ripped leatherette seat, the yellow foam of the upholstery dirty and crumbling. Laura sat down, pulled a fashion magazine from the pile, and began leafing through it.

A short while later the door opened and a man dressed in motorcycle leathers and crash helmet came in and went up to the desk. "Anything else for me?"

Sharples whispered something to him and the man turned to look at Laura. He turned back to Sharples and more whispered words were exchanged. Finally the man took off his helmet and walked across to where Laura sat.

Even with his sweat-soaked hair flattened to his scalp Laura could see he was very good looking. He had a smooth, tanned face, set with hazel eyes and a mouth that seemed permanently fixed in a smile. "I understand you're waiting to see me," he said. His voice had only a trace of a Dorset accent. It seemed cultured, educated. Coupled with his looks and obviously toned physique, she could easily see why Maggie had been attracted to him. Though the way he treated Maggie, the "pig" description of Laura's was still apt, she thought.

Laura got to her feet and stretched out her hand. "Laura Craig," she said.

He shook her hand. "Mark Jameson," he said. "But then you probably already knew that. How can I help you?"

"I'm a friend of Maggie Kennedy," she said and watched as the mention of Maggie's name wiped the smile from his face. She continued quickly. "She told me you used to be the chauffer at Dunbar Court, for the Charteris family."

He turned away from her and went back to the desk. "Give me that Bridport delivery, Harry. I'll take it now."

Sharples handed him a large manila envelope. Jameson tucked it down inside the front of his leather jacket, glanced back at Laura coldly, and strode out of the office.

"Shit!" Laura said under her breath and followed him. As she passed Harry Sharples he chuckled softly. "And you can fuck off," she said and the smile was on her lips and in her eyes this time.

Jameson was straddling his bike and pushing off the stand when she caught up with him. "I just want to talk. Five minutes of your time. That's all."

He was about to slip the helmet over his head. "Maggie Kennedy's bad news," he said. "I'm well shot of her."

"This isn't about Maggie," Laura said. "I wanted to ask you about your time at Dunbar Court."

He looked at her steadily, but didn't put on the helmet. Laura seized her chance. "I hoped you might give me some background information on the Charteris family."

"What are you, a reporter?"

Laura saw the same greedy look she had witnessed at the McMillans'. "No nothing like that. Richard Charteris and I are friends . . ." Hell, she had nothing to lose. "I'll pay you," she said. "Twenty quid for half an hour of your time."

"And this concerns me how?"

"Can we go somewhere to talk?" she said.

"I've got a delivery to make."

Laura thought quickly. "I could take you in my car. You'll get the job done, earn a bit extra, and keep dry."

He considered this for a moment. The drizzle had taken a breather, but black thunderheads were gathering farther to the west, rolling in from the sea. He shrugged. "Okay," he said.

"Great," Laura said. "I'm parked just up the road."

"So what do you want to know?" Mark Jameson said.

Laura was concentrating on the road. She'd chosen a scenic route to Bridport, eschewing the major roads in favor of country lanes. She hoped, the longer she had Jameson in the car the more information she would be able to get out of him. "Well, to start with, Maggie told me you left the Charterises' service in less than amicable circumstances. Do you feel like telling me what happened?"

It was an important question. She wanted to establish how much bitterness he felt toward the family. This would color his answers and she wanted to be able to filter the truth from anything he said. It was the first time she'd used her journalistic training in an interview situation, but she remembered the ground rules from her time on the paper. Her old editor used to say, "Get the facts. Don't worry about the truth. The truth is subjective. The facts are the true measure of a story."

She glanced at Jameson's face. He was smiling slightly and staring at the road ahead. "I worked for them for five years," he said. "My father was chauffer at Dunbar Court for thirty years. When he retired he recommended me for the job. I should have known it wasn't really the right thing for me. I haven't got much time for aristocracy and privilege, but at that time I'd just been made redundant from Fontwell's, the paper manufacturer in Poole, so I needed the gig. To be fair to them, both Catherine and Richard are not your typical aristos. Catherine especially is very down-to-earth, but then she never really grew up in that environment. So the job was better than I'd been expecting."

"So, why did you leave?"

"Richard sacked me," Jameson said bluntly. "Probably it had something to do with the fact that I was sleeping with his mother."

Laura swerved slightly as she looked at him sharply. "Sleeping with her?"

"Why not? Catherine's extremely beautiful and I've always had a weakness for beautiful women. There's something else about her too. She never seemed comfortable playing the Lady of the Manor. She used to tell me about the things she got up to as a teenager.

She's had a colorful life, that one. I think she missed the lifestyle she was used to and found Dunbar Court oppressive. You're surprised?"

"Shocked actually."

"Why?"

Laura thought. She wasn't sure why the revelations surprised her so much. She had to admit Catherine was beautiful, and it was only natural for a woman like her to need male company. "But you were the chauffer, I just can't see Catherine and you as a couple."

"And if I were a gamekeeper it would be shades of *Lady Chatterley's Lover*? Is that what you're saying?"

"Something like that."

"All women need sex," Jameson said. "You're a snob."

"I'm not!" Laura said hotly. "I hardly know Catherine, but she doesn't seem the type for an affair."

"Keep the servants in their place. That's what you mean. That's the position my father would have taken. Bowing and scraping, yes, ma'am, no, ma'am. Well, that's not me. Catherine came to me and made her feelings perfectly clear. I was only doing what any red-blooded male would have done in those circumstances. When it's offered on a plate like that I'd be a fool to turn it down."

Laura was silent for a moment. Whatever had Maggie seen in him? There was an arrogance and chauvinism about him she found distasteful, but then Maggie had always had a peculiar taste in men. She wondered too why Jameson had reacted so strongly at the mention of Maggie's name. "Bad news," he had called her.

"So was that the only reason for your dismissal?"

she said. She didn't want to antagonize him before she could learn anything else.

Jameson laughed. "It was certainly a factor, but there were others. Catherine is a woman of esoteric tastes. It was something else we had in common."

"Meaning?"

"Pills, weed, a little coke occasionally. More often than not we were off our faces on one substance or another. We had a ball, but Richard took a very dim view of his mother's behavior, so I was made scapegoat. Easier that than confronting the real problem."

Laura sat in a stunned silence. None of this was what she'd been expecting to hear. She was finding it hard to reconcile her image of the serenely elegant Catherine Charteris with the picture of a sex-mad junkie that Jameson was painting. "I don't believe you," she said at last.

"That's your choice. I'm just telling it like it was. Let's face it; I've got nothing to gain by lying. Whether you believe me or not is up to you. I couldn't give a toss either way."

"All right," Laura said. "Let's change tack. Did Catherine ever talk to you about her brother? The one who died."

Jameson shrugged. "She might have done. I can't say it registered if she did."

"Okay, what about Richard? How did you get on with him?"

"Very well, at first. He's okay, Richard. I know he sacked me, but to be fair, I did give him cause. But no, on the whole he's decent enough."

Laura drove and thought hard. The conversation was really leading her nowhere. "Do you think your father would know anything about Catherine's brother?"

"He probably did, but he died three years ago. Ironic really. All those years working, and then he dies before he gets time to enjoy his retirement. It's a mistake I won't be making."

Once they reached Bridport, Laura found the street Jameson needed and waited while he made the delivery. When he got back in the car he said, "You seem disappointed. What were you expecting to hear?"

"I don't know," Laura said. "And that's the problem. I'm fumbling around in the dark." She shook her head. "I'll drive you back to Dorchester."

"Fine by me. Sorry I couldn't be more help."

CHAPTER TWENTY-ONE

By midday Maggie was feeling even worse. Her temperature had soared and she was starting to feel shivery. She'd sent a colleague, Barry Hayes, out to handle her appointments, and another, Paul Foster, was engaged in a long negotiation with an extremely fussy client who had quickly established himself as the bane of their lives.

The telephone rang. She picked up the receiver. "Kennedy's Estate Agency," she croaked. Paul Foster glanced across at her and grinned, holding his throat in mock-sympathy until his client glared up at him from the house details he was studying.

There was silence on the other end of the line. No, not quite silence. There was the drone of an engine. Whoever was on the phone was calling from a mobile while driving. "Hello?" she said, and waited. Nothing but the drone. And then the line went dead. "Suit yourself," she said to the phone and cradled the handset.

The door to the street opened and a young couple

walked in. She'd been watching them covertly for the past ten minutes while they scanned the properties for sale in the window. She cleared her throat. "Hello," she said with a smile. "How can I help you?"

Half an hour later the couple were still there and Maggie's desk was awash with paper as she showed them one property after another. They were newlyweds, living with the girl's mother, but the need to find somewhere of their own was evident from the barely concealed bump of pregnancy swelling the girl's midriff.

"You see, the problem is, we don't have very much to spend," the husband was saying. He looked young, barely out of his teens. The girl was about the same age, but already had a careworn look about her, as if she were carrying the weight of the world along with the baby. Maggie felt sorry for them, but was growing impatient by their inability to reach a decision.

"Well, perhaps we should tackle this another way," she said. "What is your ceiling, the absolute limit of what you can afford?"

The girl named a figure. Maggie smiled ruefully and scooped up the papers on her desk, shuffling them into a pile. "Right, well, all of these are out of your price range. When you said you wanted a three-bedroom semi I thought you might have some idea of current market values." She softened the barb with a smile. "Perhaps a flat?" she suggested.

The young couple looked at each other. He pulled a face.

"We really wanted a house," the girl said.

Yes, and I'd like to drive a Ferrari, but it ain't going to happen—at least, not this side of Christmas, Maggie thought. She said nothing but gave an eloquent shrug instead.

"You'd better show us what you have," the young man said sulkily.

"But, Lance—" the girl began.

"Beggars can't be choosers," Lance said sharply. "And the sooner we're away from your bloody mother's the better."

The young woman sagged in her seat, a petulant expression on her face.

I need this, Maggie thought and pushed herself away from the desk, pulling open the bottom drawer of the filing cabinet and taking out yet another sheaf of property details. All she really wanted to do was to go home and curl up in bed with a few favorite magazines and a glass of hot milk laced liberally with whiskey and honey.

Outside on the high street a dark blue BMW drove slowly past, the driver peering in through the agency window. By the time Maggie returned to her desk the car had gone.

Fifteen minutes later the couple left, clutching a handful of details and nursing a few shattered dreams. Maggie was pleased to see the back of them. The chances of them actually buying something from her were remote, and the headache was fast becoming intolerable. She took a packet of ibuprofen from her desk drawer, shook three tablets out into the palm of her hand, popped them into her mouth, and washed them down with the cold dregs of her coffee.

It was coming up to one o'clock. "Another ten minutes and I'll call it a day," she said to Paul. "Can you cope? Barry should be back by two."

"Go now," he said. "You look like shit." He'd finally got rid of the obstreperous client and was making a new batch of coffee. "Can't have you putting the clients off, can we?"

"Thank you for those kind words of sympathy," she said with heavy sarcasm.

"I mean it. You look like you should be tucked up in bed. I can manage things here. It's not exactly frantic, is it?"

"Mondays never are. I'll just make a few phone calls and then I'll go."

She spent the next few minutes chasing a couple of hesitant buyers, and then, sharp at one, she picked up her bag, said good-bye to Paul, and headed back to Charleston Street where she'd parked her car.

It was a glorious afternoon. The sky was a clear blue and the sun warmed her back as she walked, making her feel slightly better.

Although the thought of curling up in bed was appealing, there was little these days for her to go home for. It was why she didn't mind putting in extra hours at the office, and spending her evenings showing prospective clients around what, she hoped, were suitable homes.

Her own home was a hollow shell. A place to exist rather than a place to live, and when she was there she could always feel the walls closing in, trapping her, confining her.

It was different when she was in a relationship. Then there was warmth and purpose; candlelit dinners and energetic sex on the sheepskin rug in front of the fire. But she hadn't been in a relationship for months and she had to admit she was lonely. She was starting to feel that her love life was a thing of the past. Thoughts of Laura Craig drifted through her mind. She hoped her friend would be able to save the relationship with Richard Charteris.

In truth she'd always envied Laura. Laura had always seemed to cope with the loneliness of being single, whereas she was constantly falling apart. And that was the difference between them, Maggie thought. She needed to be in a relationship. She defined herself by the men she was with, only feeling complete if she had someone with whom to share her life. The relationships she'd been in, even the bad ones, gave her a security that had been missing since the death of her father. He'd been the foundation on which she'd built her life, always there to offer support and encouragement, always ready to dry her tears and to comfort her when she felt her life was disintegrating. He called her his little princess, and while he was alive that was exactly how she'd felt. Loved, cherished, protected from a hostile world by his strong arms and soothing words.

Her mother, on the other hand, had no time for her whatsoever and seemed to resent the special bond Maggie had with her father. She'd hoped his death might have brought her and her mother closer, but instead the gulf widened to a gaping chasm, unbreachable, with each of them unwilling to build bridges. They rarely saw each other these days, and when they did the meetings were tense, with latent hostility coloring each and every conversation. Acid barbs and sarcasm were how the two women communicated with each other, and any form of intimacy was treated with the deepest suspicion.

Maggie felt rudderless and more alone than at any other point in her life. Laura's involvement with Richard Charteris bothered her more than she cared to admit. Not that she resented Laura finding happiness. After the disastrous partnership with Brian Tanner she deserved a break. But if her friend did salvage the relationship with him, then Maggie's isolation would be complete. She balked at the thought, and then chided herself for being so selfish.

She unlocked the door to her black VW Golf, threw her jacket onto the backseat, and was about to slide in behind the wheel when a voice behind her said, "Hello, Maggie. Fancy seeing you here."

She turned and looked into the smiling, supercilious face of Brian Tanner. "Hello, Brian," Maggie said carefully. "Were you waiting for me? Why didn't you come into the office?"

"You were busy," he said, leaning against the car casually. "That young couple. I didn't like to disturb you."

"Well," she said. "What can I do for you? Are you in the market for another property?"

He smiled. "Possibly, but that's not why I've come to see you. I think you know why I'm here."

She looked at him steadily. "You've got to be kidding."

"What we had together was pretty special."

"And, as I told you when I finished it, completely wrong. Laura's my best friend."

"You didn't seem to mind while it was happening."

"I was going through a bad time."

"So you screwed me to make yourself feel better? Come on, I know you better than that."

"Ancient history." She made to step into the car, but he moved his weight forward, effectively stopping her from opening the door wider. "There's no need to be so hostile, Mags. Be honest, it was good while it lasted."

Maggie began to feel uneasy. Her relationship with Brian Tanner had happened at a time in her life when she was feeling particularly vulnerable. How they'd ended up in bed together baffled her to this day. One moment they were sitting on the couch, drinking wine, getting slowly drunk while they put their fragile love lives under the hazy alcoholic microscope, the next they were in each other's arms, kissing with a passion fueled by loneliness and lust.

It had been just that night, that one moment of weakness. She should have rationalized and filed it away at the back of her mind in the drawer marked *drunken mistakes*, but it was his insistence they keep it a secret from Laura that finally made her decide to end it. Had Laura found out about it would she have cared? Probably not. She told Maggie the relationship between her and Brian was over, but still Maggie wasn't prepared to take the chance. Her friendship with Laura was too important to jeopardize.

There was something vaguely different about the Brian Tanner standing before her now. He seemed more assured, as if dissolving the partnership with Laura had given his self-confidence a boost. It was in his body language. The way he stood, arms folded, looking at her imperiously, was very different to the almost shy person she knew. She'd always been aware that the diffidence was an act—a pretense to put people off their guard—but now the act had been dropped and it was if she were seeing the real Brian Tanner for the first time, and it bothered her.

"I haven't got time for this," she said. "Nothing's changed. I still feel the same now as I did then. My friendship with Laura is infinitely more precious to me than satisfying my libido."

He smiled at her infuriatingly. "I don't believe you. Come for a drink. We can talk about old times." He reached forward, grabbed her behind the neck, and pulled her head forward. He kissed her, his tongue trying to force an entry between her closed lips.

She pulled away from him and yanked open the car door savagely, cracking it against his legs. He didn't even flinch. "Don't ever try that again," she said, and slid in behind the wheel, trying to pull the door closed. But he was holding it open effortlessly with one hand, and despite using all her strength to pull it toward her the door wouldn't budge. "Do you mind?" she said.

"I'll call you," he said. "Perhaps dinner. When I see Laura I'll give her your regards, shall I?" He let go of the door suddenly and it slammed shut, slewing Maggie off balance and sending her sprawling onto the passenger seat.

She struggled to sit upright and fumbled the key into the ignition. As she pulled out onto the road she glanced into her rearview mirror. Tanner was watching her drive away, arms hanging loosely by his sides, a smug smile on his face. As she indicated to turn right out of Charleston Street she saw her hand was shaking.

When she got home she turned the key in the lock and pushed the door open. Seconds later the doorbell rang. Still clutching her car keys she sighed, opened the door. Brian Tanner was standing there. He smiled and walked past her into the house.

"What the fuck . . ."

Tanner reached above her head and closed the

door. As he turned, his arms wrapped around her. She fought his kiss passionately. His fingers snaked through her hair while his other hand unbuttoned her shirt and slipped inside, kneading her breast, thumb flicking across her nipple.

"Just like old times," he said as he pulled her through to the lounge.

"Brian, don't—"

"Don't speak," he said and ripped off the shirt, leaning her forward to let him unhook her bra, her shivering slightly as he kissed her breasts. He pulled her down onto the couch, pinning her arms, unzipping her skirt, and tugging her panties down over her thighs, stroking the soft patch of hair between her legs, parting her and slipping his finger into the moist slit. She reacted angrily, closing her mouth against his, his tongue probing, his breath coming in short gasps.

He rolled on top of her, reaching down and unzipping himself, sliding inside her, bringing himself to orgasm slowly and satisfactorily.

I'm going to hate you for this, Maggie thought, but was powerless to fight him off. "No," she shouted, "No, no—"

He grabbed her wrists, pulling her hands away. "No," he said softly, and pinned her arms to her sides, his mouth closing over hers again.

Then he began to hit her.

It left her lying on the couch. The sex had been interesting and it fulfilled a need, but now it was ready to move on. It still had much to do. It might have killed her, in the same manner as the McMillan woman and the spying Raymond, but Maggie, with her special link to Laura Craig, was better left like this.

There was conflict within the Verani. The part that was still Brian Tanner lusted for revenge against the woman that had beaten him in so many ways: Laura Craig. There was satisfaction in bedding Maggie; the desire to ruin Laura as she had spoiled everything for him was strong. Now the hatred that bled inside Tanner was proving a distraction.

The Verani that had grown from the boy David had a far deeper thirst for revenge. Decades of being locked belowground, with no contact with its own kind, no touch of the sun on its back, nothing except the water and the darkness. These had driven out any essence of humanity that might have remained from David.

The Verani was dominant, and as Brian Tanner weakened so that dominance grew. It was growing and it had a purpose: full revenge on the family that had imprisoned it—the Charteris family.

Tanner drove back to the Hooper house, parked the car on the other side of the wood, and set off through the trees.

The Verani remembered the room that had been its shelter for so long. And the trunk where it had hidden the journal. It needed to read through that again, to familiarize itself with what it had written all those years before.

It came out of the trees and stopped dead.

Someone was standing at the entrance to the cellar.

It pulled back into the shadow of the wood. It would wait.

* * *

Richard pulled up outside Brian Tanner's house. He turned off the engine and stared across at the house. He was improvising now. He didn't want to confront Tanner, but he had to find if Jim Raymond had been here. He got out of the car and walked up the drive to the front door. Taking a deep breath he rang the door-bell and waited. After a minute or so he rang again. It soon became evident there was nobody at home. He walked across to the garage, a freestanding, pre-fabricated concrete building with a corrugated as-bestos roof and a green-painted up-and-over door. There was a grimy window set in the side of the build-ing. He rubbed at the glass with a handkerchief and peered inside.

The garage was empty.

There was a path running along the side of the house with access to the back garden through a rose arch. He tried the back door, but like the front it was securely locked. The windows on the ground floor were protected from prying eyes by heavy drapes, pulled across, shutting out the sunlight. There was a concrete patio with steps at the front leading down to the lawn, and more steps at the side that disappeared into a dark hole with a stout wooden door at the bot-tom, the entrance to a basement room. Leaves had congregated at the bottom of these steps, forming a brown, spongy carpet that gave slightly under his weight.

To the right of the door was another window with dusty glass. Silver snail trails streaked the window and the corners of the frame were garlanded with powderwhite spiders' webs, hanging with dust and the occasional skeletal insect. Using the handkerchief again he cleaned away a small circle in the dust and looked through.

The room behind the glass was lit by a single light-bulb hanging from a web-festooned cable. Boxes littered the floor, and more were stacked on shelves lining the walls, along with pots of paint and empty wine bottles. Pushed against the far wall was a shape about six feet long and two wide, covered in a blue tarpaulin. He checked the door—locked but loose fitting in its frame.

In a shed at the bottom of the garden he found a small spade with a strong beech handle. He took it back to the basement door and forced the blade between the door and the jamb. Leaning on it with all his weight he levered the door until, with a crack of splintering wood, it sprang open.

He paused in the doorway, listening to see if the noise he was making was attracting any response. When he was sure that he hadn't been heard he stepped into the basement room.

The smell hit him almost immediately, musty and stale, but with the undercurrent of putrefaction. He moved a box out of his path with his foot and a cloud of bluebottles rose into the air, swarming around the light, flying at his face. He swatted them away, waiting until they settled again before venturing forward.

He didn't need to lift the tarpaulin to know what was beneath it. He could tell from the way the flies landed and buzzed around it, but he took a deep breath, crouched down, and lifted a corner of the tarpaulin, dropping it again immediately when he saw Jim Raymond's sightless, milky eyes staring back at him.

"Shit!"

The flies swarmed up again and he retreated to the far corner of the room, covering his nose and mouth with the begrimed handkerchief. Again the flies danced around the light before settling once more. He knew it wasn't enough to know that Raymond was dead. He had to find out how he'd died. He moved forward slowly, reached down, gripped the corner of the tarpaulin, and yanked it to one side. Then reeled away and vomited in the corner of the room.

Jim Raymond's naked body was covered in flies and maggots. His stomach was punctured in a dozen places and the flies were congregating on the wounds, feeding on the sticky, congealed blood, laying their eggs in order to swell their number.

Half of the body looked normal—the arms and legs as well muscled and toned as they had been in life—but the torso was a bony shell covered in skin. The stomach was hollowed out and the rib cage prominent. There were no muscles to be seen under the skin, only thin, threadlike ridges to show where they had once been.

Richard could only imagine the agonies Raymond would have suffered before he died. What kind of monster could do something like this? But he knew the answer to the question before it had even finished forming in his mind. He also knew there was nothing he could do for Jim Raymond now, but he could try to ensure that Jim was the Verani's only victim. It was obvious to Richard who the host body was. The immediate worry was that Brian Tanner wasn't at home.

Richard walked back to the car, rang Laura, waited while the phone on the other end of the line rang unanswered, and then he disconnected and slammed the phone down on the seat beside him. Where the hell was she? He started the car, turned sharply in the road, and headed back to Dunbar Court. And throughout the drive one thought rattled around in his mind. Jim Raymond's death was his fault, his responsibility. His family's curse was being visited on others now, and he knew it was down to him to put an end to it once and for all.

CHAPTER TWENTY-TWO

Catherine steered her car one-handed along the narrow lane, heading toward the old Hooper house. With her other hand she absently ruffled the neck of Socrates, who sat alert in the passenger seat. She'd had to get out of the house. Even now she found the atmosphere there oppressive—almost as if her father were still alive, pacing the halls. As a child she'd gone out of her way to avoid him, hiding behind curtains and under tables if he entered a room; listening out for his heavy tread on the stair and trying to dodge into rooms before she was seen. Sometimes, if she was with Elizabeth the maid, the young woman would join in, turning it into a game, hiding themselves in cupboards, trying hard to stifle their giggles, while Father worked just the other side of the door. But as she got older, the game became harder to play, and escape became paramount. Spending much of her time at Tom Hooper's house was an escape of sorts.

It was a safe haven where she could go and play

and just be herself, without fear of upsetting her parents. Tom was a patient, kind man, who seemed to have all the time in the world for her. He'd listen to her when she told him what had happened at school, giving her advice when she needed it, at other times keeping his counsel, and just letting her talk a problem through. It was the kind of relationship she should have had with her father; the kind of relationship she always wanted to have with Richard but never would. Richard would never truly understand her, and she couldn't blame him for that. Because of what had happened in the past, she'd lived so much of her life within her own head it was hard for her now to live any other way.

Two miles down the lane she pulled into a small turnout and opened her purse. The cellophane packet was small, two inches square, half filled with white powder. From the glove compartment she took a pocket-sized map book and laid it on her lap, shaking the contents of the packet out and dividing it with a credit card into three straight lines.

Socrates watched the ritual curiously, pressing his face forward. She tapped him on the nose. "There's nothing for you here," she said. The dog retreated, resentment in his eyes, grumbling in his throat. She rolled a twenty-pound note into a tube and used it to snort up the lines, feeling the delicious rush as the cocaine coated the membranes of her nose and worked its way into her bloodstream. She should stop this, she thought. And perhaps she would, once the issues with David were settled once and for all. But now she needed the rush and the crutch the drug offered her.

She sat for a moment while the cocaine did its work, revitalizing her, filling her with a feeling of self-confidence she knew in her heart was spurious, but a feeling she embraced all the same. Leaning her head back against the headrest she wondered what she was going to say to Laura Craig should she be at the house. How could she begin to tell her what she knew?

"Oh yes, my brother, David—the one I told you was dead—well, actually he's not. Instead he's transformed into some kind of monster."

Socrates looked at her with sad eyes as she spoke the words aloud.

"Well, how does it sound, dog?" she said. "Do you think she'll buy it?"

The dog barked excitedly at being spoken to directly, wagging his tail so it thumped softly on the leather seat. "No, neither do I."

She wetted a finger and dabbed up the remainder of the drug and rubbed it on her gums, then put the map book back into the glove compartment and started the engine.

Laura suddenly felt tired. The last week had been a kaleidoscope of mixed emotions. Incredible highs and crashing lows. Sitting in the restaurant with Richard now seemed a lifetime away. She'd watched him as they'd eaten the delicious food, noticing the laughter lines that spread out from the corners of his eyes, listening to his easy conversation. She'd been mesmerised. No one had ever filled her with such a feeling of completeness. There had been other men in her life, but none with the charisma, the magnetism of Richard. He was a thoughtful and considerate lover, bringing her to climax after climax before finally finding release himself. And afterward he'd kissed her, stroking her hair, his strong arms encircling her, making her feel safe, and wanted. Nobody had ever felt that way before.

"All the things you mentioned . . . I'm sorting them out for you."

Richard's words floated back into her mind out of the dim recesses of her memory. Lying in his arms at his London flat, him speaking softly to her as she drifted off to sleep. How could she have forgotten about it until now? And what on earth did he mean by it?

The emotional seesaw she'd been riding on for the past few days tilted the other way and she felt a sudden surge of anger sweep through her, remembering how, the very next day, Simon Lawson phoned her to say the McMillans were dropping their claim. How many strings did Richard have to pull to get them to do that?

How dare he? No one, not even her father, interfered in her life like that. She prided herself that she was quite capable of dealing with her problems by herself. She didn't need Richard's helping hand, no matter how well meaning it was.

It was the excuse she needed. She checked her mirror, turned off the main road, and headed toward Dunbar Court.

Richard's Mercedes was parked at the front of the house. Laura took a deep breath and walked purposefully up the stone steps and rang the doorbell. After a few moments Richard, rather than the butler, opened the door.

"I'd like a word," Laura said, her voice tight with controlled anger.

Richard smiled at her with a warmth that had been missing on the journey back from London. "I've been trying to phone you all morning," he said, leading her into the study. "I was just about to come over to the house." The relief he felt was overwhelming.

There were two shotguns lying on the desk. A matched pair of Purdys. "And you thought you might need those?" she said acidly.

He glanced down and frowned. "No. These are for something else," he said, missing the sarcasm. "Excuse me one moment." He opened one of the drawers in the desk and took out a box of cartridges and counted them quickly.

"The other night, just before I went to sleep, you said something about sorting my problems out for me."

"Did I?" he said distractedly.

"You know damned well you did! I would have thought you have enough on your plate here."

"Meaning?"

"Meddling in my affairs," she said.

He put the box down on the desk next to the shotguns. "Really?" he said.

Richard seemed so disinterested, Laura felt like she'd been hit in the stomach; all the air jettisoned from her body, making her gasp. Oh, Christ, how could she have been so stupid, so gullible? Tears pricked against the backs of her eyes. This wasn't the way she wanted it to go. She didn't want an argument with Richard. She wanted to feel his arms around her, to feel his strength, to wallow in his protection. After all these years of fighting her own corner, of locking horns with life and meeting it on her terms, she'd now found someone to whom she could easily relinquish control.

Her mouth opened and closed as she tried to find the words to adequately explain what she was feeling. Richard came around the desk and took her in his arms, kissing her and holding her so tightly she found it hard to breathe.

"I'm sorry," she said, when he let her go.

"There's nothing to be sorry for. You're quite right. Sometimes I am high-handed and thoughtless. It's me who should be apologizing."

"Why were you coming to see me?"

He frowned. "There's something we need to talk about."

Laura bit her lip pensively. "Sounds serious."

"Believe me, it is. Come through to the drawing room. I don't know about you, but I could use a drink." He took her hand and led her from the room.

Laura sipped her whiskey and tried to take in what she'd just been told. Eventually she shook her head. "I'm sorry," she said.

"I know. It took me a while to understand it properly. It was only when my mother showed me all the research she'd done on the Verani that I started to believe it. Now it seems the only possible explanation."

Laura snorted. "No, I don't mean I'm sorry about what you say is happening to your family. I mean, what a lot of crap."

Richard was shocked. He had lived with the family legend for so long, he had known as soon as he read his mother's notes how true it all was, and he wasn't prepared for Laura's disbelief.

"I mean, let's get this into reality, shall we? Jim Raymond was the one who persuaded McMillan to drop the claim, and now he's dead?"

"Yes."

"Oh, Jesus! You can't imagine how great that makes me feel. Were you good friends with him?"

"No, not really. Jim didn't have any friends. The nature of his work precluded it. But we did have a mutual respect for each other. I'll miss him."

"Too late now. Why on earth did you have to make up this story about a family curse and Catherine's brother? If you want to dump me, then just do it."

Richard changed tack. "Look, the reason I was coming to see you was to persuade you to move in here for a while. If Tanner is stalking you, then it's only a matter of time before he shows up at the caravan. You'd be much safer here at the Court."

Laura thought about it for a moment. Richard was right. She had no desire to be at the site on her own. Despite her astonishment at the story he had told her, the fact remained that Tanner did frighten her. "Will you drive me back there? I need to pack," she said. "And I think I should suspend work on the site, at least for the time being." She got to her feet and walked to the door. She paused with her hand on the doorknob. "I think I should tell you, I'm frightened by Tanner."

"Yes," he said, wrapping an arm around her shoulder and pulling her close, kissing the top of her head. "So am I." Though it was what Tanner had become that really frightened him.

"I mean I'm frightened about Tanner, of course I am. Not just him . . ."

"The Verani escaping . . ."

Laura shouted, "Christ! Don't start that again. Look, I'll stay here, frankly because I don't want to stay at the site. I mean I'm frightened for you and Catherine. If you believe this—"

Richard put his finger to her lips. "Don't say any more. Leave it."

Catherine stood at the entrance of the cellar, hesitant, remembering the last time she'd climbed down that ladder and the horror awaiting her below. She could see a light burning down there, enabling her to see the concrete floor and the black-coated walls.

"Hello," she called. A moment later a tall, good-looking man with a shock of unruly black hair and piercing green eyes appeared at the foot of the ladder.

"Can I help you?" Shaun Egan said, peering up at Catherine curiously.

"I was looking for Laura Craig. I'm Catherine Charteris."

Shaun nodded slowly, recognizing the name immediately. "She's not here. I think she went into town."

"I see. Will she be long?"

He shrugged. "No idea."

"I'll wait, if that's all right."

"Fine by me," Shaun said and moved back into the cellar.

Catherine took a deep breath and climbed down the ladder.

Shaun came out of the back room. "I said you could wait, but not down here," he said, spreading his arms wide to usher her back up to the surface.

"It's been a long time since I was down here," Catherine said, sidestepping Shaun and going to look down into the well.

"Then you know this place? I'll have to ask you to

leave," Shaun said. "It's not safe down here. The building work."

Catherine laughed sharply but without humor. "It's a little late for health and safety regulations, Mr. Egan. Know about this place? It has haunted me all my life. The question is, what do you know?"

"Come through." Shaun beckoned Catherine into the back room. "So how does all this concern the Charteris family?" he said, following through the doorway.

"This was where they kept my brother, David, locked up," Catherine said.

Shaun handed her the journal. "So this belonged to him, your brother?"

Catherine took the book and flipped it open, recognizing her brother's handwriting instantly. "Yes," she said, flicking the pages over and starting to read. Her eyes filled with tears as David's voice sounded in her mind, reading aloud the words on the page. She sniffed back the tears and sat down on the bed, nodding her head slowly.

Cathy came to see me today, and it was terrible. I wanted so much to hug her, to tell her everything was all right. But of course, it's not all right. It will never be all right again. I'm finding it hard to control myself now. When Cathy was here I felt I wanted to hurt her, but I can't understand why. The feeling was so strong, so powerful. It boiled up within me and had Tom not come down when he did I hate to think what I might have done.

What have I become, that I could even contemplate hurting my dear Cathy?

Catherine wiped away a tear and looked up at Shaun, the anguish plainly written on her face. She turned over a few pages and read on, struggling with handwriting that had become erratic and scratchy.

I killed Muminah today.

I didn't want to, but the hunger was so great.

Muminah gave herself to me freely. She was even smiling as I pulled her close toward me. She was whispering to me. I couldn't understand the language, but it was as if she was trying to soothe me, to tell me I shouldn't be upset about what I was doing to her. Things came out of my stomach, spikes. Spikes as sharp as needles, and I could feel them as they stabbed into Muminah's body. I could feel them driving deeper and deeper, and I drank, and drank, draining her, and filling myself up.

Father tells me that what happened was not my fault, but a result of this sickness, this Transition. I want to believe him but I hate myself now and I hate what I've become! I just pray that I'll be better soon. Once the Transition has passed, Father tells me I will be my old self again. I do so want to believe him. I want to go back to the house, back to school. I want to feel the sun on my skin and hear the birds singing in the trees. Fishing in the lake, playing with Cathy—all the things I've missed so much. He says it will be soon, but I'm finding it harder and harder to believe him. I can barely breathe the air in here and I'm spending most of my time in the water of the well.

This is the last entry I shall make in this diary. I can't even hold the pen properly now. I hope, one day, someone will find this and realize that I couldn't help myself. I'm not a bad person, honestly I'm not.

Catherine closed the book and hugged it tightly to her chest. She got to her feet like an automaton. "He didn't know," she said, shaking her head. "That bastard lied to him. David thought he was going to get better!" She started to cry, her shoulders heaving as the sobs racked her body.

Shaun wrapped an arm around Catherine. "I'm sorry," he said gently. "I'm so sorry."

"He was my brother, did I say that?" Catherine said through the tears. "Where he describes the Transition. It sounds horrendous, but what about the mechanics of the change from human to Verani? You see, only the males of the . . . only the males undergo this Transition. The females remain human—I guess so they can perpetuate the race. That's not to say the females are held in any less regard. After all, without them the race would die out. My God, poor, poor David." Her voice dissolved into tears.

Shaun said softly, stroking her hair like he would if comforting one of his own children, "He wouldn't have known what was happening to him. He was young. I'm sure he wouldn't have suffered." Christ, he thought, I sound like a bloody doctor.

Catherine accepted the handkerchief from Shaun and dabbed at her eyes and nose.

Shaun was thinking back to Dean McMillan, grabbed by the ankle while submerged in the water of the cellar. He mentioned the accident at the site to Catherine.

"Richard would say it was the Verani looking to transpose itself into a human host. Remember this journal was written in the late fifties, which means the Verani has been stuck in there for over fifty years. Dead, it has to be dead . . . poor David." Her voice caught on a thorn of emotion and for several minutes she was unable to speak. When she looked up her voice was remarkably calm. Unnaturally so. "Not so much a problem, this length of time, as Richard would no doubt remind me, they are able to enter stasis—a kind of hibernation. But once awake from this the drive to reproduce would be very strong. And you say you drained all the water out of the cellar?"

"Apart from the water in the well, yes."

"Then it had probably retreated down there. It was probably down there all the time you were knocking the wall down to get through to the shelter. You see this stuff on the walls? It looks like a black weed? Slimy, thin filaments, masses of them that form a sort of hairy black carpet, which is how it gets its name— Devil's Hair." Her voice sounded like a recording, stark and mechanical, as the effects of the cocaine she had taken finally kicked in and her grief and sorrow fell secondary within her emotions to the tenuous high.

Shaun thought about the patch growing on his shoulder and started to feel slightly sick. "Yes," he said carefully. "Yes, I ripped a lot of it down to gain access. I noticed something just before you arrived."

"What's that?" Her mind was beginning to clog up with emotion. It was as if she was approaching overload; as if the roller coaster that had been her life for years was rushing to one final, steep, far too steep, incline.

"The Devil's Hair. It's stopped moving."

She nodded distractedly, going first to examine the walls. "It's dying," she said. "Look."

"What does that mean?" Hope burned in his mind. If it was dying on the walls, perhaps the patch on his skin was dying too.

"I think it means that the Verani is no longer here," she said. Suddenly she felt incredibly tired. The drug had worn off, the escape from her reality only temporary. The true depths of her sadness overwhelmed her. Her legs buckled and she had to grasp on to Shaun to stay upright.

"Shit!" Shaun said and then thought for a moment. He tried to get Catherine's attention. The last thing he needed was her getting hysterical on him down here. "But I thought you said it could only live in water."

Catherine nodded absently. "Yes, that's right."

"So how could . . ." Shaun stopped midsentence as the thought hit him. "The human host?"

"I was thinking the same myself. But the question is, who?" She shook her head to try to free her thoughts. God, she needed to sleep; years wouldn't be enough.

"Dean McMillan?" Shaun suggested. Then he swallowed. The thought that was really bothering him was, But what if it's me?

Catherine tried a half smile but it was forced. A picture of David, the young boy she had known, flooded her mind and she collapsed into Shaun's arms, crying uncontrollably.

"Perhaps it'd be better if we went up to the house. Come along," Shaun said, and led Catherine, sobbing, back to the ladder, watching her carefully as she climbed up to the surface.

* * *

From his position in the trees it watched its sister emerge from the cellar. Older now, barely recognizable, but it *was* Cathy. It waited until they'd filed past the house and then ran across the open ground, slid the board to one side, then climbed down the rusting iron ladder. At the well it paused, looking down into the water, a hundred memories pressing into its mind; waves of bitterness and hatred rushing through its thoughts.

It walked through to the back room and knelt down by the trunk, opening the lid. For a moment the wave of memories threatened to engulf it as it fingered the piles of old comics, the painting set, the steam engine. What had happened to the boy who had looked upon these things as his treasures?

Dead.

The answer reverberated around its mind.

Lost forever in the stagnant water of the well, where darkness reigned and anger and hatred festered.

It lifted everything out of the trunk, piling it on the floor.

The journal was gone.

It didn't matter. Its memories would suffice. They would strengthen its resolve; would give it purpose.

It replaced everything in the trunk and lay down on the bed, closing its eyes and focusing on the past. And it remembered the last time it had lain here.

The Shelter—August 1959

Tom Hooper shouldered the air rifle and shot a tranquilizer dart into the exposed shoulder of the Verani's sleeping body. The desiccated body of David next to it twitched as if in sleep, and the Verani sunk deeper into unconsciousness as the drug took effect.

"How long have we got?" William Charteris said.

"An hour at the most," Hooper replied.

"Where did you get that thing from anyway?" Charteris said.

"A friend of mine. He's a vet. Does a lot of work for the zoo."

"Didn't he ask what you wanted it for?"

"He's ex-army. He didn't ask questions."

"Fair enough," Charteris said, moving into the back room of the cellar. "We'd better get him down the well."

"Are you sure about this?" Hooper said.

"Once he's down the well and we seal it over, it will be an end to this nightmare."

Hooper hesitated in the doorway. He'd held his tongue for years now, but he couldn't remain silent any longer. "And how will you explain his disappearance?" he said.

"David will die from a sudden illness. There will be a funeral and an empty casket will be interred in the family crypt."

"But you can't hope to carry off such a pretense. What about a death certificate? What about Helen?"

"People have their price, Tom—even doctors. And one of the major benefits about having wealth and influence is that their price is always affordable. A death certificate will be forthcoming and no one will ask any questions. I will play the part of the grieving father, and I shall play it well. There will be only sympathy and kind words. And as for Helen she will do as I say. David's life has brought her nothing but suffering. She'll not shed any tears once he's gone."

Tom Hooper shook his head. "But David's your son," he said quietly.

Charteris glared at him. "My son was a bright, lively boy, full of enthusiasm for life. That . . ." he said, gesturing to the unconscious form on the bed, ". . . that thing is not my son. Now, are you going to help me get him into the well or not?"

Hooper shrugged and rested the air rifle against the wall.

The body was slippery with the slime that oozed from its pores. Finding purchase was difficult. After several fruitless attempts they gave up and hauled it off the bed using the blanket on which it was sleeping. Together they dragged the body across the floor to the lip of the well.

They'd brought the steel plate and pile of concrete blocks down earlier. They could have sealed the well then, but not long after they'd carried the last of the blocks down the ladder the Verani surfaced and pulled itself out of the water.

Charteris and Hooper climbed up the ladder quickly and shut the trapdoor, slamming home the heavy iron bolt. It was no longer safe to remain in the cellar. Memories of finding Mary's body still haunted them, and neither of them wanted to suffer the same fate.

Charteris sank to his knees and tugged on the blanket, rolling the body gently into the water. David's husk was more easily carried to the well, and then together the two men slid the steel plate across the wellhead and spent the next ten minutes building a pile of blocks on top of it.

Charteris rubbed his hands on his trousers to remove the dust and nodded his head in satisfaction. "That should keep him down there," he said.

Tom Hooper wiped away a tear from the corner of his eyes. For the first few years of David's life he'd played father to the boy. It was a role he'd taken to naturally, making him regret the years in the army when his career meant more to him than personal relationships. He'd forgone the chance to marry and have children of his own, and now it was too late. David, for those few brief years, had filled his life with a happiness he knew he could never recapture, and knowing that he'd never see the boy's smiling face again broke his heart.

He couldn't believe that Charteris felt nothing. It wasn't natural, but then he'd witnessed the way the man treated his wife and daughter. It was if something had died within him that day in the cave—as if his heart had been ripped from his body and been replaced by a block of ice.

Only David had been able to cut through the frozen demeanor. Hooper had seen the love in his employer's eyes when he'd looked at the boy; heard him laugh when they played together. But now even that had been taken from him, and the barriers reerected, as difficult to breach as the steel and blocks that now covered the wellhead.

"Right," Charteris said. "It's done. I'll leave you to your work."

"I still can't see why you want to seal the room," he said. "If the cellar's to be flooded . . ."

"Memories," Charteris said. "Allow your old friend one indulgence. That room contains the remnants of my son's life. I can't bear to see them destroyed. If I know they're sealed in there I can draw comfort from the knowledge and I can remember my son as he once was, not the monster he became."

"You always knew what his destiny would be," Hooper said. "We both sat in that cave and listened as it was spelled out to us."

"But I clung to the hope that it might not happen. A false hope as it turned out. Now, please do as I ask and seal the room."

Hooper would have argued further, but could see from the blank look in his employer's eyes that further talk would be wasted.

"And I want the cellar filled to the top. It will discourage anyone in the future from venturing down here," Charteris said as he climbed the ladder to the surface.

"As you wish, sir," Hooper said sullenly, and started to move more blocks into the doorway separating the two rooms.

He worked quickly, mixing the mortar, heaving the blocks into place. From time to time he'd stop and listen, but there was silence from the well.

He slotted the last block into place and stood back to examine his workmanship. Every seam was filled. No gaps for the water to seep through. Satisfied, he gathered up his tools and moved to the ladder. As he passed the well something thumped on the underside of the steel. David was awake.

He shivered slightly. In Hooper's mind the only proper and merciful solution to this problem would have been to kill David. A bullet in the head, swift, simple, and final. He'd always hoped that that's how this would end. In his view it was the only humane course to take. William Charteris's decision to leave David alive down here carried with it, not only ramifications for the future, but also difficult moral questions Tom Hooper had no answer for.

What was done here today, he thought, would one day have to be paid for. And God help those upon whom this curse was visited.

He climbed up the ladder and went to find the hose.

CHAPTER TWENTY-THREE

Catherine cupped her hands around the mug of tea, drinking the steaming liquid with small sips. She'd stopped crying now, but her eyes were red-rimmed, and she dabbed at them occasionally with a tissue. They were sitting on packing crates in the center of the lounge in the old Hooper house. Plaster dust covered the floorboards and the room was still far from finished. From elsewhere in the house came the various sounds of activity as the workmen carried on with their daily tasks, oblivious of the drama unfolding around them.

The sound of a car pulling up outside drew Shaun to the window. He watched as Laura and Richard got out, and then tapped on the glass to attract their attention.

"What are you doing here?" Richard said as he saw Catherine sitting on one of the crates.

"I came to see Laura," she said. "Laura, I think you deserve an explanation. I'm afraid I wasn't entirely honest with you the other day."

"It's all right," Laura said. "Richard's told me everything." She went across and crouched down in front of the other woman, taking her hand between both of hers. She thought about telling Catherine how crazy she found the story about David, but she could see how upset Catherine was already. Her eyes had a nervous edge to them as if it wouldn't take much to push her to hysteria. "I *do* understand," Laura said. "Had it been my brother I probably would have acted the same. Are you all right?"

"Fine," Catherine said, sniffing back a tear.

Laura looked at her skeptically.

"No, really. I'm all right now," she said, smiling wanly.

"What has she been saying?" Richard said to Shaun. Even now the inbred urge to protect the family honor was strong.

"Nothing that I'm sure you don't already know," Shaun said.

Laura and Richard exchanged looks.

"It's true," Catherine said. "Shaun has David's diary. I've been reading it. It's awful. My poor David."

"Well, I suppose that's going to save us some time explaining things," Laura said. "When did you find the diary, Shaun?"

He couldn't miss the undertone in her voice. When he answered he avoided her eyes. "A few days ago," he said.

"And you didn't think to show me?" She was clearly annoyed.

"You had a lot on your mind."

"Still, I would like to have seen it. What do you think about all this?" Shaun was as practical as it was possible for a man to be. Laura knew he would have as much skepticism about it all as she did. Between them perhaps they could talk some sense into Richard and Catherine. Perhaps then they could unite to do something about Brian Tanner.

Shaun could tell from Laura's tone that she didn't believe what she had been told. "Let me show you something," he said. With one fluid movement he peeled off his sweatshirt and turned so the others could see the growth of black fungus on his shoulder.

Laura took a step backward and the color drained from her face. "Oh, you poor man. I had no idea . . ." She gathered herself and came up beside Shaun, peering closely at his shoulder. "How . . ."

"When I was down in the cellar. The walls were covered with this stuff. I had to scrape a load of it away from the block work before I smashed through to the shelter. I think some of it must have got down inside my shirt. It started as a small spot at first, but it's been growing steadily ever since."

The growth now covered much of his shoulder and was starting to creep down his back and upward to his neck. Catherine came next to Laura and looked at the growth from every angle, then prodded it with her fingernail. "I'm sorry," she said. "May I?"

"Go ahead."

"Devil's Hair is a form of parasite. Each hair is a small, living organism and has roots that spread far and wide in search of nutrients, rather like a fungus. The roots literally suck the life from anything they come into contact with and feed that life force back to the hairs, which in turn are eaten by the Verani. I've only ever read about this, and I thought it was just fancy. In one paper I read the author was trying to claim that the deserts of the world were formed by the Devil's Hair sucking the life from all vegetation, all plants and flowers, indigenous animals, what have you. Nonsense of course, but I think there must be an element of truth there somewhere."

She prodded again and scraped off a little with her fingernail. She wiped it on her sleeve. The fine black filaments looked like tiny but thick worms. The fibers were moving, pulsating. Shaun could see clearly that each hair was moving sinuously, rippling like seaweed caught in a current. They writhed and twisted; it gave him the distinct impression that the Devil's Hair was aware of their presence, was sniffing them out as another potential source of food. He felt sick. This monstrosity was growing on his skin. He could almost feel the fibrous roots burrowing into his flesh. "How do I get rid of it?" he said. "I've tried scraping it off, but it just comes back, if anything thicker than before." The sadness in his eyes was impossible to disguise. "Well?" he said to Catherine. "Shouldn't this be dying like that in the cellar?"

Catherine shook her head slowly. "I honestly don't know. This stuff provides food for the Verani. I've never read of it attaching itself to a human host like this. My guess would be that the only way to stop its spread would be to find the Verani and destroy it. That might get rid of the Devil's Hair, it might not."

"And if we can't find the Verani, this stuff will continue to spread?"

"Yes," she said. "I suspect it will."

"And it's drawing nutrients out of my body all the while it's growing?"

She nodded. "Have you been feeling unwell at all?"

"Tired," he said. "I've been feeling very tired."

"It will get worse," she said. "This is only a small

patch covering a relatively limited area of your skin. As it grows it's going to suck out more from you, until—and this is only speculation—until your body won't be able to sustain it."

Shaun frowned. "I hear what you're telling me. If we don't destroy the Verani this stuff is going to kill me."

"We can't destroy the Verani. I'm so sorry." Catherine sounded so calm, so in control yet clearly so close to losing it that it chilled them all.

"What do you mean "can't"?"

"David."

She said the single word so quietly that Laura was uncertain what she had said for a moment. When she realized Catherine was talking about her brother she knew with sudden clarity that all this was true. It was all happening; no matter how much she wanted to dismiss it, no matter how much she wanted to shout at them all to help her get rid of Brian Tanner, she realized she was locked into the madness.

Laura drew in her breath, and only when she exhaled did she speak again. "Richard, I didn't believe you at first . . . No." She brushed away his attempt to speak. "It hardly matters now. This is serious, and we need to work together." Laura was concerned more about Catherine, who was showing every sign of losing control.

"Right." Richard pulled up another crate and sat down. "You know part of the story," he said to Shaun. "I think Laura and I had better tell you the rest. Is there any more tea in the pot?"

When he'd finished there was silence in the room. Catherine was standing by the window, staring out at the garden. The others had been watching her throughout Richard's brief summation. She hadn't moved once since she had taken guard at the window. If she was looking at anything in particular it was something only she could see.

"So there you have it," Richard said. "Any opinions?"

"It's imperative the Verani is destroyed," Shaun said.

"But how—" Laura said.

"The only way we can stop this spreading is to attack it at its source," Richard said.

"Do you know that for a fact?" Laura said. "Go on, Shaun."

Shaun spoke quietly, but they were all listening intently. "This journal gives an incredible insight into the mind of a Verani. You read how the desire to be in the water of the well became almost pathological. The water drew him like a magnet, and he was submerged in the well at every opportunity."

Richard took over as though they had rehearsed it, though he was remembering words spoken years ago by his grandfather. Words Catherine had reinforced, had embellished only hours ago. He coughed and his voice caught more than once. The strain, the way his mother was struggling to cope, was becoming a huge burden on him. "When the Transition is complete they have to spend virtually all their time in water, so I suspect their lungs atrophy, making them unable to breathe air in sufficient quantities for them to stay alive for any great length of time. Which brings us to the question of reproduction."

Laura shook her head. "We don't have to worry about that, do we?"

Richard placed his hand on her shoulder. "In

Mother's notes it says the females remain in human form, so the only way for the male Verani to mate with them was to find a surrogate to carry their seed. Which was what, I think, made them so feared. According to the legend they can take over the body of a human host—don't ask me how—and using this body they can mate with the females to produce the progeny. But eventually the human body dies and then the Verani has no choice but to return to its natural environment—water. Sounds gruesome, doesn't it?"

"I still don't see how that has any relevance to whatever we have to do next," Laura said.

"It say's there in the legend that the image of the Verani cannot be captured. No artist has ever produced a picture of one. There were never any photographs of David, simply because he was impossible to photograph. It stands to reason that more modern technology would be just as impotent."

"I'm sorry, I don't know what you mean," Shaun said. He looked at Laura, but she shook her head in puzzlement as well.

Richard got to his feet and started pacing the floor, thinking the theory through. "The night of the party Laura swears someone was in the maze, and later that Brian Tanner appeared on the terrace with her. We checked the CCTV tape afterward, but there was no sign of him, of anyone, just a shadow that seemed to flow from the terrace to the garden. Nothing else."

"I don't see the significance—"

"What if Tanner found his way into the cellar and encountered a fully grown Verani, awake after hibernating all those year?"

"Then surely he'd have been killed?"

"What if it's using Tanner as a host? It would explain why he was there that night but the cameras couldn't pick him up. It would explain where the Verani is. And it would explain why Jim Raymond's body is in Tanner's house."

Richard told them quickly about finding Raymond's body; sparing them the full gruesome details. "That's the other reason Verani are feared."

Silence settled in the room for an instance.

The silence was broken by Catherine hammering on the window. For a moment they thought she had seen something outside, but when she spoke they realized her horrors were all locked within her. "Richard thinks Tanner is the body the Verani has chosen," Catherine said. It pained her every time she had to say the word or even think it. *Verani.* To her mind, confused and emotional as she was, it was her brother they were talking about. Even though she knew, deep down she knew, that David, certainly the David she had known and loved, was dead, still it grieved her to think of what agonies he had endured. The thought that was prodding at her, giving her hope however unrealistic it might turn out to be, was that the presence of the Devil's Hair had somehow kept David sustained through all those years.

Laura sat down. What would it mean to her if Tanner were being used? Then she realized. "If Tanner hates me as much as he does . . ."

"It might be enough to drive the Verani to find you," Richard said.

"I'm sorry," Shaun said. "The only suggestion I have is to destroy its shelter."

"The well?" Richard said.

"The entire cellar, I think."

Richard nodded. "We need to stop it going to

ground. I don't think the body it inhabits, even if it is Tanner, will sustain it for long—especially if it gets to mate. If that happens, then the deterioration of the host happens very quickly, and the Verani has to return to its natural habitat."

"Water," Laura said.

"Exactly. The obvious thing for it to do would be to return to where it feels safe. The well. If we can, in some way, prohibit that, then I think we'll have a better chance of catching up with it and destroying it."

"I would have thought we could just seal up the cellar," Laura said, standing and beginning to pace the room. "Fill it with concrete, seal the well forever. Shaun? Possible?"

"It'd take an awful lot of concrete, but I agree, it would work."

Catherine wheeled away from the window. "I need some air," she said, walking to the door. "It may have escaped everyone's notice, but it's my brother you're talking about destroying."

She stormed from the room. Seconds later they heard the back door slam.

"Shall I go after her?" Laura said.

"No," Richard said firmly. "She knows it has to end, and end here. She can't go on pretending any longer."

"Shaun, how long would it take to organize the concrete?" Laura said.

"Give me a few moments and I'll let you know." He took his phone from his pocket and punched in a number.

Laura sat, shaking her head. "That poor woman. Perhaps we were a little insensitive."

"There is one more thing," Richard said.

Laura looked at him, wondering what further family secrets were about to be revealed.

Shaun interrupted. "The host body."

"Meaning?" Laura asked.

Shaun nodded to Richard, who spoke. "The Verani has most probably taken over a human body, Tanner, to allow itself access to a female with which to mate. I can't be sure, but I would guess that as the Verani was imprisoned for all those years it would possess a huge capacity to seek revenge. Added to that Tanner's urge to, as he sees it, get even with you . . ."

"The host," Shaun prompted him.

Laura suddenly realized. "Brian Tanner hates me enough to want it to be me the Verani mates with."

CHAPTER TWENTY-FOUR

Catherine stood just outside the back door smoking a cigarette. She looked out over the decimated garden and from there to the hole in the ground. She pinched out the cigarette and walked slowly across to the entrance of the cellar. Laura had spoken to Pat Donnelly and told him to clear the site for the weekend. He had started to protest, saying he had to clear it with Shaun, but Laura was very persuasive, and in any case Shaun shouted out at him to "move yer arse, Pat." The site was empty within the half hour. Consequently no one took any notice of Catherine as she slid the board covering the opening to one side. She glanced back at the house. Through the window to the lounge she could see the back of Richard's head, and Shaun, pacing up and down, speaking into a mobile phone.

When she was sure nobody was watching her, she climbed down the ladder. The lamps were still alight, but one of them was low on oil, the flame guttering. She approached the well.

She was still clutching David's journal to her chest. She held it out over the torpid water for a second, and then let it drop with a splash. The book floated on the surface, spine splayed out, pages open. The water soaked into the pages, making the ink run, smearing it into pools of sapphire blue. "Oh God, David," she said. "Why couldn't you have just stayed down there? You would have been safe then."

"Because it stinks down there. And it's very, very lonely."

Catherine spun round as Brian Tanner moved out of the shadows of the back room.

"Hello, Cathy. It's been a long time."

Catherine took a step backward.

"Don't worry. You're safe. I won't hurt you."

"You're not David," Catherine said, glancing around and trying to judge how much distance there was between herself and the ladder.

Tanner smiled. "Well, no, the body's not, I agree. But I am David. I am your brother."

"Prove it," she said.

Tanner frowned for a moment. "How to prove it to you," he said quietly.

He advanced on her so quickly Catherine didn't have a chance to move. His fist lashed out and caught her on the point of her jaw. Her legs buckled and she pitched forward. Tanner caught her before she hit the stone floor and hoisted her effortlessly onto his shoulder. "Proof enough," he said and climbed the ladder.

He'd climbed out of the opening at the top when his leg locked at the knee, making him stumble. At the same time a searing pain coursed through his body and he had to bite his lip to stop himself crying out. Catherine had become a deadweight across his shoulder, and he staggered toward the trees, confused, not sure what was happening to him.

His knee finally freed and the pain abated, but he was struggling for breath. As he pounded down the undergrowth he could feel the sharp thorns of bramble tearing at his legs. Once he stumbled and crashed into a tree, nearly dropping his burden. His shoulder took the impact and sent another spasm of pain arcing through his body.

He'd left the car just the other side of the wood, but it seemed like miles away. His breath came in short, painful gasps and he could feel a burning sensation that started at his chest and worked its way down to his pelvis. Ahead was a clearing and he tried to stop as both knees locked, but his momentum carried his body forward and he fell facedown on the patch of scrubby grass that covered the clearing. Catherine tumbled from his shoulder and fell to the ground, rolling over twice before coming to a halt against the stump of a felled oak.

He lay there for a moment, disorientated, in agony, his strength gone. Eventually he pushed himself to his knees and knelt in the clearing, swaying slightly as images of barren deserts and high sand dunes swept through his mind.

He looked down at his arm. The skin was split from elbow to wrist, bright blood pouring from the wound. Inside the split he could see something other than flesh and bone. Something dark and glistening that pulsed with a life independent of the torn flesh surrounding it.

"Not now," he said under his breath, but he knew instinctively what was happening to him.

The Verani was reverting, discarding the body that had been its shelter for the past few days. Within the hour it would need to find water if it had any hope at all of survival. Without the host body's lungs it would no longer assimilate enough oxygen from the air to enable it to breathe.

Catherine groaned and opened her eyes. For a moment she was dazed, confused. Then she remembered the cellar and panic surged through her. She sat up and looked about her.

Not more than three yards away Brian Tanner was kneeling on the grass, swaying backward and forward. She scrambled away, ducking for cover behind the tree stump. She looked back at him, but he gave no sign that he'd seen her. He gave no sign at all that he was even aware of her presence.

"They reckon they could have it here by tomorrow afternoon," Shaun said as he switched off his phone.

"No chance for today then?" Laura said.

Shaun made a point of looking at his watch. "It's five o'clock. It was lucky they were still there. I'd better go and work out how much we need. They're hanging on there for me to phone them back with quantities."

As he approached the cellar the first thing he noticed was that the board covering the hole had been moved to one side. He was sure he'd replaced it earlier before going back to the house. He looked around. There was no sign of Catherine Charteris. With a sigh he lowered himself down into the hole. What was she playing at? He was halfway down the ladder when he heard the scream from the wood. Within seconds he was running toward the trees, nearly colliding with Catherine as she broke from the shadows of the wood.

She was white-faced, tears pouring down her cheeks. She made to run past him, but he stretched out his arms to intercept her. "What's wrong? What's happened?"

Catherine was gasping for breath. "In there," she panted. "David . . . in the wood."

"What did he look like?"

From Catherine's garbled description Shaun recognized Tanner. "Okay. Go back to the house. Tell them what you saw. I'll deal with this."

Catherine's eyes were wild, and she was shaking her head, trying to draw breath into her lungs. He shook her by the shoulders. "Go back to the house," he said again, more firmly.

With a sob Catherine started to run again.

Shaun looked into the trees. "Right, you bastard," he said softly, and started to move deeper into the wood. Catherine had left a trail of flattened bracken in her wake. He moved forward cautiously, alert for any movement, any sound, but the wood was still and silent, as if it were holding its breath.

A hundred yards in, the trail grew indistinct as the bracken gave way to dry and dusty earth. It was impossible to see from which direction Catherine had come. "Damn it!" Shaun said under his breath, his eyes searching the woodland floor, looking for any telltale sign. Ahead of him, on the trunk of a hornbeam, he saw a small smear of slime, glinting like silver in the afternoon sun that filtered through the canopy above his head. He approached the tree cautiously, reaching out and touching the slime, rubbing the sticky liquid between his fingers. It smelt foul, like decaying meat. Moving around the tree he made his way through an area where rhododendrons were growing in profusion, their dark green leaves providing ample cover for anything that might be hiding among them. The hairs on the back of his neck began to prickle and a thin bead of sweat trickled down his spine, making him shiver.

CHAPTER TWENTY-FIVE

In the house the others listened to Catherine's tearful and rambling account of what had happened with a growing sense of foreboding.

"And Shaun's gone into the wood?" Laura said.

Catherine nodded.

"Bloody fool!" Richard said. "He should have come back to fetch us. He doesn't stand a chance on his own. You two wait here," he said to the women. "I'm going after him."

He ran out to the car, opened the trunk, and took out one of the shotguns, grabbing a handful of cartridges and stuffing them into the pocket of his jacket.

"Give me the other one," Laura said, appearing at his side.

"I told you to wait in the house," he snapped at her.

"And I told you to give me the other shotgun . . . and some cartridges. Shaun's my friend," Laura said belligerently. "Besides, I don't take orders."

He looked at her steadily for a moment, seeing the

determination in her eyes. Then he shrugged and took the other shotgun from the trunk. "Have you used one of these before?"

"My father used to take me shooting when I was a kid. I can handle it."

"Okay," he said, thrusting a handful of cartridges at her. "Let's go."

"I'm not staying here on my own." Catherine emerged from the front door. She was still pale but had stopped crying. "Don't leave me on my own."

"Okay," Laura said to her. "Bring Socrates. We might need him. But stay behind the guns. The last thing we need is a bloody shooting accident." The only one we want to shoot, she thought, is Brian Tanner.

They reached the clearing.

Shaun was lying facedown on the grass.

"Oh my God!" Laura said, and made to move forward out of the trees.

Richard grabbed her arm. "No!" he said. "Stay back."

Laura snatched his arm away. "Shaun's hurt!" she said angrily.

"We don't know for a fact it *is* Shaun," Richard said calmly.

Laura's eyes widened with understanding.

"We don't know that the Verani hasn't claimed another host," Richard said.

"And even if it is Shaun," Laura said, "the Verani could be using him as bait and lying in wait for us."

"So what do you suggest?" Richard said. He was scanning the woods for any movement.

"Do you remember the first day I met you? The accident? Remember the way Socrates reacted when we got close to the cellar? I didn't think anything of it at the time, but my guess now is that he sensed the Verani in the cellar. Didn't you, boy?" She crouched down and ruffled the dog's coat, then removed the choke chain that attached him to the lead. "Richard, you'd better give him the command."

"Go on, boy, on you go," Richard said.

The dog started forward, then stopped dead just beyond the trees. He sniffed the air and growled, a steady rumble of aggression and confusion.

"On, boy," Richard said, urging him forward.

In the clearing Shaun opened his eyes and rolled over onto his back.

Socrates barked once and ran forward. Stopping and sniffing at a pool of foul-smelling liquid next to Shaun's body. The dog sniffed it once and backed away, hackles rising, loud staccato barks booming from his throat. He looked back at his master, still barking.

"See?" Laura said. "He can smell it. And all his instincts are telling him to be wary."

Richard looked at her. "Either that or he can sense the Verani inside Shaun."

Shaun pushed himself into a sitting position. At the same time Richard raised the shotgun and aimed carefully.

Shaun swallowed twice. His throat was dry, his mouth parched. He saw Richard aim the shotgun at him. "What the fuck are you doing?" he said thickly.

Socrates started at the sound of Shaun's voice, and then his tail began to wag and he bounded toward him. Shaun shrank back.

"He won't hurt you," Laura called. "Pet him."

Shaun stuck out his hand. Socrates sniffed it, and then licked it.

"I think that answers our question," Laura said to Richard and started to move away from the trees. "Keep the shotgun ready, though, and keep your eyes open." She ran forward. "Shaun, are you all right?" She bent over him, concern etched on her face.

He stared up at her, bleary-eyed. "Yeah," he said. "Fine." He sat up, rubbing his head gingerly. Richard and Catherine were standing a few feet away.

"You were lucky," Laura said. "You shouldn't have tried to tackle him on your own."

"As far as I was concerned I was chasing Brian Tanner. I can handle him. He attacked Catherine. When I arrived there was nothing here . . . except that." He pointed to the milky pool of liquid. "He must have been waiting for me. I didn't see a thing. It all happened too fast. Have you checked to make sure he's not still here?" Shaun continued to rub his head. Laura noticed the red weal scorching the back of his neck, and another down the side of his face.

Laura touched her fingertips to his cheek. "Did you see anything at all?"

Shaun shook his head, but it only made the aching inside it worse.

"All this . . . all this mess here. It looks like the Verani is getting rid of the host body."

"Getting rid of Tanner's body, you mean," Shaun said.

Richard stepped out from the trees. "It's moved on." He'd noticed the slime trail and followed it for a short way into the wood. "It gives us something to follow," he said. "Except for one thing."

"Which is?"

Richard turned away. "It looks as if it's headed for Dunbar Court."

Laura helped Shaun to his feet and turned to the others. "So, what now?"

"It will head for water," Richard said emphatically. "It can't survive in the air for more than a day or so. There's a stream, in the grounds of the Court, just on the other side of these woods. And the trout lake of course."

"Then my guess would be that it's heading there. They can probably sniff out water. They would have to in order to survive," Laura said.

"Let's get back to the Court," Richard said.

Laura stared at him. "Are you mad? That's heading straight for danger."

Richard placed both his hands on her shoulders. "I'll understand if you want to go back to the Hooper house. Your car is there, you and Shaun could get away."

"We could get help," Laura insisted strongly.

"Who would believe us?" Shaun said quietly.

Richard nodded. "He's right, but even so you can both get away. I have to finish this; it has affected my family for too long." He looked across at Catherine, who gave every impression she was staring into space but he knew she was listening. "I'd be happier if you were safe, Laura."

Laura thought for a moment. She glanced at Shaun, who shook his head imperceptively. "It's me Tanner is after. I'm staying with you."

* * *

As soon as the changes began inside his body Tanner knew his life was ending. The brief glimpses of clarity that had stayed with him, that had dragged him through the past few hours, were disappearing.

With shaking hands he tore at his shirt. The thin cotton was restricting, tight around his chest. The thin slits on his abdomen were opening and closing rapidly, the thin spines, now pale coral and anemic, danced in and out of the opening, seeking sustenance and finding none.

He pushed himself to his feet and stood for a moment, staring up at the sky, and then his eyes rolled backward in his head, he opened his mouth, and a thin, keening sound escaped his throat. At the same time his body split, ribs cracking and snapping, bursting out from skin that tore like tissue paper.

Tanner drew on every last ounce of strength he had to fight off the Transition. It was useless. The flesh was peeling away like rotted skin from a vegetable. He had long since lost his will for life, that was irrelevant. All that had mattered for days was Laura Craig, and his desire for revenge.

At thought of Laura he felt a residual emotion inside. It wasn't a will to live, to prolong his existence; it was hatred pure and colorful. With this hatred he began to resist the Verani.

The Verani felt the surge within it and knew instantly what it was. It had chosen its host body well. This human was possessed of an evil that was to be admired. Even now the Verani could use this final power from the human to get closer to the family it was sworn to destroy.

It was a disfigured Brian Tanner, tatters of flesh hanging from his limbs, head distorted with mis-shapen appendages, trails of slime cascading behind him, that moved slowly toward Dunbar Court; moved slowly toward Laura Craig.

Chapter Twenty-six

Richard took Socrates' lead from Catherine and led him across to the pool of slime, letting the dog sniff it again. Socrates pulled against the lead, growling and snapping. "He may not be a bloodhound, but he can still follow a trail. You should see him when he gets the scent of a rabbit. Find, boy," he said to the dog. Socrates barked and put his nose to the ground, sniffing furiously. He caught the scent immediately and lurched forward. Richard glanced round at Shaun and grinned. "Let's go," he said.

The dog headed into the undergrowth, circled aimlessly for a minute or so, and then picked up the scent again, moving away from the clearing and deeper into the wood. The others had no alternative but to follow, treading down the knee-high ferns, picking their way carefully through thick patches of bramble and gorse.

"Definitely the way back to Dunbar Court," Catherine murmured. "Going home."

The farther they went into the wood the less easy

they became. The trees were growing closer together here, and it became harder to see any kind of path. Often the way through them was blocked by fallen trees, or by head-high clumps of rhododendrons.

Laura kept glancing from side to side; the Verani could be hiding in countless places, watching them, lying in wait. The truth was they had no idea how it would behave, or even what it might look like, assuming it had cast off Tanner's body, which was nowhere near certain.

After ten minutes they reached another clearing— a large grassy hollow in the woodland floor filled at the bottom with crisp brown leaves and broken branches from the trees above. Beyond that were the beginnings of the manicured lawns of the formal gardens.

"There's Dunbar Court," Laura said. Her hair was soaked with sweat and flattened to her scalp.

Richard nodded and called Socrates to heel. The dog whined in protest. Richard crouched down and took the dog's great head between his hands, whispering to him, calming him.

"How far to the lake?" Shaun said.

"About another half a mile," Richard said. "Can you take Catherine straight inside when we get there?"

"No. Not a good idea," Laura said. "We have a choice. We all go on together, or we all go back to the Hooper site, but it's not safe for anyone to stay in the open alone. Certainly not after what happened to Shaun. So do we press on?"

"Give me a minute," Catherine said quietly.

Laura dropped to the grass and sat cross-legged. Catherine lit a cigarette. Shaun took out his mobile to call Siobhan. The phone was dead and when he looked closely at it he saw a hairline crack splitting the case.

"Problem?" Laura said.

"I must have fallen on it. It's not working." He slipped the phone back into his pocket. Siobhan would be furious. There was an open evening at his daughter's school tonight and before he'd left this morning she'd made him promise to be home on time.

Since the growth appeared on his shoulder he'd avoided any kind of physical contact with her; something that hadn't gone unnoticed by Siobhan. It was starting to create an ever-widening rift between them. Missing the open evening would create yet more friction.

He explained to Laura. "She probably thinks I'm seeing somebody else," he said gloomily. "It seems so mundane, compared . . ."

"I hardly think she'll doubt you're faithful, Shaun. Siobhan's very bright, and she's certainly never struck me as the insecure type."

"Maybe, but put yourself in her shoes. What would you think?"

"I think, that for now, it's more important that we do this, isn't it?"

"Yes, it is," Shaun said. "Of course, sorry. I . . . this whole business about my back."

"No, I'm sorry," Laura said.

"For what?"

"Getting you involved. If I'd any idea about any of this I wouldn't have touched the Hooper place with a barge pole."

"Yes, but that's the luxury of hindsight. Don't

blame yourself. You weren't to know. And it was my own bloody curiosity that made me knock down the wall in the cellar. Perhaps if I hadn't done that I wouldn't have this thing growing on me. But again, it's easy to be wise after the event. Then again, some people did know what we were getting into." He nodded at Richard and Catherine. "Might have helped matters if they'd said something to us."

Richard gave them another five minutes, then said, "Let's go on."

Laura looked at Catherine, who nodded her head sharply and got to her feet. "Ready," she said.

Once again, with Socrates leading the way, they headed across the lush lawns to the lake.

Socrates stopped at the water's edge, sniffing the ground furiously, turning to bark at them in confusion.

"He's lost the scent," Laura said. "So it looks like it probably entered the water here."

"What do we do then?" Shaun said.

"It's not a large lake, but it is deep in the center," Richard said. "He's going to be weak after being in the air after so long, so I suspect he would take the easier option and go into the deep water to rest."

"Possibly," Shaun said, looking around.

"Think about it," Richard said. "This is the first time the Verani's been out of the well for almost half a century. It's going to be disorientated. Confused. My guess is it will hole up somewhere—give itself time to regroup."

"Laura, what do you think?" Shaun said.

"Sounds reasonable to me," she said. "Unless . . ."

"Unless what?" Richard said.

"Unless Brian Tanner is still in control somehow."

"Oh, to hell with it then," Shaun said.

"We've got about two hours of daylight left," Laura said.

The area surrounding the lake had been left to be exploited by weeds. For the wildlife, was Catherine's excuse to the gardeners. Head-high clumps of brambles formed thorny thickets, while snaking stems of bindweed twisted around them, the white, bell-shaped flowers decorating the thickets, making them look deceptively innocent.

The lake was roughly circular, several hundred yards across, the margins filled with water-hungry plants—clusters of bulrushes, great stands of gunnera and rogersia; flag irises, now running to seed in the late summer. The surface of the pond was partly covered by the flat, circular leaves of water lilies, while blanket weed rose up in frothy green clouds, the home for all manner of pond life. As they approached, a brightly colored dragonfly skimmed the surface, searching for food, before alighting on a rush stem to rest.

Richard crouched down next to Socrates, removed the choke chain, and slapped the animal on the rump. "Go on then. Home, boy."

Tail wagging, the wolfhound ran instead to the water's edge, barked once, and started to circle the lake. Laura and Richard walked after him, alert for any movement, their eyes flicking from the surface of the water to the trees, to the thick growths of gunnera. There were so many places for the Verani to hide, if it wasn't in the deep water.

The dog was sniffing at the ground by the edge of the lake. By the time Richard reached him Socrates was staring out at the water and growling deep in his throat.

"Good boy," Richard said.

Laura stood a few feet back, examining the surface of the lake for any movement.

The dog ignored Richard, his attention fixed on a spot on the water, several yards away from the bank. Laura followed the dog's gaze. A few small bubbles were breaking on the surface, just to the right of a mound of blanket weed. As Richard reached down to slip the choke chain over the dog's head again the water started to boil.

Socrates barked ferociously. Richard made a grab for the dog's ruff, but Socrates lunged forward, shoulder deep into the water, and swam out toward the bubbling water.

"Socrates, no!" Richard cried out, but could only watch helplessly as something dark broke the surface of the water and wrapped itself tightly around the dog's neck, pulling him effortlessly out into the center of the water. Socrates thrashed in the water, yelping, keening, but the Verani was too strong, lifting the dog out of the water, and then plunging him back down beneath it, once, twice. A few moments later Socrates disappeared from view for the third and final time.

Richard looked away from the pond. Laura took his hand. "Come on! Run."

CHAPTER TWENTY-SEVEN

Within minutes of sinking beneath the surface of the lake the Verani could feel the restorative powers of the water working on its body. The pain where the host body was changing was intense—a white-hot fire that engulfed the body, clouding thought, blurring vision. But now, with the coolness of the water surrounding it, the pain was ebbing away and tissues were regenerating. The mud at the bottom of the lake was a soothing balm, and the Verani was content to lie there while it healed.

Only the pain in its mind matched the pain in its body. It was certain it had seen the human father's face staring back from the woods, kindling a hundred emotions, reawakening the feeling of betrayal and the anger at being shut away for so long. This father had tricked the boy David, telling tales of an illness that would eventually be cured, when in fact it was nothing of the kind.

Not an illness but a birthright. And the Verani had years of living alone, submerged in the stagnant wa-

301

ter of the well, to search the race memory to discover exactly what it was. It was all there in the genetic blueprint. Memories of shifting sands, of barren desert wastelands, and soothing cool oases. There were others, a whole race that called themselves Verani and who had a long and noble history.

The Verani rolled over in the mud, letting it coat its body. It would rest for a while, and once the strength had returned fully it would go again to the surface, but this time prepared. It would seek out the man who had rejected it and shut it away. It would seek out the whole family and destroy it.

Memories mingled with rage: vistas of sweeping deserts, scenes it had never witnessed for itself but which were so much a part of its heritage that they had become its own. Faces of dark-skinned humans, swathed in white cloth, some leading others in chains, others chanting, dancing around, yet seeming to pay homage to its ancestors.

There was a pale moon in the sky, casting little light in the grounds, but stirring shadows and shapes so that the entire milieu seemed to be moving; the darkness alive with constant shifting movement.

Another spasm of pain racked its brain. The host body was still alive. Whatever was driving the human that had been Brian Tanner was a primal hatred. The Verani could see through the human's eyes and experience the depth of the anger whenever the young female was there. That was good. If the human body remained a little longer, then it could be put to productive use.

With a huge effort the Verani heaved Brian Tanner's body out of the mud, and swam to the surface.

* * *

They hadn't got far when the surface of the lake, erupted in a tidal wave of rushing white water and weed. Laura turned to see what was emerging from the lake, but the black shape was too obscured by the water.

Shaun took Catherine's hand. "Come on," he urged and all but pulled her toward the house.

"Run," Richard said breathlessly.

When he turned for the others he could see that Shaun and Catherine were already on the terrace at the rear of Dunbar Court. Catherine was handing Shaun some keys, which Richard guessed were the ones that would open the french doors to the drawing room. Why on earth didn't the staff, Payne at least, hear the commotion and do something? Then he remembered. Generosity of spirit had prompted Catherine to give everyone the two days of the weekend off, as they had worked so hard at the party. Dunbar Court was completely empty.

But Laura?

When the lake began to subside she could see that even though he was clearly damaged, it was still Brian Tanner that emerged. There was only one of them that he was interested in. So she ran. She ran away from the others, she ran away from the house. In close proximity to the lake was the maze. She ran there.

The yew was over seven feet tall, far too high for her to see over. As she entered the maze and ran purposelessly along its tracks she could only hope Tanner had seen her and would follow. Moments later she knew her idea had worked; the crashing and thrashing of the foliage told her something was blindly following her scent.

She ran then, pushing stray strands of leaves and branches away with her hands, conscious that the heavy sound of pursuit was getting closer. There were noises like footsteps and she imagined Brian Tanner's face contorted with rage and the effort of running; then there were noises like a great body being dragged along the ground and Laura had to fight against the images in her mind of what might have overtaken Brian.

She came to a crossroads in the maze. A junction in the green walls where she could choose left or right. The noises behind her were closer. She chose left. It was a dead end.

"Shit, fuck."

There was no time to turn back, the walls of the maze were too thick for her to break through, whatever was following her was too near, she could hear that. She could try to turn back the tide, but even as she panted in an effort to regain her breath she knew that was impossible. She recognized Brian Tanner as he lolled down the avenue toward her. He was still wearing that same leering look on his face, and his clothes were just about hanging on his body, but there were huge changes. His skin broken and black, the clothing torn, and through the rips she could see that the flesh of his stomach was crisscrossed with small red slits. Bloodied, like raw meat, the edges of the slits moved, and from inside the slits, sharp, coral-pink spines emerged, protruding viciously, their tips glistening.

"Fancy me now?" The voice was slurred as though it was from a mouth that was under water.

Laura had no idea whether there was any humanity left in the Brian Tanner that remained; there hadn't been a great amount in the original, she thought, but her instincts took over.

She pressed her back against the end hedge of the maze and cast her eyes downward. "I treated you badly, Brian, I know that."

"Humility from the Ice Queen, how quaint," Tanner mocked. "Do anything to save yourself, would you? Suck on this like you sucked my cock." A thin sharp spine flicked out toward her, but she ducked and it retracted into the now heaving mass of the body.

Tanner's face was undulating as though immense forces were playing behind the skin. His body was rippling in a way that made it seem as if all his muscles, all his veins and arteries were quivering.

With a visible effort Tanner lurched toward her. "I hate you with a passion, Laura. As much as I loved you, and I did, I despise you. I'm dying, I can't hold this, this thing, off any longer, but at least I can take you with me."

Laura screamed. Tanner lunged forward to grab her. The slimy flesh of his body slithered against her. His head opened from the top of the skull and thin protruding spikes thrust out quivering in the air before moving to Laura's face. Tanner had come so close; touching distance. In the end he had failed. As in life Laura had deserted him, and there was no coming back. As the Verani asserted its full dominance the echoes of Brian Tanner reverberated away into the memories of time. Only the tattered remnants of the body existed.

Then the bushes in front of her burst open as the Range Rover smashed through the hedgerows of the maze and spun around a few feet from her. In turning it caught Brian Tanner, thrusting him to the ground.

Richard yelled, "Get in!"

Shaun leaped from the side of the vehicle and pulled Laura to her feet. "Come on, girl, move yer arse." Between them they both scrambled into the Range Rover.

Laura jumped into the passenger side, Shaun in the back, and Richard spun the wheel. "I'll try to run it over. What the . . . where is she . . ."

Catherine had opened the back door and was climbing out. She was calling out, "David, David."

By the time Richard had maneuvered the car around, there was no sign of Catherine. She had disappeared into the darkness of the maze. There was no sign of the Verani either.

"I was sure I hit it."

Laura was pointing at the ground. "What's that?" Illuminated in the headlights was a shriveled and bloodied blanket of skin. They were looking at all that was left of Brian Tanner. Before anyone could speak Catherine came running into view. Shaun pushed open the door and helped her inside.

"Where the hell did you run off to?" Richard shouted.

"Just get us back to the house," was all Catherine said.

It was already getting dark as dusk crept up onto the terrace.

CHAPTER TWENTY-EIGHT

The drawing room was dark, with only a couple of lamps switched on to break the gloom. Catherine was slouched moodily on a couch. Shaun tried to get her to drink some water, but she pushed his hand away. It was only when Laura stroked her hair that she offered a small smile.

"Thank God," Laura said. Looking at Catherine. "So, why the hell *did* you run off?"

Richard shut and locked the doors behind them. "I could ask you the same question about running into the maze."

Laura patted Shaun on the shoulder. "I had a good idea. . . ."

"Not one of your 'good' good ideas?"

Laura gave a tight smile. "Sort of a decoy idea?"

"And that comes into the 'good' category, does it?"

Laura flopped into a chair. "Best I could come up with at the time. So, what now?"

Catherine ground out her half-smoked cigarette in

an onyx ashtray and stood. "Did you see . . . I mean, what did it . . ."

Richard put his arm around her shoulder. "Still looked pretty much like Tanner, so far as I could see," he said gently.

Outside in the grounds the dark had taken hold. Dusk had disappeared and in its place were pools of shadow, hulking shapes of trees and bushes made unrecognizable by the blackness of the night.

Darkness surrounded the room, peering in at the windows, rattling the door handles, adding an air of isolation to the small group.

"We could make a break for it in the Range Rover," Shaun suggested.

Richard shook his head. "Possibly, but to be honest I don't much fancy it. We have no way of telling how quickly it might be able to move—"

Catherine gave a strangled sob.

"I'm sorry, Catherine," Laura said. "But it's no use pretending. It was Tanner's discarded body back there. I think the Verani has taken over."

A small tear escaped from Catherine's eye and trickled down her cheek. She dabbed it away impatiently with a tissue.

"Something occurred to me," Laura said. "I think we're in bigger trouble than we first thought."

"It couldn't get much worse," Richard said.

"Oh, but it could. In fact I think it already has. The fact that Tanner's body is being discarded—assuming it is—can mean only one thing. The Verani has mated."

Richard closed his eyes and swore quietly. "Of course," he said. "But who?"

"That's something we'll probably never know."

The room lapsed into silence as they all retreated

into their private thoughts. None of which were pleasant.

In the room the four occupants were conscious of their fear. Each was aware of small sounds outside the french doors. They could imagine crawling creatures slithering below the windows, scratching at the glass to be allowed in. They could believe they could hear whispering behind the drapes, feel a cold draft of night air on their shoulders, and if they turned around . . .

"Can you hear something?" Shaun asked after a while.

They all listened. There was a scuffling sound coming from above them.

"Does this room have a flat roof?"

Richard shook his head. "Not flat as such, it's a pitched and tiled roof."

Shaun snorted angrily. "Never mind the building specs. Is there space up there for something to get onto?"

"Yes."

"Right." Shaun stood. "I'm going to take a look. I would guess the front landing will give me a good enough view over this room?"

"It will but I'll come with you."

"Far be it from me to order a lordly gentleman about, Richard, but you'd be best occupied right here."

"He's right, Richard," Laura said.

The house was darker than Shaun expected. He found his way across the vast entrance hall and stumbled up the grand staircase. The front of the house was fed from a long hallway from which opened several doors. Most of these he found to be bedrooms.

Shaun was looking out the window, trying to see if there was anything on top of the drawing room roof, when the door to the bedroom, the door he had carefully closed behind him, opened.

A table lamp was switched on and in its warm glow he could see Catherine. She was smiling. She was unbuttoning the front of her dress.

"Catherine?"

"We may not have much time, Shaun. I know you want me."

She was naked underneath the dress. Her breasts were visible now, the nipples already erect.

Shaun held out his hands in a dismissive gesture. "Catherine. No, I . . ." Then he watched as the dress fell in folds around her feet. Watched as she reached out her arms for him. Watched the flesh of her stomach crisscrossed with small red slits. The edges of the slits moved, and from inside the slits, sharp, coral-pink spines emerged, protruding viciously, their tips glistening.

"You *do* want me . . . don't you?" Catherine leaped across the room before Shaun could move.

It held Shaun aloft, slammed him against the ceiling, stunning him, and then drew him toward the needle-sharp spines that protruded from its body.

Shaun screamed as three of the spines punctured his back. They threaded through his body like hungry worms, piercing his liver, seeking out the nutrients in his kidneys. Shaun screamed again as the mouth-slits in the body of the Verani started to suck the life from him. His body squirmed and shook as it began to drain him.

It was Shaun's screams that alerted the others.

Richard was the first to push open the bedroom door and run in. He had already raised his shotgun in readiness to shoot, but what he saw froze him to the spot. Laura moved to his side, her own shotgun ready.

Catherine turned to face them and if she recognized her own son she gave no sign.

Laura lifted her shotgun, pointed it at Catherine. Before she could fire the gun Richard grabbed the barrel and forced it toward the floor.

"You can't."

Catherine lifted Shaun away from her, threw him against the wall, and rushed out of the room.

Laura and Richard ran to where Shaun lay, motionless on the carpet. There was no movement, but Laura could see from the steady rise and fall of Shaun's chest that he was still alive. His shirt was drenched in blood.

Richard took him by the arm and tried to drag him into a sitting position, but it was hopeless. Shaun was a deadweight.

"Laura, I need you to help me lift him."

"He shouldn't be moved," Laura said, but together they carried Shaun to the bed, laying him down gently.

Laura was sitting on the floor, next to Shaun, watching him intently. She looked shaken, scared, as she had every right to be. She still managed to smile at Richard as he crouched down beside her.

"Are you all right?" she said.

He shook his head. "My mother . . ." was all he could say.

Laura stroked his hair. "It must have happened at the maze."

"The new host. It means she has a few days left, that's all."

As far as Laura was concerned Catherine, the real Catherine, had already died. Once the Verani had taken over she was lost. "I feel like a rat in a trap," she said quietly.

"You and me both," Richard said grimly.

CHAPTER TWENTY-NINE

Laura knelt down next to Shaun. She took her shirt off and used it to swab away the blood, much of which began to soak into her camisole. "I can't see how much damage has been done to him," she said as Richard came over to join her.

"Well, his arm's definitely broken. Can we roll him over? I want to see what those spines did to him."

"What are they anyway?"

"It's how they feed," Richard said. "It was going to suck everything out of him." His voice sounded as if he was reading from the notes his mother had researched, and in a way he was. There was only one thought keeping him sane at the present: how he could stop Catherine suffering any more.

Richard had a mental flashback to the basement of Brian Tanner's house and Jim Raymond's hideously wasted body. He shuddered.

They rolled Shaun onto his front and pulled up his sweatshirt. There were three puncture wounds, each no more than a quarter of an inch across. Blood seeped from them, but they didn't appear to be life-threatening.

"We've got to get out of here and get him to a hospital," Laura said, and then noticed the look in Richard's eyes.

"Are you okay?" Laura said, putting an arm around his shoulder solicitously.

Richard looked at Laura. They moved across to one another and in an act as primal as the instincts of the Verani haunting them, their lips locked and pressed together in a passionate desperate cry for help. Their faces merged together like raindrops on a windowpane, separate but entwined.

In truth Catherine had little experience in the kitchens, having enjoyed a pampered existence where others helped her with most of life's mundane tasks. That might have mattered if she had any intention of preparing food. The kitchen just happened to be the room the Verani stopped in as it ran to the ground floor of the house.

Catherine knew enough about the layout of the rooms in Dunbar Court to know that the kitchens led through a side door onto the rear terrace. Once the door was opened the night poured through with all its cold embrace. Although she shivered she was hoping, anticipating, in what was left of her humanity, that the Verani would find the exit enticing. If it left the house, perhaps back to the lake, then her son might be safe.

But the Verani was too strong now. With Catherine taken, there remained only Richard. Too late in years to exact revenge on those that deserved it most, it would be some consolation at least to kill Richard.

It would happen soon enough. If it waited here eventually Richard would come. It was good at waiting, it had years of practice.

"We can't wait here," Laura said.

"What do you suggest?"

Laura studied his face carefully before replying. The wrong word here and she would be on her own. "We intended killing the Verani while it was Brian Tanner. We still have to kill it, even if . . ."

Richard pulled away from her embrace. When he stood she thought he was walking out on her. Instead he picked up his shotgun. "Come on then. What *are* you waiting for?"

They searched the rooms on the first floor, before checking the ground floor. Eventually they came to the kitchens.

Catherine was sitting at the pine table, calmly waiting as if ready to prepare tea.

Richard and Laura entered the room together and then separated. Laura with her back to the ovens, Richard against some cupboards.

Without warning Richard raised his gun and fired. The blast hit Catherine full in the chest.

Black jellylike flesh poured out of the chest, hitting the floor with a soft plopping sound. After it came long, coiled lengths of scaly black flesh that uncurled on contact with the floor. Next the legs, articulated, long, covered in leathery skin. The rasping sound stopped as the skull split open and the Verani's head emerged into the shade of the room.

Catherine was disintegrating with soft popping noises as bones broke, muscles snapped, and sinew and ligaments tore from their anchors. Like someone shrugging off a sodden raincoat the Verani hauled itself free from the carcass and stood in the center of the room, a shimmering mass of lashing coral spines.

The head was large and misshapen, great saucer eyes placed on each side, like a lizard's, but coal black and glistening. The mouth that split the head midway was nothing more than a lipless slash, but when it opened to take in air, Laura could see row after row of jagged teeth, yellow and sharp. A thin red tongue flopped over the teeth, flicking backward and forward, as if tasting the air around it.

And then the Verani turned to look at her and she screamed.

At the sound of her scream the Verani lurched forward, lashing out, slapping savagely at the pine table that was Laura's only cover. With a cry she pushed herself away from the table and backed against the oven. With a cry of rage, the Verani lashed out again, but Laura had already made her decision.

"Richard," she yelled. "Get out. Now."

"No chance."

"Richard, do it. Get out now."

Richard shook his head, and raised his shotgun to his shoulder. "Only if you come too."

"Right behind you." Laura had her gun raised as well. "I promise I'll be right behind you."

"Together. Otherwise one of us will get trapped."

The Verani had pushed the table aside. Before it could get any closer, Laura ran to the terrace door. Richard ran to the internal door.

He raised his shotgun. The Verani turned to look at him. Laura knew he would hesitate. She wasn't angry that he did, not even disappointed, it was inevitable he wouldn't be able to finish it.

It was he who fired the vital shot though.

Richard's final shotgun blast hit the ceiling in the center, smashing wood and plaster, but most importantly distracting the Verani.

Laura took careful aim. Both barrels needed to hit the head. She was fairly certain she could kill it with a shot to the head.

She was right.

The Verani was advancing on Richard when Laura fired. The Verani briefly howled as the first shot hit. The second shot killed it.

It was over.

Dunbar Court—Present Day

Siobhan kissed Laura on the cheek. "I hope you'll both be very happy," she said.

"Of course they'll be happy," Shaun said. He'd hoped to come to the wedding on foot rather than being pushed there in a wheelchair, but he had several months to go before his broken pelvis would knit together enough to stand his weight.

"Thank you both for coming," Laura said. "I really appreciate it."

"Wouldn't have missed it for the world," Shaun said. He was smiling, but there was still a hunted look in his eyes. On the death of the Verani the Devil's Hair had dropped from his skin, leaving no trace it had ever been there. He still felt guilty. One day he would sit down with Siobhan and explain to her what had really happened to him that day; but not yet. It was still too soon. His body would mend in time, but the mental scars he'd carry for the rest of his life. Laura saw this in his eyes, and he saw similar emotions in the depth of hers.

It had been an exercise in damage limitation, she thought. No more, no less.

There was little left of Catherine, but what remains there were Richard buried in the grounds of the Court before any official investigation began. No one would ever find them, and that was as it should be.

The story was put out that Catherine had returned to her old ways and left the country, probably for Europe, but possibly South America. She disapproved of Richard's relationship with Laura apparently, was one version, though another suggested it was the plans for the old Hooper place she disliked.

Richard's status in the community meant there were few official inquiries of any consequence.

Marjorie McMillan found the body of her son when she brought Jamie home after a wonderful day spent at Monkey World. For weeks afterward a tearful Marjorie told anyone who'd listen that her son would be alive today if that bitch of a wife of his hadn't left him. Fuel was added to her argument by reports from a local pub that Jenny McMillan had been seen drinking and sharing an intimate conversation with Brian Tanner, a local property developer, who, coincidently, had also disappeared.

Eventually the bodies of Jenny McMillan and Jim Raymond would be found at Tanner's house, leading to a police investigation and a worldwide search for him involving Interpol and the FBI. But he would never be found, not unless the lake at Dunbar Court was ever drained, and that was unlikely, as Richard had begun to fill it in.

Tom Hooper's house was to be demolished. Laura

had lost heart with the renovation. Finishing it would stir too many memories—memories that were best left buried. There would be other houses to work on in the future if she had a mind to, but at the moment she was content in her role as wife to Richard and as the new mistress of Dunbar Court.

"So I suppose it's Lady Laura now, is it?" Shaun said.

"Bit of a mouthful," she said. "I think I'll stick to plain Laura." She looked across the room at Richard, who was deep in conversation with her parents. He felt her eyes upon him and looked back at her, smiling. She returned the smile, but was hesitant, uncertain. Actually until Catherine's death could be officially recorded Richard could not inherit Dunbar Court, but as it was his home it was natural they would live there.

It was her decision to marry here at the Court, and they'd arranged the wedding quickly, inviting only their closest family and friends. Now halfway through the day she was feeling sad. She wondered what her relationship with Catherine would have been like. She suspected they would have become good friends.

"A penny for them," Maggie said as she drifted by in search of another glass of champagne.

"Pardon?"

"You were miles away," she said. "Mind you, if I'd just married Richard Charteris I daresay I would be lost in dreamland too."

Laura squeezed Maggie's hand affectionately. "One day you'll meet him. I'm sure your Mr. Right is out here somewhere."

"Yes, but he's probably halfway up the Amazon,

or climbing Everest. I suspect our paths will never cross." She kissed Laura on the cheek. "Go on, circulate. It's your day," she said.

She found a waiter carrying a tray, plucked off a glass of Bollinger, and went to stand by the french doors, looking out over the garden.

The day had started with a shock for Maggie Kennedy. She cast her mind back to this morning, standing in the bathroom watching in panic as the indicator on the pregnancy testing kit turned blue. Positive.

It took her a while to face up to the fact that she was pregnant, that inside her, Brian Tanner's baby was starting to grow. When the shock abated she gathered her thoughts.

At least she would never be alone again.

PANDORA DRIVE

TIM WAGGONER

The small town of Zephyr, Ohio, is home to a very special young woman. Damara is reclusive—and she has the ability to make other people's dreams, fears and fantasies all too real. But this isn't an ability that she can control, as many people in town are beginning to learn. For some, dreams are becoming living nightmares. For others, their deepest fears are suddenly alive and worse than they ever imagined.

As Damara's powers sweep like a wildfire through the town, her neighbors' long-hidden desires are dragged out into the open—and given life. But as the old saying goes, be careful what you wish for, because in this case...it could kill you.

DOUGLAS CLEGG

THE ATTRACTION

The signs all along the desert highway read "Come See the Mystery!" But some mysteries should remain buried forever. Like the mummified remains of an ancient legendary flesh-scraper, whose job had been to scrape the flesh off the bones of human sacrifices…

When a car filled with teenagers gets a flat tire, the kids figure they have time to check out the Mystery. Behind curtains lies a small, withered corpse with very long fingernails. Above it, tacked on the wall, is a sign: "Do Not Touch. Do Not Feed." But it has to be a hoax, right? How could anyone know that the flesh-scraper is hungry for flesh?

AFTER MIDNIGHT
RICHARD LAYMON

Alice has quite a story to tell you. That's not her real name, of course. She couldn't give her real name, not after all the things she reveals about herself. All of her…*adventures*. She wouldn't want the police to find her, now would she?

It started out so nice. Alice was house-sitting, enjoying having the whole place to herself. But everything went wrong that first night, when she looked out the window and saw a strange man jumping naked into the swimming pool. Alice just knew he would be coming to get her, like all those other men before. But she would never be a victim again. Not after she remembered the old Civil War saber hanging in the living room…

DEATHBRINGER

BRYAN SMITH

Hannah Starke was the first to die. And the first to come back. In the small town of Dandridge they all come back. The buried claw their way out of their graves. The recently killed get up and kill. As the dead attack the living, the numbers of the dead continue to grow. And the odds against the living get worse and worse.

In the middle of it all stands a dark, shadowy figure, a stranger in town with an unspeakable goal. If he is successful, death will rule Dandridge and the terror will continue to spread until all hope is lost. Who can defeat an army of the living dead? Who can stand face-to-face against the...

DEATHBRINGER

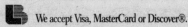